AF398436

DISTORTED MINDS

GUNILLA FAGERHOLM

TRANSLATED BY: GUNILLA FAGERHOLM

(FROM ORIGINAL SWEDISH TITLE: "FÖRVRIDNA SINNEN")

BOOK COVER: ELA SAWOSKO

PRINTING: BoD – BOOKS ON DEMAND, STOCKHOLM, SWEDEN

PRODUCTION: BoD – BOOKS ON DEMAND, NORDERSTEDT, GERMANY

ISBN 9789177859901

"IN EACH OF US THERE IS ANOTHER WHOM WE DO NOT KNOW"

(QUOTATION BY CARL GUSTAV JUNG, psychiatrist, psychologist, author, historian and mystic)

A WARM THANK YOU!

TO MY FRIENDS LINDA BOLLINGER AND MARTIN WIRTH

AND TO

MY HUSBAND, BERTIL LINDSTRÖM

FOR THEIR SUPPORT

<u>PERSONS APPEARING IN THE STORY</u>

<u>Living in the USA</u>
Jenny Johnson, a 19-year old Swedish-American girl,
living in Mora, Minnesota
Johan, Jenny´s father
Anton, Jenny´s brother
Wally, Jenny´s grandfather, dead
Sonja and Mikael, Jenny´s lovely neighbours
Peggy and Monica, Jenny´s friends
Nicklas Burger, lawyer, living in Minneapolis, Minnesota
George Burger, Nicklas´ retired and senile father
Maja and Yngve Hermansson, a bored childless couple,
living in Eire, Pennsylvania

<u>Living in Dalarna, Sweden</u>
Sven Martinsson, young police assistant in Mora, Dalarna
Ida Martinsson, Sven´s mother, living in Orsa
Lars Hellström, Sven's boss
Jonas, another police assistant, not too bright
Doctor Larsson, doctor at Mora Hospital
Nurse Gertrud, not the most charming woman in the world
Nisse Nilsson, old cross-country skier with a big heart

<u>Living in Mariestad, Sweden</u>
Peter Petersson, kind truck driver
Anna Petersson, his wife

<u>Living in Uppsala, Sweden</u>
Sture Blomkvist, raving over help to Africa or … ?
Ove, Sture´s son, with a low IQ but a kind heart.

<u>Living in Torrevieja, Spain</u>
Short-tempered Agnes Rojales, according to her own
opinion the most beautiful woman in the world

<u>Living in both Australia and Mora, Dalarna</u>
Anders Torstensson, gold- and opal digger
David Torstensson, Anders' son

<u>Living in Australia</u>
Riki, aborigine boy
Riki's grandfather and grandmother

PROLOG

Mora, Minnesota, USA – 20 June 1973

The June breeze is softly shaking the leaves in the softwood grove close to the lake. An angler covers his eyes with one hand in order not to get blinded by the afternoon sun. Happy laughter is heard from a canoe on the verge of capsizing. Down at the lake shore a group of people are having a picnic while their dogs and children are playing. Others have brought their garden chairs and enjoy the heat, leaning back in them. Everything is so idyllic. As it always is when summer has arrived to stay here in the little town of Mora in Kanabeck County, Minnesota USA, so far away from the crisis and problems in the rest of the world. Today nobody is interested in listening to the radio reports about the Watergate affair, in which focus is now being increasingly centred on President Nixon. A piece of a poster, almost torn in half, is fluttering from a birch. It says that there will soon be an opera performance in town – the Threepenny Opera by Bertolt Brecht.

Who would ever have believed that this marvellous summer day, before sunset, would be turned into a horrendous tragedy? There is, however, a sign of an approaching catastrophe. At the town limit a blue car is heading towards the centre at top speed. The driver's one and only errand in Mora is to refuel at the gas station, close to the tennis courts, and maybe also to have a short nap before continuing. The car is to be

delivered at the airport tonight and thereafter the
driver will fly back home to Europe.

CHAPTER 1

Mora, Minnesota, USA – 20 June 1973

The white two-story building, high up on Lincoln Drive 23 in Mora, is almost vibrating with youthful joy. Through the wide-open windows you can hear the happy voices of teenage girls, once in a while intermingled with the hoarse voice of a teenage boy.

The elderly couple – Sonja and Mikael from number 29 – are passing by with their dog on their habitual early evening walk. They smile at each other and stop when 19-year old Jenny comes dashing down the kitchen staircase, halting in front of them.

"Where have you been?" she eagerly asks. "I´ve missed both of you so much!"

"We´ve been visiting our son Tom and our grandchildren in Saint Paul for a few days, but now we´re back home again, as you can see", answers Mikael.

"Sweetheart, I´m so content to see you this happy. Are you throwing a party?" wonders Sonja. She loves Jenny as much as if she had in fact been her own daughter, but that is of course natural since Sonja has been taking daytime care of both Jenny and her brother Anton for many years. Sonja´s exterior appearance mirrors her lovely motherly disposition. She is rather short and sturdy, has red round cheeks and the kindest eyes, you could find. Comfortably dressed, but far from modern. Mikael is totally different. He is tall and lean like a pole. His hair is quite long and you could see him wear a rear-facing cap all year round but he too has such kind eyes.

"Now, listen to this. Dad has finally given me permission to go to the disco in Brunswick Township tonight. And afterwards my friends Monica and Peggy are allowed to stay the night at my house. Their parents have also given them permission to do this. It´ll be such fun!"

"Oh, how wonderful for you! The years do pass so quickly. You girls have been longing for this moment for such a long time. I'm happy for you. Will Anton join you?" asks Sonja.

With laughter Jenny says:"No, he´s too young, but he´ll do something else, something very nice, tonight. He´ll actually play a tennis match in front of a scout looking for talented tennis players for a college. If Anton succeeds he could get a scholarship to study there. Sorry, now I have to go back inside. Anton is helping us putting up the disco lamps. Us girls, we have to warm up a little before the disco."

"Jenny, wait a moment. Would you like to accompany the two of us to the Opera next week?"

"Of course. Wonderful. I like opera much better than noisy jazz and hippie music. What will they be performing?"

"The Threepenny Opera."

"Lovely, that is one of my favourites. Listen. I know a few lines:

Then one night there's a scream in the night
And you say, "Who's that kicking up a row?"
And ya see me kinda starin' out the winda
And you say, "What's she got to stare at now?"
I'll tell ya.

There's a ship
The Black Freighter
Turns around in the harbor
Shootin' guns from her bow…

"That's all I know."

Jenny makes a gesture as if to receive applause.

"And which language will you be speaking tonight?" asks Mikael.

"Swedish of course. We always speak Swedish when we are together. That way we're also able to comment on others without anybody understanding, but it is, of course, important to be careful as there are so many Swedish-talking people up here in the old Swedish settlements. Now I must really rush, see you later." Jenny gives both Sonja and Mikael a quick hug and then runs back up the kitchen stairs on light feet.

Inside the house the joy is now almost ecstatic. Illuminated by the disco light the girls are wildly dancing around, clad in only panties and bras. Anton, embarrassed by seeing them almost naked, has retreated into his room in order to prepare himself mentally for the evening's tennis match. Seeing his sister that way is no big deal. He has seen her naked since early childhood but it is worse with Peggy. He is somewhat in love with her, which makes it worse. She should not be dancing half naked with anybody, not now nor later tonight. And Jenny is so stupid telling everybody that he is too young to go to the disco. He just has not time enough to do that too. Tennis is actually far more important than girls!

An hour later there is a sound at the entrance door. Jenny's father Johan has returned home after work.

"Hi girlies! Having fun?"

A joint "Yes" comes from the three of them.

"And girls, I've bought you a bottle of red wine to share. And I've also talked to Steve, in number 32. He'll drive you to the disco and also back home. And he'll keep an eye on you during the night. OK?"

Johan laughs as three pairs of girls' arms are hugging him. He is so happy that Jenny has met Monica and Peggy. Both are sensible girls. Having them as friends will prevent Jenny from getting into trouble.

"Anton, hurry up! We're short of time. We mustn't arrive too late for your match. It would give the wrong impression!" calls Johan to the upper floor. Then he walks out of the house to start the car.

As Anton hurriedly passes them on his way to the car, the girls give him "break a leg" kicks in the ass. Having waved goodbye to him, they return inside to start their makeup. But first of all they are going to enjoy the wine for a moment.

Seating himself in the car, Anton looks at his father.

"Dad, this morning Jenny once more behaved in that strange way, making me unhappy."

"What happened?"

"She started scolding me about a stain of butter being on the table cloth. She was probably herself the guilty one for it being there. Then, when I said I didn't cause it, she became almost mad. And then when I opposed her, she started to cry and accused me of trying to start a fight with her."

"Listen, my son, that is typical premenstruative trouble. That's something girls suffer from before their monthly menstruation. Unfortunately, we men have to cope with that."

"But Daddy, she grabbed the knife!"

"Maybe she was going to cut herself a new slice of bread. The knife is on the table for you to use. As a matter of fact, I was the one leaving butter on the table cloth yesterday evening. I'll explain that to Jenny and she'll most certainly ask you for forgiveness."

Dad parks the car down at the tennis courts. He and Anton arrive early. Nobody else has yet come so they wait on the pavement outside the entrance. The street is empty, except for an unfamiliar car parked at the roadside a bit further away. The driver seems to have been asleep but awakened by their arrival. Her eyes widen as she keeps staring at them, as if she cannot believe what she sees. Yes, her eye sight is OK. She instinctively reacts like a cobra. Turning the ignition key, she steps on the accelerator. A few moments later the street is once more deserted. The only thing you could hear is a light swish of a car, disappearing in the far distance. Streaks of blood are dripping from the edge of the pavement.

Jenny looks at the kitchen clock. Steve should have been here five minutes ago. Hopefully he has not had a flat tyre ... or found himself out of petrol... She discards the thought. "We´re going to the disco, tralalala..." Now there is suddenly a call at the door.

"Steve is here now!" Jenny tries to make herself heard through the music that Monica by now has turned up to maximum Steve is however not there. Instead of Steve, Jenny can see Peggy´s father, who is a police-man. Also Mikael and Sonja are outside, standing on the landing. All three of them seem so serious – as if they would be going to a funeral. Jenny does not notice that. She is soon going to be the disco queen.

"Have you come to see how beautiful we are? How kind of you!" Laughing Jenny makes a small pirouette.

At that moment she finally notices their grave faces. What is wrong with them? A few seconds of awkward silence pass. Then she asks, in a trembling voice:"Has anything happened?" As Sonja, without answering Jenny´s question, takes Jenny into her arms, Jenny suddenly understands. Something is terribly wrong!

"Oh, my sweet little darling… Something so terrible has happened… An accident." Sonja frenetically swallows in order to keep herself from crying. "Your Dad and your darling Anton… They were both hit by a car, and they´re both dead. Dearest darling Jenny, I´m so very sorry!"

Jenny remembers how Dad and Anton had happily walked down to the car just a while ago. They were going to Anton´s match, and she had given him a "break a leg" kick.

"No, it can´t be true!" she whimpers. "Anton has to play an important tennis match tonight."

Seeing Sonja´s tears run down her cheeks, Jenny suddenly understands the hideousness of the situation. Sonja has been telling the truth. Sonja would never lie about such a thing. Jenny wriggles out of Sonja´s embrace.

At that moment the world stops… and Jenny Johnson is feeling how she is rapidly sinking into a big black bottomless hole…

CHAPTER 2

Mora, Minnesota, USA – 15 July 1973

Jenny lives as if being in a vacuum. The world surrounding her is so distant. When somebody talks to her, she is barely capable of hearing it. Her thoughts are just whirling around in her head like in a whirlpool. She is not interested in anything. Does not want to know anything at all about the accident – that is not essential. Dad and Anton will never return, even if the accident is investigated. And the police have already told them that they have no traces of the perpetrator and that they are so busy with a lot of other cases. The car had already left for the state boundary when the victims were discovered.

Jenny no longer wants to see her friends Peggy and Monica. And she is no longer interested neither in her looks nor her dressing. She is completely changed. Has no interest in life. She just wants to die.

Jenny is staying at Sonja´s and Mikael´s home until the funeral. They have insisted on not leaving her alone in her now terribly empty home. To them it feels as if they had a small distant and apathetic child in their home, and they are terribly concerned about Jenny´s state of mind. Their attendance to the opera performance is of course cancelled.

The funeral, organized by Mikael and Sonja, is very beautiful and emotional. Lots of people from Mora are attending. Everybody wants to honour and say farewell to Johan and Anton. Not one eye is dry during the ceremony – except for Jenny´s. She cannot even cry any longer. She is feeling paralyzed and emotionless. She cannot believe that her Dad and brother are lying in the coffins up there in front of her. Most of all she would actually prefer to leave.

Jenny moves back into her own house after the funeral. She wants to test being alone. She needs peace and quiet for a while. She wants to gain perspective to what has happened. And with Sonja around all the time, like an anxious hen, that is not easy.

Jenny loves Sonja – she truly loves her. At the same time, she however wishes her own mother would still be alive. She wanders around in the house, searching for anything that could give her a picture of her own real mother, whom she does not remember herself. She has done that so many times during her childhood but she has never found the tiniest trace of her Mum´s existence. Not one photo, not any keepsake at all. Jenny once asked Dad why, but he just looked miserable and tense and would not give her any answer to her question. Jenny´s interpretation of Dad´s reaction was that he was grieving Mum so much that he did not want to be reminded of her. Deep inside, Jenny felt that this was unfair to her and Anton. They both could need some keepsake of their Mum. But at least for Anton that is not a problem any longer.

When Jenny tries to ransack her mind for memories from the years she had spent with Mum, she feels how a wintry darkness starts growing inside her. Icy winds penetrate her soul. And sometimes she even hears a female voice that after a very mocking and mean laughter, says the words:"You just wait!" This is repeated 24 hours a day and is awfully scary. Jenny is getting more and more nervous. It is as if she is constantly expecting to hear that voice again and she cannot concentrate on anything else. She has, on several occasions, searched the whole villa in order to find out from where that voice emanates, but there is no explanation to be found. She is completely alone in the house. Completely alone with an evil voice without a body!

Jenny and Anton talked about Mum as late as only a few months back. Jenny then asked Anton if he knew which illness had killed Mum. Anton told her that he had asked Dad for the name of Mum's illness. Dad had just muttered that Mum had been sick in her head. And that it was as well that she had died. Anton was a little astonished by Dad's voice, when he said that. It had sounded so cold and unengaged. And Anton, just like Jenny, came to the conclusion that Dad was so upset by Mum's death that he did not even like to talk about her.

During the time Jenny has been living alone in her villa, Sonja has, by bringing her food, been keeping Jenny under a certain observation. Sonja gets increasingly worried when she notices how quickly Jenny is changing. Her face has turned so thin, she is hollow-eyed, her skin is greyish and she hardly ever talks. And she is very nervous. Sonja really tries to talk to Jenny but she very seldom gets any real replies. Then, one day, Jenny has a break-down and tells Sonja about nightmares and about the strange threatening female voice that she is constantly hearing, during the day as well as during the night. Quite frightened by this, Sonja realizes that Jenny, immediately, should get help from a psychologist. Without professional treatment to get Jenny on an even keel, the dear girl might succumb.

During her talks with the psychologist Jenny explains that she must leave Mora. She can no longer bear seeing objects that remind her of Dad and Anton. The psychologist agrees. It might be better for Jenny to leave home, in order to get some perspective to everything that has happened to her. Right now she is building a wall of ice around her and that is not good.

But where could she go? She wished her grandfather Wally were still alive. She could have gone to him! But he, too, had died, six months ago. The psychologist suggests different alternatives which are thoroughly discussed. Jenny wants a job at which she would get a lot of time to think about the deaths of her family members and also about her own future. She finally decides to spend a year at sea, working as a cabin cleaner and kitchen assistant on an Atlantic cruiser. Mikael, having been a shipmaster for many years, knows a lot of people at the shipping companies. He is certain that he, without difficulty, could find Jenny a job on a ship.

Before long, Jenny gets an offer for a job as cab cleaner and kitchen assistant on the Atlantic cruiser *RMS Queen Elizabeth 2*, on the route between Southampton and New York. The company also promises to help Jenny, if needed, to a change of ship so that she could continue to far-off countries. She immediately accepts the job, and for the first time in months you could even see a faint smile on her lips. She has always loved the sea and big heavy waves.

Before Jenny can leave she has to meet her father's lawyer, Nicklas Burger. He tells her that the estate inventory will take considerable time. For that reason Jenny has to give Mikael a proxy so that he, if needed, can represent Jenny. Jenny was born during a visit to Sweden that her parents made in order to see Jenny's grandmother, who at that time was terminally ill. Therefore Jenny automatically got a Swedish citizenship, in addition to her American one. Nicklas Burger advises Jenny to use her Swedish passport during the voyage. It could save her many of the problems that Americans could face abroad, due to the now 10 year old Vietnam War. The world is not so American friendly these days.

With only a few possessions in her duffel bag, Jenny travels with Mikael and Sonja to New York where Jenny will embark.

"Sweetheart, do you promise to write us once in a while? We'll miss you so much," exclaims Sonja, while they are standing on the quay close to the enormous ship.

"Yes, I promise," answers Jenny. "But it could take considerable time for a postcard to reach Minnesota. I'll miss both of you enormously. You two are wonderful!"

Saying farewell, the three of them are hugging each other, shedding quite a lot of tears. Finally Jenny breaks free and leaves, walking up the gangway, without looking behind. She is now alone on her way into a big world, about which she actually knows nothing. In a low voice she is humming a part of the ballad about Jenny the Pirate, composed by Brecht. When she had made up her mind about going to sea, she had decided to learn it by heart,

"You people can watch while I'm scrubbing these floors
And I'm scrubbin' the floors while you're gawking
Maybe once ya tip me and it makes ya feel swell
In this crummy Southern town
In this crummy old hotel
But you'll never guess to who you're talkin'.
No. You couldn't ever guess to who you're talkin'..."

CHAPTER 3

New York, USA – 25 July 1973

Jenny continues humming as she hands over her travel documents to a short woman in an impeccable hostess uniform. The humming gets to an abrupt end as the woman, in a harsh voice, says:"Miss, please stop singing. Listen to me. You're part of the crew and are not allowed to embark here. This entrance is for passengers only. Please leave the queue and return ashore. Then follow the red arrows marked "CREW ONLY". And please make space for embarking passengers. And, Miss, smile at them! Here priority number one is always to smile."

Jenny forces her way back along the gangway, all the time smiling at passengers embarking with hand luggage, pets and small children. She does not receive any smiles in return, just pushes.

She follows the red arrows leading 50 metres further down the quay. There she finds another and much smaller gangway. It does not rise up towards the ship's entrance deck but down into the dark space between the ship's hull and the sea. Down there, only a meter above the water surface, is a small door leading into the ship. Inside Jenny finds herself at the end of a very long corridor, at the very end of a long queue. In it there are all sorts of people, except Westerners. She is standing out from them all because of that. Everyone is looking at her. A nice woman from Latin America asks Jenny if she has been lost and needs directions to find her way.

"No, thank you. I belong to the crew", answers Jenny smiling.

"But Miss, this crew is only for cleaning and service staff", says the woman.

"That is exactly what I am", answers Jenny. She is beginning to feel irritated.

A startled silence is spreading along the queue. Only quiet whispers can be heard here and there. People at the head of the line start moving towards the back stopping behind Jenny. Maybe out of kindness, maybe in order to see and hear better without having to turn around. Soon Jenny finds herself at the head of the queue.

"Next person. Please hand me the documents. Do you speak English or do you need an interpreter?"

"I´m an American citizen."

"I did not ask about citizenship. Do you speak English?"

"Yes."

Jenny is now so frustrated that she wants to scream. She finds it increasingly difficult not to show how irritated she has become.

"First language?"

"Swedish."

"In this bag you'll find a uniform that you must use onboard. So please, go over there and change your clothes. Leave your own clothes in the bag and leave it with my assistant. Then continue to the next room. Did you bring any drugs or alcohol?"

"No, only a bottle of wine I received as a gift."

"Leave that in the bag. The crew is neither allowed to drink alcohol nor to use drugs onboard. Nor to have sex relationships with the passengers. Show your arms. I'm looking for pinpricks. You may keep your long beautiful hair, but it must be covered for safety and sanitary reasons. And Miss, remember that you must always smile. That is our priority number one."

After three similar conversations about rules and formalities in different rooms, Jenny is now boiling inside out of sheer humiliation and fatigue. And she is starting to get a headache. But now at last she is an employee and onboard the ship, in a uniform similar to the one the girls wear back home at Mora Tourist Information Office. When Jenny is doing her chores, she will wear overalls.

Among all things she has been informed about, she has learned that her first introductory lesson starts at exactly 5 a.m. Leisure time can only be spent in the cabin, the assistants' recreation room or on designated parts of the very lowest of the ship's decks. There is a small space outside, at the ship's stern, where they are allowed to be but it is normally so crowded that you can hardly find space enough for standing. The best way to get outside is to find outside chores, according to a Philippine woman, who has been working on the ship on earlier voyages. Staff breaking any rules or fraternizing with the passengers during leisure time will be expelled in the next port.

On their way to the cabin that Jenny will be sharing with three other girls from different countries, they meet some young, bearded men in nice black uniforms.

"Hi sweetie", says one of them, "are you Jenny from Mora, Minnesota?"

"Yes, I´m. Hi!" answers Jenny. "Are you Swedish? What is your name?"

"Erik. I´m an assistant steward. I saw in the ship records that you would be here. No, I´m American but my ancestors came from Örebro and I´ve been studying Swedish. I work in the Staff Section, so if you have any problems or questions you can come to me. I have number 0112 on the intercom. See you."

"That is really a cutie", whispers the Philippine woman to Jenny. "He is yours, but keep him hot for us too. You need a partner on this ship if you want to survive."

The cabin is rather big but with four bunks there is not much private space. There are however at least four basins in the shower room. In the floor centre there is a round coffee table that could be used for card games. Each girl has a rather high bunk, fastened to the wall, with its head end facing separate cabin corners. Beneath the bunk there is a cupboard for private belongings and below the foot end there is a small writing table. One chair per person.

Without a moment of hesitation and before any of the girls have time to react, Jenny, to her own big surprise – she usually does not act in such a perky way – rushes up to one of the bunks and jumps into it. The cabin's only small glass valve facing the sea is at the head end of that berth and Jenny has immediately discovered that. Jenny closes the curtain. She can hear the other girls mumbling disappointedly in the cabin. The Philippine woman is saying that you normally choose your bunk in age order. And then she adds that Jenny will probably not be lasting long onboard. Therefore she does not want to make difficulties.

CHAPTER 4

The Atlantic Ocean – 25 July 1973

Jenny falls asleep very fast on her first night onboard, totally exhausted by all the events. She is dreaming about her grandfather Wally. About how he emigrated from Mora in Sweden, but how he in spite of that was always considering the Swedish traditions and language as very important. How Granddad told them about the Vasaloppet cross-country skiing race in Sweden and that the skiing trails follow the route Gustav Vasa had used, when he escaped from the soldiers sent out by the Danish king. Granddad had himself participated in the race and socialized a lot with the most famous skiers.

Granddad wanted his family members to meet all the Swedish tourists visiting the area in Minnesota, famous for its old Swedish settlements. Jenny and Anton as well as Dad – and even granddad Wally himself – had on many occasions acted as tour guides back in Mora. They had often invited the visitors for dinner or to spend the night at the Johnson home. Being hosts they always spoke only Swedish with their guests. That was a good way to keep the Swedish language alive and to avoid getting an American accent. Most of their friends in Mora also had Swedish ancestors and it was an unwritten rule that they only speak Swedish when coming together.

Granddad had passed on the Vasaloppet interest to Jenny's father, Johan. To participate in it in Mora,

Minnesota was high up on their wish lists. And then they had finally been able to do that - but only once. ONLY ONCE! Jenny presses her face deep into the pillow. It is so horrible to remember. She forces herself back into sleep in order to continue remembering.

For several years people in Mora, Minnesota, had been preparing for an American Vasaloppet. It was to be a copy of the Swedish one. Granddad's Swedish friend Nisse Nilsson, a famous skier had come over to the USA a couple of times to be part in the discussions about the setup of the race. And then the day had finally come, the day when the American Vasaloppet was to start for the first time. It was the second Sunday in March 1973; approximately six months ago. Both Jenny's Dad and Granddad had registered. Jenny's Dad tried to dissuade his father from participating, since Granddad Wally's heart had been troubling him a lot. And that same morning it was disturbing him more than ever. His chest was tight and he found it difficult to breathe, but that was only due to the excitement he was feeling before takeoff, he said. Granddad was a tough and stubborn old man.

The race was very thrilling. Dad and Granddad were, during the whole race, always found up front among the best skiers. Lots of friends from Mora, having been invited for the first race, were supporting them in a very lively way. Dad at all times kept a little behind Granddad, probably to check how he was feeling. Granddad Wally crossed the finish line as number five and Dad Johan as number seven! What an achievement – Granddad was after all 64 years old.

At the evening banquet in Mora´s Community Hall the participants were thoroughly celebrated. The five first crossing the finish line were given a possibility to speak to the guests from the podium.

When the turn came to Granddad to speak, at first he did not want to climb the podium but the cheering made him change his mind. So he went up there, white in his face, and immediately broke into a huge smile telling the audience how happy he was having finally been able to participate in the Vasaloppet, also here at home in Mora, Minnesota. He had already taken part in the original Vasaloppet in Dalarna, Sweden. And, imagine, he had today beaten his own son Johan with two placements! He smiled at his own joking boast. Then he thanked the present guests for all the support he had been receiving. A big applause exploded. He turned to leave the podium. Then he staggered, moved one hand to the chest and fell to the floor. A swish of dismay was heard from everywhere. Jenny cried out in despair. Together with Dad and Anton she rushed forward onto the podium and up to Granddad. A doctor, who had been among the guests, also came running. Somebody pulled the drapes.

”I´m so sorry but it seems Wally has had a massive myocardial infarction. I´m afraid that there isn´t much we have time to do.” The doctor, a close friend of the family, had tears in his eyes.

Dad, Anton and Jenny were jointly hugging Granddad, as he was fighting for breath. He could only utter one word at a time:”I´m so happy having had you all, my

dear family… Your sister must get the purse, Johan."
Then his voice died away and he was gone. Dear beloved Granddad.

CHAPTER 5

The Atlantic Ocean – 12 October 1973

Jenny has now been working well over two months as a cab cleaner and kitchen assistant onboard the *QE2*. The ship has made a few trips between the USA and England, and she is getting used to the job. It has not been a nice time. She actually finds the work degrading, picking up pornographic magazines in the cabins of the men and condoms in those of the women. In the galley she has to clean every piece of kitchen-ware until it shines, while the chefs are lustfully studying her behinds and even her more intimate parts. Yes, even the female chef is doing that. And the constant invitations. And the tampering. And the excuses. "Sorry, there´s so little space here. Could you please put your feet a little more apart so that I can get closer?"

In order to stand the dissatisfaction, Jenny starts to fantasize about herself being the cleaning woman Jenny in the Threepenny Opera. While she is moving the mop on the floor Jenny tries to remember the story of the opera and the different persons. Evening-time she sometimes joins the crew to listen to Chef Matthew and his stories about skirmishes with pirates in the waters outside Singapore and the Horn of Africa. She is actually quite envious of him for his experiences. That kind of life would certainly have suited Jenny!

She hardly ever talks to anybody and absolutely not to her cabin mates. They have already given up on her. In the beginning, they smiled at her and asked her to join them. When they, later on, understood that she did not approve of their doings, there were no longer any invitations. It was always the Philippine woman who took the initiative to the strange things they were doing. "Girls, time for a shower", she used to say. She and the other two girls then undressed until they were only wearing their underwear. Carrying a bath towel they entered the shower room. And then the panting and the giggling began.

When Jenny, being late from her work in the galley, on one occasion enters the cabin, she does not notice that her cabin mates are in the shower room, so she opens the door to it. The girls are sitting in there on the floor, in a small ring, passing between them something. Anton had shown her a photo of such a thing, so she knows what it is. It is a hookah, a small tube of burnt brick used for smoking hashish. The shower is on and the evacuation fan is at high speed in order to minimize the smell of hashish. When the girls come out of the shower, they snigger at her disapproving face, start laughing loudly at their own grimaces and in different other manners behave very strangely. Collective lunacy, Jenny thinks. This should actually be reported.

But Jenny does not report the incident. Unfortunately! Instead she crawls into her bunk, puts the pillow close to the valve so that she can lie comfortably with her face close to the glass and look out at the outside storm. The waves almost hypnotize her. She can hardly see where the waves stop and the sky starts. Out there, down under the surface, there is an unimaginable depth, and immediately above the wave crests a similarly unimaginable sky is taking over. Through her small valve, she can admire how everything is seamlessly connected.

In a low voice she starts reciting, for herself:

Then one night there's a scream in the night
And you say, "Who's that kicking up a row?"
And ya see me kinda starin' out the winda
And you say, "What's she got to stare at now?"
I'll tell ya.
There's a ship
The Black Freighter…

But those stupid girls behind her back do not understand anything. They have the Universe in front of them. Instead of admiring it, they laugh at their distorted images in the mirror and start giggling stupidly at their own grimaces.

"No, they're not even worth being shot at. I, actually, feel sorry for them." Jenny falls asleep.

Jenny's space in the gang does not continue unoccupied. A few cabins down the corridor a somewhat older German kitchen assistant is staying. Her name is Britchen Bauer and she calls herself a hippie and admits to being gay. At first she tries a few times to make up to Jenny but tires of that and then starts talking with the Philippine woman. On one occasion Jenny hears her laughing. It is probably at her. She has never heard a meaner laughter. Britchen soon starts joining the girls during their hashish sessions in the shower room. And in the ward-room she sits at their table, on Jenny´s empty chair. Jenny herself has already long ago moved to a table with some Russians that are not very interested in conversation. Or maybe they do not know English.

The atmosphere in the cabin is getting even worse, when the ship is on its way to Southampton in England. One night Britchen enters the cabin, noticeably drunk. She walks up to Jenny´s bunk, demanding to have it starting at that very moment. Jenny will have to transfer to Britchen´s old cabin. It is the joint wish of the girls that the two of them switch places. Jenny of course refuses and draws the curtain. She ought not to have done that! The cabin gets silent. Everyone, except for Jenny, has left. Jenny has difficulties falling asleep that evening. She can hear the others enter the cabin to go to bed. No words are uttered. And Jenny does not notice neither that the girls hide their hookah nor where they hide it.

 A question crops up in Jenny´s head: Could this really be a coincidence? That she has now lost her whole family. Firstly Mum died a long time ago and now the rest of her family. Three persons in half a year. And she has now herself been transferred to the lowermost deck of an Atlantic cruiser, on top of everything? Has maybe some kind of curse or retaliation been put on her family?

No, of course not, thinks Jenny. The answer is obvious. It must be by accident. There are no superior potencies. Every person decides about his own life. Also Pirate Jenny and herself! The Threepenny Opera is more or less about that fact.

This straight answer, coming from within her, has the effect of an unexpected turning point for Jenny´s thoughts, moving her development forward. She herself bears the responsibility for her own life. If she does not react, she will continue forever bouncing back and forth on the Atlantic Ocean on the lowermost deck of an Atlantic cruising ship in the company of her tiresome cabin mates. Dad and Anton will never come back, whatever she does. So now it is time for her to take command.

But maybe fate anticipates her command. At 5 a.m. there is a knock on the cabin door, and assistant steward Erik steps in. Everyone immediately sits up in their bunks, as if in attention.

"Jenny Johnson is to report immediately to the Captain", he says in a harsh voice. "I´ll be waiting outside the door while you´re getting dressed. The cabin is to be searched." He turns to the other girls:"Please stay in your bunks, ladies. You know what all this is about. We´ll first search the whole cabin and then you can stand up, without anything in your hands, so that we can also search your bunks."

The Philippine woman pouts and folds up the quilt, so that she is lying there for anyone to see. "Come to Mum, my little boy. It is so cosy and warm here." Then she grins and covers herself with the quilt.

Accompanying Erik up the elevator to the captain´s office on the top deck, Jenny asks him:"What´s all this about?"

"I can´t tell you yet. However it seems that there have been several severe complaints about your behaviour. You should know that the Captain´s name is Julius and that he is Swedish. You should only call him Captain. And don´t speak, unless you´re told to do so."

They enter the captain´s office cabin. He is seated behind a big overloaded desk. A secretary is standing near the bookshelf.

"So this is Jenny Johnson from Mora, Minnesota. I´m the captain of this ship. Are you feeling at home onboard?"

"Yes, Captain!" answers Jenny smiling, obeying the ship´s rules. Though inside herself she wants to answer ´No´. That she is feeling uncomfortable all the time.

"Then I must ask why you´ve caused two serious complaints in 24 hours."

There is a signal on the intercom and he stops talking.

"Captain speaking!"

"Sir, we found it, where they had told us."

The captain turns back to Jenny:"I said two complaints but now they´re three. The first one is threatening people, carrying a deadly weapon onboard."

"What?" Jenny turns quite pale.

"The kitchen assistant Britchen Bauer has reported that when she came into your galley, you were there waving a chopper screaming that everyone was going to die."

Jenny cannot help smiling a little in spite of her distress.

"I sang, Captain. I was singing. I´m interested in opera, and I sang a strophe from the Threepenny Opera. That is the one about Pirate Jenny. It goes like this:

By noontime the dock
Is a-swarmin' with men
Comin' out from the ghostly freighter
They move in the shadows
Where no one can see
And they're chainin' up people
And they're bringin' em to me
Askin' me,
"Kill them NOW, or LATER?"
Askin' me!
"Kill them NOW, or LATER?"

Noon by the clock
And so still at the dock
You can hear a foghorn miles away
And in that quiet of death
I'll say, "Right now.
Right now!...

Scratching his head, the captain continues:"It might be true. What about the chopper? You´re not allowed swinging that one around."

"It was one of those pat irons that you use for minute steaks. It had been thrown on a shelf, so I put it in the right drawer. Maybe I was waggling it in the air like a conductor before putting it down."

"You seem to always have an answer, girl. Unfortunately the two other remarks are worse. You´ve been accused, by three persons, to have tried to persuade them to smoke hashish in the cabin. What´s your answer to that?"

"That´s a lie. They don´t like me. They want me out of the cabin. They´re the ones smoking hashish. I don´t even smoke tobacco."

"You just gave me the standard answer. I have heard that reply at least fifty times in this room but here only evidence counts."

"They can´t have any evidence."

"Yes, they can. That´s the reason why I myself is signing this third remark about you. During a search of the shower room made a moment ago a hookah was found hidden under your basin."

Jenny starts to cry heavily:"I'm innocent."

"Yes, that´s quite possible. The girls down there are not easy to handle. I must follow the rules. If we had already been in English waters, I would have been forced to call for the police. And if I don´t follow the rules, I´ll have to go back to sailing ships from Stockholm to Åland."

Talking, he starts scrolling through a bundle of papers. "Here I see that you came onboard at the request of the shipping company in New York and that you´re a trainee. Why on earth are you then staying at the lowermost deck with the cleaning women?"

"I´m sorry, Captain, but what´s a trainee?"

"Don't you know that? Strange. Trainees are practicing in a special program for future supervisors and bosses. We have a lot of Swedish and American trainees onboard. They stay on the deck above yours. Erik here started as a trainee. We never put Westerners on the lowest ranked employments. Their union agreements are too expensive for that. Somebody onboard has coded your employment papers in the wrong way."

"Does that mean that I should be staying on the deck above the present one?"

"Exactly, you can move upstairs on the spot, if you want to. That does not change anything in this issue. You´ll have to disembark in Southampton. Wait a moment… I can see in the documents that we´ve promised to get you another job on a different ship so that you can go on to Singapore. Please, organize that, Erik. And give Jenny a good recommendation letter, because there´s something fishy about this whole story. And make sure that it will all be done correctly."

"Oh yes, Captain!"

"And Jenny, please forgive me. I think you´re a nice and smart girl. Of the kind I´d like to have onboard as supervisors. I must however prioritize peace onboard instead of justice. I´ll take care of that gang down there as soon as I find the time."

After the meeting with the captain, Jenny experiences a complete revulsion towards continuing at sea, so she decides to drop out of it. She could travel to faraway places later on in life. Now the most essential thing for her is to go to Dalarna. To see by herself the area that Granddad Wally had been so fond of. It is not important to her that the Vasaloppet is still several months away; it goes off in March every year. As her family is now dead, she has no longer any dates or times to watch out for.

In order to reach Sweden and Mora, Jenny must first get from the harbour of Southampton to the one in Felixstowe. From there she can go by a Tor Line ferry to Gothenburg in Sweden. That trip only takes 24 hours. And from Gothenburg she can continue hitchhiking towards the north. She could be in Swedish Mora within a few days.

Jenny leaves the ship as soon as it has anchored without saying good-bye to anybody,. The October weather is grim, and a strong wind is coming in from the sea towards the harbour. Jenny has fortunately dressed sensibly in order not to be cold during hitchhiking.

Between the ship´s berth and the port gates the distance is more than one kilometre. And it is only over there that you could find cars with drivers accepting hitchhikers. Jenny puts the duffel bag down onto the quay and starts thinking. Taking command over your own life must certainly include being allowed to receive help. If people want to help her, she should not be stupid enough to decline that help. You should not, under any circumstances, be like Britchen Bauer who is just walking around taking things for granted without even asking. Jenny is fully aware of the fact that lots of people would love to help her. Maybe because lots of them consider her so beautiful and sweet. That is a lousy fact but it is true. Beautiful women get help, whilst ugly women go to Heaven.

Jenny is not in any hurry, so she decides to wait for help. And after only a few minutes help comes. It comes from above.

She hears a dark, manly, voice talking to her:"Where are you heading, Jenny? Wait for me. I have some good news for you."

Jenny looks up. From the deck, right above her, where the valves are a little bigger than on the lowermost deck, a head is sticking out. It is the beardy guy. His name is Erik, she remembers. "Wait, I´m coming out to you."

Within a few minutes Erik comes hurrying from the gangway. A duffle bag is swinging in his hand.

"This is the situation. The captain has thrown that report into the waste paper basket. He understood that it was all a setup from the other girls. You can't however stay onboard, because then the girls would go to the union, and then we would be facing a big quarrel. But we've arranged another job for you. With a ship transporting cars down to Singapore. The only problem is that the ship in question will be leaving from Bremerhafen in Germany within a few days. You'll have to take the ferry to Bremerhafen and that ferry leaves from Felixstowe north of London. And that is far from here."

"But…" says Jenny.

"Now listen. Do you see that small beautiful car over there on the quay? It belongs to our ship. We use it to drive important passengers to the ship. Since we placed you on the wrong job and therefore on the wrong deck of the ship, captain thinks that I should drive you to Felixstowe, so that you don't have to hitchhike."

"But… it's a Rolls Royce. Do you mean that I could go in that one?"

A short while later they are on the road. The Rolls is cosy with fittings of wood veneer, leather and velvet. Most beautiful of all is the rear seat but Jenny prefers sitting in front so that they can talk.

"Now I'm going to tell you something nice. The ship you'll be working on belongs to the Wallenius shipping company. It is shipping cars to Singapore and Australia."

"Oh, I would really like to visit Australia. My granddad used to go there."

"The ship´s name is Mac the Knife."

"But Mac the Knife is the other main character in the Threepenny Opera…"

"Yes, the Wallenius Company baptizes all their ships with names from different operas. Aniara, Isolde, Bohème and so on."

"Mackie also has a song of his own, the Cannon Song. It´s very good but I don´t know it – yet."

The conversation comes to a halt. Jenny is thinking of something the Philippine woman said: in order to survive onboard you have to be a couple, that is to have a boyfriend. I suppose that is applicable for your entire life, thinks Jenny. She glances at Erik. If she had a boyfriend, he would probably be like Erik – good-looking in a manly way, strong, kind and full of action. Imagine, that man sitting here is driving me across England without expecting anything in return from me. It would be wonderful to have a man like that! "Do you have any girlfriend?" she gently asks. "Somebody who is waiting for you ashore."

"Oh no, certainly not", he answers with a heartfelt laughter. "I´m a true thoroughbred stallion. As gay as any man could be. I´ve no girlfriend but I´ve a boy-friend. He is the ship´s second officer."

Towards the evening they drive down to the Felix-stowe port, stopping outside the ferry line's ticket of-fices.

"Now you´ll get a good treatment. You´re after all ar-riving in a Rolls Royce. Good bye, Jenny. We might be seeing each other again."

"Good bye and thank you. Say hello to the captain and forward my thanks to him."

When the car has disappeared, Jenny turns her face upwards to look at the black rain clouds in the sky. Some rain water is running down her face. She whis-pers:"God, if you exist then I thanks you for your help. Now I´ll try to do everything alone and in my own way. So Singapore is not for now."

Jenny buys a one-way ticket to Gothenburg.

Immediately she is onboard the ferry, Jenny is forced to rush to the toilet. The cubicle is very tiny, so she puts her duffel bag in the washroom outside, where all the basins are. She will just have a quick pee. Nothing could happen to the bag in the few seconds that will take, could it? But when she comes out of the cubicle the unbelievable has happened. The duffel bag is gone. Jenny gets so miserable. Apart from all her clothes, the bag also contained both her American and her Swedish passports. Thank God, that she had put the money in her waist bag. At least she still has her money.

I hope there is a good and cheap shop in Mora, where I at least can buy some new underwear, Jenny thinks. This has anyhow not been a good start. How could she have been so naive and stupid? She is almost feeling sick by all the mood changes she is experiencing. One minute she is enormously happy about going in a Rolls Royce. Next minute she is depressed for having lost her passports. One minute she thinks she is Pirate Jenny, loving violence. Next minute she is poor orphaned Jenny seeking her roots in Swedish Mora. Can you really be that unstable without being mentally ill? But then she remembers that her psychologist had explained that the human soul processes a loss in very many different ways. Maybe that is what is happening to her now?

CHAPTER 6

Gothenburg – Mariestad, Sweden – 13 October 1973

Fatigued and crestfallen Jenny is standing on the quay in Gothenburg watching the trucks leave the ferry. She is comfortably dressed in a green hunting outfit and has tied a red scarf around her neck. Her boots are heavy. The copper-red hair, arranged in a pony tail, is covered by a cap. How lucky she is, having changed into those clothes already onboard the ship in Southampton. If she had not done that, also these clothes would have been stolen by now! In one hand she is holding a sign, on which she has written "Dalarna". In spite of the thick and warm clothes it is obvious that Jenny is very pretty. Therefore lots of truck drivers stop in front of her offering her a hike to Dalarna or any other place she prefers. With such a companion in the truck, they would not be in any hurry to reach their destinations. There is almost a traffic jam around Jenny, who is feeling extremely embarrassed by this commotion.

Suddenly a very loud and continuous honking is heard from the back of the truck queue. The noise does not stop until the trucks, having stopped in front of Jenny, are driving off leaving her behind. A very big truck drives up to Jenny. An elderly man jumps onto the ground and walks up to her. Oh Dear, he really looks like the pub owner of Night Owl back home. With a belly as big as the pub owner's and of the same small height. Oh, what chalk-white hair he has. It goes extremely well with his bright blue eyes. He really looks pleasant and nice. Jenny suddenly feels ashamed. It is probably rather rude to stare in that way at another person. She smiles apologetically when the man stops in front of her.

"Hello, my friend", says he, having discreetly spat out the snuff. "Be careful with those truck drivers! A young girl like you could easily find herself in trouble. Do you want a lift? I see that you're are on your way to Dalarna."

"Hi to you too", answers Jenny, finding the old man sympathetic. "But you're also a driver. How do I know that you're not as dangerous as them?"

"Oh, there I got the answer my question deserves! But you're right. Don't go with me either, until you're sure about me and who I am but we can solve that in an instant. You just wait a moment. By the way, my name is actually Peter, Peter Pettersson. My wife and I live on a small farm just outside Mariestad. All the drivers here know me, because I'm also active in the union. That's why they left. They recognized my car horn. I have been honking at them so many times before."

Peter climbs into the driver seat and starts the com-radio. Jenny can hear him calling his truck company on the radio. Then he asks her to listen extra carefully, when he tells the girl at the switch board his ID-number and his address and also what Jenny looks like. "We're on our way to Dalarna but it'll soon be dark.

Therefore I think we had better let the girl stay the night at my and my wife´s house in Mariestad. Could you please call my wife and alert her about that. That way, the young girl can also have a nice dinner. My wife loves having guests."

As soon as the operator has noted all this down, Peter switches off the radio, jumps back onto the ground and says:"Agreed? Do you feel safe now?"

"Yes", answers Jenny. "But you still don´t know who I am. Isn´t that true?"

"Yes, you´re right about that. OK then. You´ve been abroad. What´s your name?"

But suddenly Jenny once more is feeling uncertain about Peter. And she must be in charge of her own destiny. Must not let anyone else take the command! He seems so nice but she will only give him her first name now. The surname will have to wait.

"OK, Jenny – jump into the truck. Let´s continue home to my wife. Don´t you have any luggage?"

"No, unfortunately not. My duffel bag was stolen on-board the ship. I can´t understand how people can be that mean. I´ve informed the receptionist onboard and they´ll look for it or at least keep an eye open. I can manage in the meantime. I guess I´ll have to buy some clothes once I´ve arrived."

Peter is for a while concentrating on steering the big truck through heavy evening traffic, out of Gothenburg and onto E20 leading to Mariestad, but then he turns to Jenny and kindly asks her: "Can you tell me a little about yourself, Jenny? It can´t be helped but I´m somewhat curious. Why is a young girl like you standing hitchhiking in the port of Gothenburg? Do you work at sea?"

"Could we talk about that later, Peter? I´m rather down right now and almost crying because of my stolen things. But… I come from the surroundings of Mora."

"Oh, little one, don´t worry. I´ll not pester you with questions, but remember that if you want to tell me more, I´d be happy to listen. And don´t forget that my wife, Anna, is a very kind person. She has comforted many lost souls during her life."

It is pitch-dark outside when Peter turns into a gravelled courtyard in front of a white house. As soon as he has turned off the motor, a short white-haired woman walks up to the truck to welcome Jenny.

"Welcome, dear", she says with a smile. "My name is Anna. I´m so happy that you´ve accepted to stay the night with us. We get guests so seldom – and almost never youths. I hope you´re hungry because I´ve prepared a lot of food."

Anna shows Jenny the room where she will be staying for the night. It is a small chamber that has been beautifully furnished. A lovely painted basin with its appurtenant pot sits on a small sideboard. A blue-white bedspread covers the wide bed. Curtains in matching colours are covering the small windows. Jenny is convinced that she will sleep very well there.

Outside the small chamber, a white balcony is stretching along the whole facade. A small door with paned windows leads to it. Anna points at the door, saying:"Promise that you´ll step out onto the balcony tomorrow morning. The view from it is fantastic. You´ll see a large portion of Lake Vänern from it. Alas, it´s dark now so test it in the morning instead."

"Thank you but no thank you", says Jenny. "I react so strangely on balconies. As soon as I try to walk onto one of them I feel so scared. It is as if a cold icy wind is lying in wait for me. It wants to sweep me over the rail. So I have come to realize that balconies are not for me. Unfortunately! I´ll have to be content with the view I can see from within the room."

After the abundant and very delicious dinner the three of them spend some time in the snug living-room. Both Peter and Anna have a lot of very funny and thrilling experiences to tell Jenny about. After a while Jenny can feel how her eyes are involuntarily closing.

"I´m so sorry, but I´m so tired. Would you be disappointed if I go to bed already?" asks Jenny.

"Oh, dear child, how thoughtless of us keeping you awake at this hour. I can see that you´re very tired. Go to bed at once, my love. Sleep well! And I promise you a nice breakfast."

Jenny gives Peter and Anna a good-night hug, enters the chamber and crawls down under the lovely duvet. Within five minutes she is fast asleep. Completely without nightmares or voices.

CHAPTER 7

Mariestad – Evertsberg, Sweden - 14 October 1973

Early in the morning, Anna serves a wonderful break-fast, which is a completely new experience for Jenny: pancakes with cloudberry jam. She eats so many that her belly afterwards is protruding. Then Anna hands out two lunch boxes with beef stew and a bundle of ready-made sandwiches.

"I think that you now have enough to get you through the day." She smiles contentedly. "And Peter, make sure you eat the stew together, before parting. You know how to keep it warm in the truck. And you can give Jenny the sandwiches to eat during her trekking."

Satisfied and happy, Jenny hugs Anna. What a wonderful woman. She feels almost reluctant to part from her. She reminds Jenny so much of Sonja back there in America.

Anna puts a slip of paper with a telephone number on it into Jenny's hand. "Here's our telephone number. It could be useful in case you're in trouble and need help. Call us and we'll come with the car as soon as we can. I understand that you're not feeling well. That something very horrible has happened to you, but that you're not yet ready to talk about it. I want you to know that I'm willing to listen to you. And that I'd so much like to help you."

After a few more hugs, Peter and Jenny climb into the truck and leave. The morning is chilly and Jenny is happy to have her warmest clothes on.

A couple of hours later, Peter drives into the small village of Evertsberg and stops on a parking lot. He points at a wide trench beyond the parking lot. ”You can see the trail of the Vasaloppet over there, but now we'll eat some meat stew so that you're warm and satisfied, when you leave. By the way, are you sure that I shouldn't drive you all the way?”

”Yes, dear Peter. What I have to do means so incredibly much to me. And it's so important that I do it on my own. Don't worry, I bring both a map and a compass!”

Jenny has decided to walk in the Vasaloppet trail from Evertsberg all the way to Mora. During that walk she will think intensively of her father and brother. Maybe even speak to them in a loud voice, saying good-bye to them. Here in the Vasaloppet trail she might be able to concentrate on that task better than she had been able to do on the ship. Now she will remember happy moments but not be afraid of also remembering the sad ones. She will try to find inner peace. Maybe she might, one day, regain harmony, so that life can go on?

CHAPTER 8

The Vasaloppet trail, Mora, Sweden – 14 October 1973

With a sense of melancholy, Jenny waves farewell to Peter, as he is driving out of the parking lot. Oh, she really likes him and his wife Anna so much!

But something troubles her. Despite the fact that she trusts Peter and Anna, she senses a quick flicker passing through her body, like a warning. Had it not, after all, been Peter who had advised her to start her hiking here, very far away from honour and probity in a country without policemen in the countryside? But Peter had, after all, given her alternative starting points. He had however pressed a lot for his own proposal. Jenny is moving uncomfortably. She really has to stop being so suspicious. There are actually good people too – not only mean ones like the girls on the ship. She finds it strange that she has become such a negative person mentally. That she sometimes is feeling that certain persons ought to die. That they have no raison d'être. She never used to be like that – before the death of Dad and Anton. But… maybe it is because she finds it so unfair that they, being such nice people, had to die. While other nasty individuals were allowed to stay alive.

Jenny shakes off her concerns. No, now she had better get going. She still has many kilometres to walk. And she is sure she will manage. In Minnesota, Jenny was known as a real nature girl. She has climbed mountains, walked for many miles in rugged terrain and lots of other similar things. So this could not be any worse than what she has been doing earlier in her life.

Jenny jumps down from the high road edge onto the Vasaloppet trail. It is dangerously slippery. As soon as she has gotten used to the slipperiness, she increases her speed. Sometimes the trail is so muddy that she instead chooses to walk at the side of it, but there it is so difficult to make your way. The spruce forest is both high and dense. The wide Vasaloppet trail is on both sides trapped by forest. It looks a bit strange. Like a scar in nature.

After an hour of arduous trekking Jenny is already feeling hungry again. She sits down on a tree stump and devours one of Anna´s sumptuous sandwiches. Liver pâté with pickled cucumber. Oh, it is heavenly!

Life suddenly feels easier again. She will soon get to see the area that her granddad and dad have been talking so much about. Jenny looks at the sky. She has a feeling that dad and Anton and also granddad Wally are sitting up there waving at her. She waves back and shouts at the top of her voice:"Dad, I´m going to participate in Vasaloppet in March, and I´ll do that in your place!"

Jenny continues walking after the food break but the trail suddenly becomes awfully muddy. Why did not Peter tell her about that? It is now quite impossible for her to find her way. At this time of year it becomes dark very early so she will have to hurry up. Is she really on the right track? Maybe she has come too far away from the trail, the trail she ought to follow? The forest is now so dense around her that she is no longer sure from which direction she has come. Now Jenny is in command of her own life but ever since she decided to take command herself, onboard the American cruising ship, small mistakes have occurred in an ever increasingly mean environment. Things that have made everything harder and harder for her. Now she is lost in an unknown, cold and muddy Swedish forest. Could life become harder than that? She misses her American Mora. She will go straight back home! This adventure must come to its end!

But a bit further on, Jenny can suddenly see lights shining through the windows of a small cottage. How good! She can walk up to it and ask in which direction she can find the trail. She is feeling her way through the thicket, approaching the cottage. And then she hears hens cackling wildly. What is happening? The door is abruptly opened and an angry woman´s voice yells: "Now you bugger of a fox! Now you´ll not have free hens any longer! You´re going to die!" A burst of rifle fire comes from the vestibule. Jenny throws herself down onto the ground. She can feel a considerable sting in her left arm. Has she been hit?

Jenny is completely panic-stricken. Under no circumstances she dares approach the cottage – not even to ask for directions. The woman´s voice had sounded absolutely mad. No, this is not good, thinks Jenny. I have to get away from here. If I´m walking in the wrong direction now, I could change it tomorrow during daylight.

Having calmed down, Jenny is soon on her feet again. She continues walking for about an hour on the path she had earlier chosen. When she notices how tired she is, she sits down beneath a spruce at the edge of a long ravine to rest for a while,. The wounds on her left arm do not appear serious. For safety´s sake, she cleans them with some water out of the flask she carries in her waist bag. The woman seems to have been using a shotgun.

Jenny has by now once more found the Vasaloppet trail and decides to stick to it. She keeps walking for a couple of kilometres. She suddenly realizes how amateurishly she has been behaving. She had forgotten that she had a compass in her waist bag. But now the waist bag is gone. She had opened it in search of cotton, after she had been hit. She must have forgotten to put it back on. Jenny quickly searches her pockets in order to see what she still has left. First her duffel bag was stolen on the ferry to Gothenburg and on top of that she has now lost her waist bag. In her pockets she can now only find a bundle of Swedish banknotes, some coins and a slip of paper on which part of a telephone number is written.

Jenny´s nerves are completely on edge. She is weeping, her nose is running and she is feeling very lonely but then, being the winner she is, she puts on a stiff upper lip,. She believes that she, by now, must have had her part of misery. She is at the bottom. So from here on she should only get positive experiences.

At that very moment she hears a suppressed roar from the forest line in front of her. The small hairs on her arms rise. She recognizes that sound so well from Minnesota. It is a bear! An enraged bear, judging from the sound of it. She immediately forgets everything she has learnt about how to act if she met furious bears. Should you stand still or should you run? She cannot remember anything at all. She sees a high boulder diagonally behind her. She throws herself towards it to get some protection. Falling, her head hits hard on a sharp stone and everything is darkness.

CHAPTER 9

Mora, Sweden - 14 October 1973

Mora's youngest police assistant, Sven Martinsson, recently graduated from the Police Academy, is anxiously sauntering about in the living-room of his small studio, located in the outskirts of Mora. Darkness is taking over outside. He has been feeling nervous the whole afternoon. Actually ever since lunch time, when the hunting team had shot the bear. He is quite sure that the rest of the team were all behind him, when he fired. There was absolutely nobody in the shot line. But still… He believes that he, in the corner of the eye, has glimpsed something red around five metres to the right of the furious bear. A horrible thought strikes him. Could another human being have been up there? What if he had accidentally shot someone?

Sven is feeling that he has to do something immediately. If he waits until morning, the person, who could have been shot, might die? Sven sits down at the telephone table, calls Criminal Inspector Lars Hellström, who is on call service today, and tells him what might have happened. At the same time, he however says that he is not completely sure. Hellström agrees. They have to leave immediately for the hunting ground and search it thoroughly.

Within a few minutes, Hellström stops at the parking lot outside the street door to Sven's apartment, and honks. He has been very meticulous and chosen the station's biggest car. He has also brought some extra men as reinforcement. The car is equipped with a big light bar on the roof and there are some extra strong headlamps in the car.

With the accelerator pressed to the bottom, Hellström drives along the winding roads up to the hunting spot. Having arrived, the men put on their headlamps, set the compass and start trekking through the now pitch-dark forest.

Suddenly Sven shouts:"There's the boulder where I was standing when I shot the bear. Search around that big boulder, a little more to the right! The bear appeared exactly there."

The men scatter around the bolder. They search among the thickets in the light of their headlamps.

Hellström suddenly cries:"There's somebody here. A woman. I can't see if she's alive. Please help me with the light!"

The men gather around the person Hellström has been pointing at – a young woman with a red scarf, lying unconscious on the ground. Sven leans forward to check her pulse. "She's alive, but the pulse is very slow. I think she's in a state of hypothermia. She must immediately be taken to the hospital."

Hellström has been foreseeing, also bringing a stretcher in his big car. The stretcher is rapidly placed beside the girl. Being extremely cautious, the men transfer the girl to the stretcher; place it in the car and at high speed drive to the hospital. At their arrival, the hospital Emergency Room team takes over.

CHAPTER 10

Mora, Sweden - 15 October 1973

Sven is sitting on a chair beside the still unconscious girl. He is very tired but also feeling somewhat ridiculous. Arriving at the hospital a little earlier he had met the physician, Doctor Larsson. Sven had been full of self reproaches. He had exclaimed:"How serious are her shot wounds? I didn´t understand that she was there, quite close to the bear. Is she alive? I´m feeling horrible knowing that I´ve shot a person!"

Doctor Larsson had astonished looked at him and then asked:"Do you usually shoot bears with a shotgun?"

Sven had been staring at the doctor for a long while until it suddenly dawned on him. "Do you mean that the shot wounds come from a shotgun? I´m so relieved. Then I wasn´t the one shooting her. I´ve not been able to sleep a wink during the night because of the worry."

The girl has an ugly wound at the temple. All the medical examinations however show that she has not got any brain damage. But probably a very bad brain concussion, which is probably the cause of her being still unconscious. Her body temperature is now normal once again. Otherwise she only has some minor injuries on her left arm, caused by the shot, and a sprained ankle. "And her hair colour is authentic", adds doctor Larsson.

Sven is looking at the young girl, wondering who she could be. They have only found some money and a torn piece of paper in her pockets. Otherwise nothing that could tell them who she is. He does not recognize her either, even though he knows most of the young people in the area. Poor girl. How old could she be? He estimates her age to between 18 and 24 years. After all, there must be someone missing her! He hopes that she will soon wake up and tell her name as her family ought to be very worried.

The following morning Sven notices that the girl is regaining consciousness. The eye lids are fluttering and she murmurs something. To hear better, Sven bends forward. He hears that she is saying one time after the other "Mor". Oh, poor little one, she is apparently missing her mother. But how could they get in touch with her, not knowing who the girl is?

Sven goes into the corridor and asks for a telephone. He calls the police station and enquires whether there have been any calls about missing persons. No such calls have been received. He tells this to Doctor Larsson, who asks Sven to stay with the girl and try to calm her down. It is important for her recovery that she does not get too agitated.

The girl now is in and out of consciousness. Each time she awakens, she seems a little more alert. She touches her forehead a lot. The ER nurse, called Gertrud, gives the girl an intravenous painkiller to help her with the headache. Criminal Inspector Hellström pays a quick visit. Having received a report of the progress, he tells Sven to stay with the girl for as long as the doctor thinks necessary. "Health care faces a bigger lack of personnel than the police", says Hellström. "We have to help them." Then he leaves.

Sven is terribly hungry and takes a lunch break. As he returns to the girl's room, he immediately notices that the girl seems to be in a much better state. The eyes are clear and alert. And nurse Gertrud has brushed the girl's hair. She definitely looks much healthier but she does not seem to be in a very good mood. "Is it really necessary for so many persons to disturb me? I've a headache and want to sleep", she mutters.

"Hi", says Sven approaching the bed. "My name is Sven and I'm a police assistant here in Mora. You had an accident yesterday and you're now at Mora Hospital. What's your name?"

"I don't know. I've already told the criminal inspector, who was here a moment ago, asking the same question." Her gaze becomes introvert – as if searching for an answer within herself – and she continues, at first tentatively but then getting increasingly alarmed:"I, I... I actually don't remember. I don't know. Oh, how terrible, I don't know my own name!"

"Calm down and don't be afraid. It will return. You have, after all, had a bad brain concussion and been unconscious since yesterday. It's not that strange that you can´t remember right now, but earlier you called for your mother. Can you tell us anything about her?"

"No, not my mother, Mum. I might have said 'Mora, Mora'"

"What do you mean by that?"

"I was wondering why Mora is so important to me. There´s something I have to do here, but I can´t remember what that is. But I guess I´m from Mora. Don´t you think so too? The nurse showed me an old tourist pamphlet and it looked so familiar with Vasaloppet and all that. Has anyone asked for me?"

"Your memory will most certainly return sooner or later", comforts Sven. "But now we´ve to make some plans. The police have checked. There have been no calls about missing girls here in Dalarna. If we don´t have any news within the next few days we might have to widen that check to include the whole of Sweden. Doctor Larsson has asked me to spend a lot of time here with you. It´s important we talk with each other as much as we possibly can. That way we might find clues as to who you are. You must however tell me if you have to rest, because your headache will probably continue for a while. Does that seem OK, so far?"

"Oh yes, and I must repeat what I said already at the start. Please, leave now so that I can get some rest. I´ve a headache. And you´ll have to find out who I am. After all, you´re the police aspiring officer and you should know how to do that".

"I'm a police assistant. I've passed the Police Academy."

"Oh, I'm sorry, assistant!"

"No problem. We'll soon find out who you are. But another question – I must be able to call you something. I suggest you find a temporary name for yourself."

"No, I've no idea at all", answers the girl. "What do you usually call girls, whose names you don't know?"

"Jane Doe", answers Sven seriously. "That name is used in American thrillers but also in real life, when things like this happen. Could I call you Jane?"

"Yes, of course, it sounds pretty nice. So from here on my name is Jane. But now I want to sleep. Good night, Assistant Sven."

"A pretty but rather nasty girl", says nurse Gertrud, who appears when Sven comes out into the corridor. "She must be from Stockholm. I gave her a tourist pamphlet, and she was rude to me."

"That could be a consequence of her memory loss", answers Sven. "Or she might not have had a nice mother at home, teaching her how to behave. Bad behaviour can be inherited just like mental illness."

"Yes, and you Sven have really inherited a good behaviour from your mother Ida", laughs Gertrud. Sven blushes as the nurse continues:"I, being a simple girl, would really like to have a mother-in-law like Ida…

Stupid, can´t you hear that I'm proposing to you. I´ll marry you, if I also get your mother − as the icing on the cake. She could teach me to bake buns and how to impress men."

While Gertrud keeps talking about their, in her mind quite possible, marriage, Sven escapes into the security of the lift and presses the exit button.

He is going home to his mum, Ida, to have supper. They have a regular supper meeting twice a week. Some weeks that is the only home-cooked meal Sven has.

Two days later there is a meeting between doctor Larsson, criminal inspector Hellström, Sven and Jane. The latter has become much nicer since her headache disappeared and she had had a long rest. They decide to turn to the newspapers for help. They´ll publish a photo of Jane and at the same time they´ll ask the readers to contact the police in Mora, should they recognize her. That way they might find someone knowing her.

Doctor Larsson says that it is now time for Jane to leave the hospital. She must start leading a more normal life. He wants to be close to her so that he can see how she reacts on different things. Therefore he wants Jane to stay for a few days with him and his wife at their home.

CHAPTER 11

Mora, Sweden – 26 October 1973

Four days have now passed since the photo of Jane was published in all the Swedish daily newspapers. They are almost giving up hope as nobody has called so far. Poor Jane, there must after all be somebody missing her!

Sven is sitting at his table at the police station. He has a couple of hours of administrative work to attend to. The telephone operator calls. A male voice says:"Hi, my name is Peter and I´m a truck driver. I might have something to tell you about that poor girl. She hitchhiked with me about 12 days ago. I have now been on the road for some days. When I returned home, I read all the newspapers that are piling up when I´m out driving. I then saw the photo and that is why I´m calling now."

"Wonderful. I´m so happy that you´re calling... Are you far away from Mora or is it possible for you to come here soon? I think we had better meet, eye to an eye, and that you explain the rest then."

"No, I´m actually parked right now just beyond Mora´s town limit. When I saw the story in the newspapers I told my dear wife that I at once had to go up to Mora. She completely agreed. I can be at the police station within a quarter of an hour. I know where it is."

"Excellent! Then come at once so that we can have lunch together and get to know each other!"

Within the promised fifteen minutes an elderly man stands in the door to Sven´s room. He looks very sympathetic and Sven immediately likes Peter´s firm handshake and honest eyes.

Having greeted each other they go down to the restaurant at the corner and order today´s menu. When they were both satisfied, Sven asks Peter to tell him how he knows Jane. Sven also wants answers to questions like how Jane was dressed, what she looked like and how she talked. All the answers he gets verify that Peter has actually met Jane.

"Sven, listen. You´re calling her Jane all the time. Her real name is actually Jenny and she comes from this neighbourhood – from the surroundings of Mora. She has told me that herself. Maybe I should start at the beginning. I met Jenny at the Tor Line Terminal in Gothenburg. She was standing there and a lot of truck drivers tried to persuade her to go with them. She was holding a notice board on which she had written "Dalarna". I pushed my way up to her and explained that it could be dangerous to hitchhike with just anybody. I actually suggested that I myself should drive her. To reassure her, in her presence, I contacted our company. I gave them details about myself and told them that I would take a young girl – I also described her – in my truck up north to Dalarna. I, furthermore, told them that we - because it would soon be dark – were going to spend the night at my and my wife´s house. All this was noted at my company. And then, when she jumped into the truck, I asked her if she didn´t have any luggage. She answered that it had been stolen onboard the Tor Line ferry. Well, and then we went to my home in Mariestad. We had a lovely dinner and spent the night. The following morning we continued to Dalarna. There she got off the truck in Evertsberg. That´s more or less the whole story.”

”Peter, thanks a lot for telling this. How was Jane´s – or Jenny´s – mood? Was she being unpleasant?”

”No, not unpleasant. She was very polite, but to tell the truth, she seemed very sad. When I asked her to tell me a little about herself, she said she would rather not. She told me she was not feeling very well. I got the impression that she had been going through some-thing horrible. Also my wife thought that Jenny seemed sad. Almost apathetic.”

”Yeah, it seems that you and I are talking about the same person. Are you ready to meet her? By the way, do you carry any photo of your wife?”

”Of course I´m ready. And sure enough, I have a photo of Anna but she has actually accompanied me on this trip to Mora. She wanted that herself. And she´s wait-ing for us in the truck.”

Having fetched Anna at the truck, Sven explains his plans. They walk over to Doctor Larsson´s house, situ-ated close to the hospital. The big red wooden villa is surrounded by a garden which, in spite of it now being the end of October, is still very beautiful. Sven presses the door-bell and then takes a step aside. He wants to see Jenny´s reaction when she, unprepared, meets Pe-ter and Anna.

During the very first moment Jenny only looks uncertain, but then her face is gradually changing expression. Her face is lighting up and the eyes start to shine with joy. "Oh", she exclaims, "I'm certain that I know both of you! And I know that I like you both very much and that you've been extremely kind to me. I'm sorry but I can't remember your names, so please tell me."

Anna folds the girl in her arms, hugging her hard. "Poor little girl, you must have had a really rough time. My name is Anna. My husband is called Peter. You've actually stayed overnight at our house. And you just love pancakes with cloudberry jam. I can tell you that, if by any chance you can't remember it by yourself."

Also Peter hugs Jenny, caressing her hair. "Sweet little girl, what do you want us to call you? Jenny or Jane? When we met, you told me that your name was Jenny."

"I actually don't know. The name Jenny is somehow familiar. It could be my name but it could also be the name of one of my friends. But if I, without memory loss, have introduced myself as Jenny, I think we should choose that."

CHAPTER 12

Mora, Minnesota, USA – 17 November 1973

Everyone back in Mora, Minnesota, is worried about not hearing anything from Jenny. Only a postcard from Southampton at the beginning of her absence. At first, they interpret this as a typical sign of teenage nonchalance, but when the Captain of *QE2* gets in touch informing them that Jenny never showed up at the ship bound for Singapore, Jenny's friends become very worried.

As a consequence, Mikael has contacted Jenny's father's lawyer, Nicklas Burger, to check if he has found out anything about Jenny's relatives, if any. Jenny's granddad Wally had used the same law firm. The owner at that time was George Burger, Nicklas ´father, and George was Wally's contact at the firm. In 1973, when granddad Wally died after the Vasaloppet race, George Burger however started having problems with senile dementia. So his son Nicklas took over the law firm, including George's account with Jenny's father Johan. "Young clients need young lawyers", George Burger used to say with a knowing smile.

Nowadays, the old lawyer at times appears rather normal, but he messes things up. You can no longer trust what he says. But he is still keeping his old office at the firm, he arrives every day in a cab and he believes that he is doing quite a good job.

"Dad, do you remember Johan Johnson, my client who was recently run over by a car?" asks Nicklas. Dad nods, where he is sitting cutting butterflies out of a folded paper in order to pass time. He has quite a heap of butterflies ready to use when he would be decorating the office for Christmas.

"Oh yes, I remember Wally´s son quite well", says he. "He killed his own wife. But I helped Wally clear him from the accusations in the first instance. And he ran away, hid and changed identity, when the prosecutor was going to appeal. Quite a nasty fellow, that Johan."

Nicklas cannot help laughing. "No, it didn´t happen quite that way. Wally was however your client for a long time, wasn´t he? Have you got any old documents left since that time?"

George nods. "In the cellar, a box in the space behind the boiler room. Look, this butterfly is beautiful, isn´t it?"

"Yes Dad, it´s really beautiful. But, wouldn´t it be more suitable to have elves for Christmas? Butterflies belong to summer."

"No, no. Do you think I´m senile? Butterflies belong to summer, as you say, but if there´s any time of the year when I´m longing for summer and butterflies it is, without doubt, around Christmas time. And I don´t even know if I´ll experience another summer. That´s the reason why I´ll continue with my butterflies!"

As he was listening to his dad's thoughts, Nicklas feels a stab of worry in his heart. "Yes, Dad, I think that's a perfectly good reason for your choice. I had never thought of it that way. Please, forgive me."

In the above mentioned box, Nicklas finally locates a dossier about Johan's father Wally's business with the law firm. Everything is in disorder. He also finds papers seeming rather irrelevant: about the Amish-people, about drugs and mental disorder. Also bank papers connected to a couple of major payments to an account in Switzerland. He puts those papers in a separate heap, which he leaves down in the archive. He takes the remaining documents upstairs for him to investigate.

Nicklas sits down in an easy chair in front of the electric fire and starts going through the documents taken from dad's old archive. He is browsing them in order to be able to arrange them in a sensible order. As he is looking at the documents he gets more and more confused. What is all this?

George suddenly stand at the door opening, together with the cab driver who usually drives him back and forth between the retirement accommodation and the office. "Good evening, I'm leaving now. What terrible reading you have on your lap – so much sorrow in that family. It is as if that family has been haunted. I have erased a lot in the documents. Wally wanted that done. The documents might end up in the wrong hands, maybe those of the police…"

"But Dad…"

"He also asked me to erase a lot in the documents regarding Johan´s trial. I thought you should know. So that nobody could find out the truth. When you´re as old as I, you can do whatever you want. No, now I have to rush back home for dinner. I have a new dinner partner. A lady who is only 70 years old, from the next corridor. And she´s sweet as a lily!"

Nicklas sighs heavily. When younger, Dad was a very conscientious person, who liked to erase things. This will most certainly be difficult!

After hours of work Nicklas has concluded the following:

Johan has a sister, who in her upper teens ran away from home in order to live among the Amish-people. Her name has been erased. She is actually Jenny´s aunt.

The mother of Johan and the run-away sister dies shortly after the sister´s disappearance. Everything regarding the death has been erased.

Johan and his father Wally blame the sister for the mother´s death. And they cut all connections with the sister. The father, Wally, sends her a big amount of money as an early inheritance.

Some years later Johan marries … The name has been so strongly erased that there is a hole in the paper. The two of them have a girl and a boy.

Someone, whose name has been erased, gets mixed up with bad friends. Starts using narcotics. Becomes temporarily mentally ill and, on two occasions, try to kill Johan's two children. It is unclear whether this 'somebody' is actually Johan or someone else.

Then Nicklas' father George has gone completely crazy with the eraser. You can only see a few words here and there… restraining orders regarding visitation rights… the court order has been changed… closed psychiatric care… special hospital for drug addicts in Switzerland… the children are never to know… tried to murder the children on two occasions… destroy the children's lives forever… the mother is dead… the family gets protected identity with new names… moved from Colorado to Mora, Minnesota…

Nicklas notices that his father George has carefully checked all the papers, erasing the old names of all people involved. The family has been given new identity with new names. So there is no way in which to find out the names that Johan, his children or his dad used to have before their name changes. Neither the name of Johan's sister – Jenny's unknown aunt – nor that of the children's dead mother is written down. The purpose has obviously been that neither Johan nor his family should be traceable. If Johan, as George is saying, has really killed his wife, then how could Johan still be allowed to take care of them? Has he really hid from the authorities with a new identity? That would mean that Johan is a criminal living under protected identity and a false name. Who is Johan, after all?

Nicklas is feeling completely confused by the facts he has found. Shakes his head, murmuring:"A catastrophe!" to himself, not once or twice but more likely one hundred times. He reads the facts many times. If this is known, his future as a lawyer will be finished. If he asks for document copies from court, they will laugh at him. After all, it is his own father, who has demanded that the documents be confidential. And if there is a place for that information to be stashed away, it certainly is at Nicklas´ office and not behind the boiler room of all places… Sensitive information put into that place, to which the caretaker and a lot of others have a key. It is too much! There will be headlines in the media. Who would trust the Burger Law Firm after that?

Nicklas continues reading and thinking well into the night. Then he falls asleep in his easy chair but continues thinking in his sleep. Here he has read about serious crimes, such as narcotics and attempted murders, about psychic illness and protected Identities. Information that might have shed light on Jenny´s disappearance has been erased. A young girl does not suddenly disappear without a reason. And why were Johan and Anton killed by the car on the pavement outside the tennis courts? Could Jenny have found out that her dad had killed her mum and that he after that had continued his life together with the children with a protected identity? An identity that Nicklas´ own father George has helped him get.

A maximum of five persons were given protected identity. Of those five, four are now dead. Wally, the mother, the father and the brother. Or did the mother die when she still used her old name? The fifth one, Jenny, seems to have disappeared. Maybe Jenny was the one behind the car killing? Maybe she had afterwards escaped abroad? No, in that case she would have needed an accomplice, driving the car.

What about the aunt? No, she disappeared many years before all this happened. She was probably not included in the protected identity. But we do not know her name, since we know neither her father's nor Jenny's father's earlier names.

How is Nicklas going to use this information and in which way could he continue the search for Jenny? He can hardly reveal that the family, during many years, had lived under protected identities with new names. That is confidential. And as a matter of fact, he does not even know their names before they were provided with new ones. He scratches his head while he is thinking. If he would talk with his old father, the crazy old man, it would only get worse. He will therefore, in a discreet way, have to contact one of his many friends within the police force.

He will, after all, also need help sending out an international enquiry. And that could be difficult, because if Jenny has a protected identity, he is not allowed to show the new name together with a photo in the ad. That would be a violation of confidentiality.

Nicklas wakes up in his easy chair as George returns to the company the following morning. George puts his head through the door to Nicklas´ room.

"Good morning. I can see that you´ve had a nice sleep. I forgot to tell you yesterday that I also have copies of the Johnson case, in which I haven´t erased anything. I always have, as an extra security."

"Wonderful, Dad! Give them to me!"

"Sorry, lad, I´ve mislaid them somewhere. You´ll get them when I find them."

CHAPTER 13

Erie, Pennsylvania, USA – 20 November 1973

Nicklas´ belief that Jenny´s aunt has not been covered by a new and protected identity is quite correct. Her name is Maja Hermansson and she lives, since many years, in Eire in Pennsylvania, together with her husband Yngve. Jenny does not even know that she has an aunt. Maja lost contact with her brother Johan and the rest of the family already in her late teens, when she ran away from home to stay with the Amish for some years. Johan blamed her for causing the death of their mother, Jenny´s grandmother, through her disappearance. Maja is one of the persons not knowing anything about her family´s new identities. Her relatives just disappeared from the surface of the Earth, and that is something that she still finds difficult to cope with.

The quiet atmosphere in Maja´s and Yngve´s kitchen is suddenly interrupted when Maja bangs her fist on the kitchen table, exclaiming:"No, I can´t take it anymore! I´m just thinking of them all the time. There has to be a change!"

Her husband Yngve, astonished, looks up from the newspaper. "What´s wrong with you? Whom are you constantly thinking of?"

"My brother, of course, and also his children if he has any – my nieces or nephews. I really must meet them soon. I haven´t seen my brother for more than 25 years. And if he has children, then I´ve never met them. He will soon be 45 years old. And I absolutely have to see him then. I so much want to hug him and ask him for forgiveness."

"But Honey", objects Yngve. "You know he doesn´t want to see you. That was said in such a definite way by both your father and your brother. As far as they are concerned, you don´t exist. They held you responsible when your mother died of a broken heart, because of your escape. And I think that they themselves were afraid that you in some way would harm them or any children your brother might get. You can be so aggressive. That might be the reason for their disappearance."

Tears are running down Maja´s cheeks. "I do think, however, that by now they´ve punished me enough. It was a typical teenage whim that made me run away."

Yngve understands how Maja must hurt. At the same time he, in a way, also understands Maja´s father and brother. "And, by the way", he continues,"your father was fair to you after all. You received rather much money over a couple of years. You can´t blame him for how you used that money."

"Yes, I know I acted stupidly with the money… But I want to make friends with them again. The years pass. And nobody knows for how long we´ll live."

Now Yngve feels really sorry for his weeping wife. "Do you have any suggestions on what we could do to get in contact with your family?"

"Yes, maybe… We can afford to hire a private detective, who could search for dad and the rest of the family, can´t we?

"Oh my darling! I did that already five years ago. I have been keeping it secret, because you were then still so bitter. I hired a private eye who searched for them all over the US, but there was alas not any trace at all of them. It was like they had been swallowed by Earth!"

"Oh, my God, do you mean they´re dead?"

"No, not at all! In such a case there would have been traces. No, I rather think that they´ve left the US. Do you remember telling me that your dad had an old friend in Australia? A very dear and close friend. They might all of them have gone to Australia… or to some other country."

Maja sighs disappointed. "Oh, I suppose that this means that I must wait. And keep hoping that they themselves want to contact me. No way! I´ll find them - even if they live in Australia."

CHAPTER 14

Minneapolis, Minnesota, USA – 3 December 1973

Looking thoughtful, lawyer Nicklas Burger puts down the telephone. He has just had a long telephone conversation with Jenny´s neighbour Mikael. Mikael´s wife Sonja was Jenny´s daytime caretaker for many years, having a very close relation with Jenny. Jenny´s own mother was already gone at that time, either in hospital or dead. They cannot remember. Jenny´s mother was not a person you spent time talking about.

Mikael has come up with a suggestion on how to continue the search for Jenny. It seems good. Nicklas lifts the receiver and makes a call to one of his contacts, a criminal investigator at the state police. That man has offered police resources as a help in the searches for Jenny, as soon as Nicklas has a concrete suggestion on how to do it. Now Nicklas feels that he might have such an idea.

After some small talk, Nicklas informs about the idea Mikael has come up with. ”We could investigate if Jenny has been employed by any other shipping company. The port authorities in the neighbourhood of Southampton and London should have notes in their ship scrolls about all ships having left the ports. Let us send a telex to all those companies. We could ask them to contact all ships having departed for example within 10 days after the day Jenny left the *QE2*. The captains should check that Jenny has not been among the crew being hired in the ports."

"That seems a good thing to do. The young girl could have gone anywhere. The fact that she earlier wanted to go to Singapore doesn't mean that she actually went there. Let's also ask the shipping companies to compile the answers and send them to us by telex. That way it'll be much easier for us. We can't be in direct contact with all the ships."

"But what will we do if all answers are negative", wonders Nicklas.

"Let's take one thing at a time, Nicklas. The police will keep you posted on the progress. We should also add a description of Jenny to the text. That she has long copper-red hair, green eyes and that she is tall and slender. And pretty."

"Excellent, I'll immediately call Mikael and Sonja and tell them what we intend to do. They're so worried, poor ones. According to them, the entire Mora community is engaged in Jenny's disappearance. Everybody wants to help one way or the other. The girl seems to be very popular. I myself immediately liked her, when we met at the office."

Sonja, being in their cosy country kitchen, is very happy that the state police have been involved in the case about Jenny. She usually lies awake at night thinking about the girl. She can feel that something has happened to her. Sonja has, after all, been taking care of Jenny and Anton, as if they had been her own kids, ever since the day Johan and his father Wally had moved to Mora. And now everybody is dead, except for Jenny. It is so terrible.

Suddenly a thought crosses her mind. ”But if we don´t find out anything from the shipping companies. What will we do in that case?”

”My darling.” Mikael lovingly caresses his wife´s cheek. ”Then we´ll find another way to search for her. And we´ll continue like that until we find Jenny... Dear Sonja, don’t give up. It is so important that we keep our spirits high.”

”I’ll try to be optimistic. I promise. By the way, I have heard that at Peggy´s house they´re also looking for different ways to search. It´s such a nice feeling that people are so engaged. I feel less lonely that way.”

As they are going to bed, Mikael says:”I also have another idea. To save time we could also contact all the ferries leaving England. Jenny has much money. And, on top of that she has also earned more on the ship. Imagine, she could actually have bought a ticket on a ferry? She might have gone as a passenger.”

”What a wonderful idea”, exclaims Sonja. ”But I know her economic mind, so I don´t think she would buy an expensive ticket for a long boat trip. No, I think she could have gone from England to some place in Europe. Couldn´t you call Nicklas Burger first thing in the morning? To tell him your thoughts”, she adds.

Having heard Mikael´s new suggestion, Nicklas once more calls his police contact. He asks him to point out in the telexes that the captains should also put up the information on all the crew pin-boards. A message saying that the girl could also have gone as a paying passenger.

Now there is nothing more they can do. It is only a matter of waiting for answers.

CHAPTER 15

Lightning Ridge, Australia – 17 December 1973

A letter from the USA arrives to the post office in Lightning Ridge, Australia. It is addressed to:

"The bar having most Scandinavians as guests"

Lightning Ridge

New South Wales

Australia

The bar owner, who knows Swedish, surprised reads the letter. Shakes his head but walks to the pin-board to nail it up.

Anders Torstensson and his son David have just had a hot cleaning bath outdoors in Bore Bath after a day with hard and dusty work in their mine on the opal fields. They enter the bar to eat a well-earned big steak to be had together with a couple of big beer mugs. They sit down and start with the beer. David, being somewhat restless, decides to play darts with some friends before it is time to eat. On his way to the dartboard, he passes the pin-board, stops and reads the letter. Thereafter he turns and quickly walks back to his father.

"Dad, I think there´s a letter for you on the pin-board. I was a little astonished when I read it. But I think it´s for you. Come and read it!"

Anders saunters over to the pin-board, holding his beer firmly in his left hand. Having read a few lines, he asks the bar owner if he could borrow the letter to read at his table. There he sits down again, takes a big gulp of beer and puts on his reading glasses.

"Hi to all you nice fortune hunters. I hope that you to-day have been lucky finding plenty of whatever you are looking for. Maybe you are right now in the pub having a large cool beer after today´s hard work!

I´m now going to tell you a true story that my brother and I were told in our childhood. It is about my father. In Australia he is known as Wally.

During his teens, Wally had a very good friend in Mora in Dalarna, Anders. Since both the boys were very adventurous, having finished school, they sailed for Australia. They wanted to pan for gold in Sofala River and search for opals on the opal fields at Lightning Ridge. It was a very happy time. They made many friends and they even got some gold and opals. From the start they had planned a sabbatical year. But time passed so quickly that they had been there for almost two years when Anders had a message telling him to return home as quickly as possible. His father had actually become very ill. At the moment of parting, Anders gave Wally the small purse in which they kept their joint treasures. He asked him to take good care of it. They would divide the treasure between them at their next meeting. Wally stayed for another couple of months but then also he returned back home to Dalarna.

Since I, unfortunately, lost contact with both my father and brother about 25 years ago, I do not know if Wally and Anders did ever meet again. I hope they did, because they were such good friends. Now I have to find my father and brother, so I wonder if any of you can help me locate them. Have you seen them, heard about them, know where they are, please send me a short letter. We have tried to search for them all over the US, where we have now been living for decades, but not been able to find them.

I keep my fingers crossed for you to succeed in all your endeavours to find gold and opals.

Friendly greetings,

Maja Hermansson

P o Box 23476

Erie, PA

USA

Anders looks up from the letter. Furtively he wipes away a couple of tears. Yes, this letter is really about him. He remembers the time he spent with Wally in Australia, as if it had occurred yesterday. They had had such a good time together, even though work was often very hard. And as a matter of fact, they at times, had been rather successful. What was concealed in the small purse Maja had mentioned was however far from a fortune. He sits for a long time, absorbed in memories from those days, wishing he were young again and able to relive everything Wally and he had been experiencing. Thinking about the snakes was however, not nice. Three of his friends had died from snake bites, down in the shaft. But on the other hand, he enjoys thinking of all the excitement they had felt the whole time. Would the next shovel reveal a black opal or would the next pan glitter with gold nuggets? They had indeed been living real bush-life, feeling like true adventurers. Yes, it had been a couple of wonderful years.

Wally and Anders had had a regular mail contact during the first years after Australia. Unfortunately that contact had thinned out as their lives put other demands than adventure on them. They had, however, after many trials, succeeded in seeing each other back home in Mora in 1945. At that time, they had both been married. Wally's and Inger's son and daughter had been 12 and 10 years old. And Anders' and Britt's son had been 13. They had spent a wonderful winter week together. But, alas, the possibility to repeat it had never arrived.

High hearty laughter is heard from the dartboard. Is it maybe David joking around with his opponents? He looks towards the corner where the dartboard is placed. He smiles seeing his son's sweaty but happy face. It is so wonderful that David nowadays can smile and laugh more frequently. Poor David has spent too many joyless and unhappy years.

Anders continues thinking of all that has happened. Everything has been horribly tragic. First of all, the fact that David´s wife Gunnel had had uterine cancer the year before David and she were getting married. The doctors had to remove her whole uterus. And that meant that she would never be able to get biological children. That was a big tragedy for both of them. But in spite of that, they were married in 1953. Instead of having biological children, they planned to adopt. And they were lucky.

Among their acquaintances in Örebro, which was where they had moved, was an elderly couple having a maid. That girl was "in certain circumstances", as it was called at that time. She would not be welcomed back to her employees with a child. And she very much wanted to keep her job, which she enjoyed and which was also well paid. Therefore, she decided, together with her employees, that the child would be put up for adoption. David and Gunnel heard this and asked to meet the maid, in order to get to know her better. They met and since all parties included liked each other, an appointment was made with a lawyer to organize adoption documentation in accordance with the law.

The wonderful baby boy was born in the middle of 1954. He was healthy and very cute. The thrilled parents, David and Gunnel, could within a few days hold their much longed-for son in their arms. All paperwork was finished and everything had been legitimately done. The boy was christened Sven and was adored by everyone, not least by his granddad Anders himself.

When Sven was two years old, in 1956, Gunnel one day entered the Post Office in Örebro in order to buy some stamps. Since the steps were very high and Gunnel therefore found it difficult to bring also the stroller, she left Sven outside, asleep in the stroller. Her errand only took about five minutes, but despite that, the stroller was empty and Sven gone, when she returned outside. She yelled hysterically and lots of people came to help her look for the boy. They searched all alleys, gardens and nooks but he was nowhere to be found.

The police was of course called at once and they continued the search. No result for them either. Weeks and months passed but no trails of the perpetrator were ever found. Since Sven had been adopted, they also contacted his biological mother to investigate whether she had been involved. She might have repented having put her child for adoption and tried to steal him back? No, they had no luck there either. She was working as usual at the couple´s home and was completely unaware of what had happened.

David and Gunnel were inconsolable. They loved their small son. Every morning they hoped that they would get positive news during the day. And every evening arrived with nothing having happened. When one year had passed since Sven´s kidnapping, Gunnel could not cope with it any longer. She jumped in front of the train and was instantly killed. David, who up to now had been the strong one of the couple, broke down completely. By now he had lost his two most loved family members.

Anders had been afraid that also David would kill himself. As soon as it had been possible to communicate with David, Anders, therefore, suggested the two of them go together to Australia to relax with opal-hunting. His son agreed. By now they have been there together probably ten times. Every time at least for half a year. Between the visits to Australia they share an apartment in Mora in Dalarna.

Anders sighs heavily. Life is really not easy. Within him he truly believes that his grandson Sven is still alive, in spite of so many years having passed. But how could they find him? Maybe it was time for them to test other, completely new, ways in their search? The kidnapper was probably a woman. That is how it generally works out.

CHAPTER 16

Lightning Ridge, Australia – 1 January 1974

As a start of the New Year, Anders sits down to write a letter to Maja Hermansson in Erie, Pennsylvania. An answer to her cry for help in finding her father Wally. Anders has for a couple of weeks been pondering on how much he should tell Maja. He has now made up his mind. She is, after all, Wally´s daughter so she must be told all that he himself knows about his old friend but that is unfortunately not very much.

Dear Maja,

Yes, I saw your letter at the bar here in Lightning Ridge. What a clever way to address it! All Scandinavians here have read it. But I seem to be the only one having had some, although not much, contact with Wally since our teenage adventures here in Australia. Since I do not know if you have sent a similar letter to Sofala, I have asked a friend of mine who is on his way there to check among the gold miners. If he gets to know something, he will tell me.

You and I have actually met once. I do not know if you remember it. Your family and mine spent a lovely week together in Mora in Dalarna many years ago. I think it was approximately in 1945. You were about 10 years old by that time and your brother a couple of years older. My son David was 13. We had an absolutely gorgeous time together. Your father and I had, for many years, tried to find a way to meet. It was not easy. You lived in Boulder City, Colorado, and we lived in Örebro. Wally had decided to participate in Vasaloppet that year, so time wise it fit in very well. And Wally made the race, arriving at the goal among the ten best, which was a fantastic achievement.

Since that time we have, unfortunately, not had any regular contact. A letter now and then between us with some news about our lives. Wally was completely devastated about your grandmother's death. Later on, I was also told that you had run away from home already in 1952 to live with the Amish people. Wally found that very hard to accept. He and your brother were both very worried about you. I think he mentioned that he had sent you some money, so that you would be able to get out of there, should you one day wish to do so.

Wally wrote, in one of his very last letters, that he had had a granddaughter. A couple of years later he gave me the news that he had had another grandchild – a grandson. He was a very happy and proud grandfather. But something seemed to bother him. Then his very last letter arrived. It was written at the beginning of 1958. He told me that he was very worried about his daughter-in-law's health. She had apparently, according to the doctors, had a depression caused by the son's birth, and it would not subside. By what he wrote I could understand that the situation at home was very difficult. Since then, I have not heard from him.

Well, Maja, that is, alas, all I know about Wally and his family. I will keep my eyes and ears open in case some more information about him appears.

I also want to tell you a little about my own family situation. We too have been affected by an inexplicable disappearance. And it is about my own grandson Sven. My son David, whom you met in Mora, married a very sweet girl in 1953. By that time they already knew that they would not be able to get any biological children. Therefore they had decided to adopt a child. And already in 1954 they adopted my wonderful little grandson, Sven. We all loved him so unbelievably much. But Sven, alas, was kidnapped when he was only a little more than two years old. In a very short moment, while my daughter-in-law was inside the Post Office, somebody snatched Sven out of his stroller. In spite of intense police searches, we have never been able to find Sven. And strangely enough, we have never heard from the kidnapper either. Not one day passes without me thinking of the little fellow. Sven´s mother could not live with her grief so the poor girl committed suicide after a year. David was also awfully depressed so nowadays I spend most of my time with him. We often go to Australia to spend half a year. When not in Australia, we live in Mora in Dalarna.

Maja, I suddenly have an idea. David and I will relatively soon go back to Sweden for this time. We could go back in the eastern direction instead of the western one. That way we could make a stop in the USA to meet you and your husband. It would feel much easier to talk face to face at a personal meeting. What do you think about my suggestion?

Warm greetings from Anders Torstensson

CHAPTER 17

Mora, Sweden – 3 January 1974

A couple of months have now passed since Jenny was released from Mora Hospital, but despite Jenny´s frequent sessions with the psychologist, her memory has still not returned. When she tries to remember, it is as if she had a black shiny screen in front of her eyes. Therefore, she is feeling depressed and lonely. Nothing is fun.

Doctor Larsson and his wife have prepared the little separate studio they have at the bottom of their villa for Jenny. There she can be on her own but still have access to their company, whenever she feels the need.

Jenny is still on sick leave but only half-time. When Doctor Larsson, about a month ago, realized how moody and depressed Jenny seemed to be, he said that maybe it would be better for her to mingle with people instead of isolating herself at home. Therefore he got her a halftime internship work in the kitchen of Stadshotellet. There she was to work as a kitchen assistant and she would also get a salary.

To her own astonishment Jenny soon notices that she is good at the chores. She is feeling as if she had had a similar work before. Without any problem and to the chef´s joy, she quickly and without difficulty makes both sauces and salads, peels lots of potatoes without protest, and is outstandingly meticulous at the kitchen cleaning. The only thing that is missing in her behaviour is a somewhat better mood. She is not unpleasant in her ways, more like quiet and withdrawn.

"Oh girl, a small smile once in a while would really be wonderful!" the chef says to her on some occasions. He knows about Jenny's memory loss and feels sorry for her. "You would be so beautiful if only you could sometimes smile, Jenny. You have to go places to amuse yourself so that you have nice memories to think of."

Jenny tries her best but it is so difficult to smile and laugh when everything inside you is just chaos.

Christmas time will also soon have passed. On Christmas Eve she was invited to Doctor Larsson and his family for a really traditional Swedish Christmas, as they explained it. She does not know if her earlier Christmases have been celebrated in the same way. She has no memories of them… But the ride to early Christmas mass in a sledge, drawn by horses, and enlightened by burning torches, felt like a completely new experience. It was all so very beautiful.

Police assistant Sven, who Jenny nowadays regards as her friend – actually the only friend she has – has also, like herself, been working during most of the Christmas holidays. During days off, he has celebrated Christmas with his mother in Orsa.

Lately, Sven and Jenny have started spending the major part of Sven's leisure time together. They walk, make excursions and go out for dinners. They speak for hours. It is, as a matter of fact, only when she is with

Sven that Jenny can laugh and smile. She is feeling so safe and happy being with him.

One day Jenny asks Sven to teach her how to ski. They go up to Gobshus where they want to start with some cross-country skiing. When Sven wants to help Jenny get on her skis, she immediately manages all by herself and then goes off without waiting for Sven, for whom it is really difficult to catch up with her.

Next time Sven is off-duty for a whole day he suggests, wanting revenge, that they both go slalom skiing at the slalom slopes at Gobshus. Once again they rent equipment in Mora. Jenny does not need any help this time either. They go uphill together in the lift. Standing side by side at the hilltop they count:"Ready! Set! Go!"

The two of them swish downhill like frequent slalom skiers. Maybe Jenny does it a little more professionally than Sven?

After several turns of uphill with the lift and downhill on skis, they calm down and enter the Gobshus café. That much fresh air has indeed increased their appetite, and now they are hungry.

"Please, Jenny, now you have to explain. You have never told me that you know how to ski – both slalom and cross-country. Why haven´t you done that?"

"But Sven, I simply didn´t know. When I had put on my ski boots and the skis, I just knew what to do next. I must have done some skiing in my earlier life!"

"Wonderful to hear that, Jenny. Maybe that´s another memory working its way up through the surface."

Jenny laughs. "Yes, the truth must be that I was born and brought up here in Mora."

Sven holds up his hand to stop her. "No, my friend. You were not. If you´d ever shown yourself in Mora, people would have remembered you. Your beautiful copper-red hair is unforgettable. But you must have done a lot of skiing in your earlier life. Of that I´m sure."

"I think we should talk about something else now", interrupts Jenny. "By the way, have I told you that sometimes I get like second-long – no, even shorter – memory glimpses? They´re so quick that I can´t actually quite see them."

"Fantastic, Jenny. You´ll probably see more and more memories coming together, staying in your mind each time a bit longer. And then the day´ll come when you quite suddenly discover that the blanks are gone. Have you told the doctor this?"

"No, not yet. I want to be able to give him some examples, but it´s still too early for that. But I´m anyhow feeling rather optimistic!" smiles Jenny. "But... there´s another thing that might mean something important. I know — yes I´m dead sure about it — that I HAVE TO participate in the Vasaloppet race. For some reason it´s enormously important to me. But I can´t remember why."

"Lovely. Then we must find a good way to make you look like a man. Think about that. My mum could probably help us."

For a moment Sven seems lost in deep thoughts but then he starts speaking again. "I suddenly remember what doctor Larsson said when you were discharged from hospital. It was more or less like this: At a traumatic loss of memory it could sometimes be good to confront the patient with the trauma she has experienced."

"Yes", answers Jenny, "but which trauma is that?"

"Let´s start with the place where that bear attacked you. That, if anything, must really have been a trauma. Let´s see how you react."

Reluctantly Jenny accompanies Sven to the car. It takes some time, on the unploughed forest roads, to reach the big boulder where they had found Jenny unconscious on the ground. They leave the car and go up to the boulder.

Sven tells Jenny to follow his instructions. "Now walk a short distance, diagonally to the right. Then turn around and imagine seeing a frantic bear coming towards you. Run, as fast as you can, towards the boulder and throw yourself onto the ground but don´t hit your head on something."

Jenny does as instructed. Imagining the bear, she can see it quite detailed in front of her. That must be a brown bear. It is running at full speed towards her. She gets afraid, but then suddenly it feels as if she is being transferred somewhere else. At that place she can see four grizzlies hover around in the snow. Like a bear family. And over there, at the river, she sees another one. A grizzly trying to catch salmon. For a short moment she is standing fossilized, before she runs to take cover behind the boulder.

"But what happened? You looked paralyzed. Do you remember anything?"

"Oh, I guess I did. At first I saw the angry brown bear coming towards me. But then I saw quite another scene. A bear family – but they were grizzlies – walking about in the snow. And then another one, but that one was fishing salmon at the river. How strange. Where could I´ve been?"

Sven looks confused. "You seeing that brown bear was probably a real memory from the attack. But the grizzly bears… We don´t have any in Sweden… Maybe you could have seen a documentary about them on TV? There are, after all, a lot of animal programs."

"Yes, I don´t know. But it felt so real."

Next morning Sven calls doctor Larsson to tell him about his experiment with the bear attack. He is expecting praise for what he has done but no way… Instead to his astonishment he gets a fulminatory scolding by the doctor.

”Are you out of your mind, boy? Do you think you´re a doctor? There is indeed a reason to why it takes so many years to become a doctor. What you´ve done is extremely dangerous! You´ve played with Jenny´s psyche. That could have resulted in terrible consequences, don´t you understand that?”

After a while Doctor Larsson calms down and asks Sven how Jenny is now, after Sven´s test.

”Quite well, she´s trying to remember if she´s seen grizzlies on TV, but that´s all.”

”Well Sven, you´ve been extremely lucky. And so has Jenny, of course. I´m happy there seems no harm done through your figment. It is, as you say, apparent that the bear attack is not the biggest trauma Jenny has undergone. This attack in combination with the concussion she had at the temple has however probably triggered factors for Jenny´s memory loss. But you must promise me not to run any more new experiments with Jenny, before having received my authorization.”

Sven is still feeling almost annihilated by the doctor´s criticism. ”Yes, Doctor Larsson, I do promise that. I really didn´t know that it could be dangerous for Jenny. There´s no way I would want to expose her to danger.”

CHAPTER 18

Orsa, Sweden – 15 January 1974

Sven has a bad conscience. His Mum must be missing him. She might be feeling lonely? He nowadays spends so much time with Jenny. Earlier he used to go to Mum in Orsa, as soon as he was free from work.

Mum has, for quite some time, actually seemed somewhat depressed. As if she is thinking of something unpleasant. Something she would want to tell him but that she is afraid of doing. There is like a pinch in Sven´s heart. Could she be ill? No, it must not be that. He will spend next weekend with Mum. And then he has to make her tell him why she is depressed.

Ida is overjoyed when Sven turns up in Orsa during the weekend, fully loaded both with gifts and good food. Now they will spend a long wonderful day together.

”Oh, my boy, how wonderful to see you looking so well and healthy. Tell me what you´ve been doing lately. Have you, maybe, found yourself a girlfriend? Rumours tell me that.” Ida looks jocularly at Sven.

”What rumours? There are no rumours being spread about me, are there?”

”Oh yes, at least Gertrud, the ER nurse at the hospital, is saying that. The two of you were out dancing at least once, I believe.”

”What is Dracula saying?”

"Please, Sven, you mustn't call her that. Gertrud is a nice girl and knows how to handle children. But she's maybe not so happy right now about the competition. I wouldn't be that either, if a non-residential person came to steal my boyfriend. And you should know that Gertrud would be a good choice, even though she was rather wild in her teens. They say she's related to the Pentecost Pastor."

"No Mum, you have to stop talking like that. I don't want to ruin the day talking about Dracula. If you can prepare our morning coffee, I'll tell you everything that has happened to me since we last met."

"It's true that I spend a lot of time with Jenny. You know, that young girl who lost her memory. The Doctor thinks it could help her to remember, if she has someone to talk to. And she's awfully nice."

"Yes, you do seem a little smitten, my friend. Maybe there could be something between the two of you. But I would pity Gertrud in that case."

"No Mum! I don't even know if she's married and has children. Or maybe a boyfriend. And when it comes to Dracula: she's too old for me, almost 30, and she behaves like she was as old as you – around 40. I don't need any extra mother. Forget about her!"

Ida stiffens at Sven's fulmination but then she pats him tenderly on the cheek. "Now I'll prepare us some morning coffee. We've to eat your sumptuous pastries."

Within a few minutes she is back in the living-room, sitting down comfortably in her armchair. Chatting, they enjoy their coffee and the Napoleon pastries. Then Ida looks at Sven. She says, a little hesitantly:"I have to talk with you about a serious matter."

"Yes, I´ve seen that there is something bothering you. And it has been doing that for quite some time. You´re not ill, are you?"

"No, no. It´s nothing like that. Physically I´m all right. But you´re right saying that something is bothering me. I´ll now tell you but it´s somewhat difficult to start. And to tell the truth, I´ll do it with fear."

"Don´t be afraid, Mum. I´m listening so just take it easy."

Inhaling deeply, Ida prepares herself. She coughs, clears her throat and looks tense, but then she starts. "Sven, I´ve done something horrible. It was many years ago but I have to tell you. For your sake, I can´t hide it any longer. You said you don´t want a "pretend"-mother."

Then she starts to tell, in a trembling voice. "I´ve stolen a child! Sven, I´ve stolen you."

Sven cannot believe his ears. "No, I don´t believe that. You´re dreaming that up."

"No, my friend. It is true. You see, once I had a little baby boy of my own. We lived in Örebro, the two of us. His father was at sea and was also killed there in an accident. Exactly like I told you your father was. He and I met when I was at sea working as a kitchen assistant for a year. My little boy got pneumonia. And the hospital doctors could not save him". Now Ida is desperately crying. After a moment she stops and wipes her eyes. Then she continues the story. "I was of course completely desolate. Most of all I wanted to die. By that time I had not yet begun working in the school kitchen, I was unemployed and day-time I started to sit on a park bench close to the children´s playing grounds. I could sit there for hours on end. Looking at the children, imagining that one of the boys was my Sven. Yes, the boy on the playing grounds was also named Sven. And he was of the same age as my dead son. Yes, Sven in the park — he was actually you. I was fantasizing about you."

Sven can feel how sweat is breaking out on his forehead. He is feeling quite nauseous. He is close to vomiting. He does not know if he can stand hearing more. He stands up saying:"I have to go outdoors for a while. I´ll soon be back."

Without even looking at Ida, he disappears through the entrance door. He walks two laps around the block trying to calm down, but that is difficult. What he has heard is so frightening, but he must know it all. He had better go back and let his mother continue her story.

Ida continues her account. "I had, of course, many times been thinking on how easy it would be to pick Sven up and just walk away. It would have been no more than fair, but I actually never planned to steal you. I had seen you and your mother on several occasions in town. And your mother never seemed to recognize me when we met."

Ida puts a hand on her forehead, closing her eyes for a moment. "And then suddenly I saw her one day entering the Post Office. She left you outside asleep in your stroller. I don´t know what happened to me. Only that I ran up to you and carefully lifted you up. Then I ran, with you in my arms, to my car which was parked only a few metres from there. I jumped into the rear seat with you and crept down onto the floor. You were awake at that time, but I told you that we were playing hide and seek. You thought that was fun." She pauses and then asks Sven:"Can you stand hearing more now?"

Sven silently nods. He cannot utter a word. He is feeling completely paralyzed.

Ida continues in a tired and sad voice. "There was a terrible commotion in the street, when your mother came out and saw that you´d disappeared. People were criss-crossing, looking for you. They wondered whether you yourself had gotten out of the stroller or if somebody had stolen you. Nobody peeked into the cars. Therefore we were not discovered. When it had all calmed down a little, I managed to move into the driver´s seat, without anybody seeing it. And then I went home to the flat. Sven, you were asleep by then. I had recently moved into the flat and had not yet gotten to know my neighbours. And they did probably not know that I had a small boy, two years old. Therefore nobody reacted when I came home with you. You and I continued living in the flat for a short time, but after some time I cancelled it. I had decided to move back home to Orsa, where I had inherited a cottage, which had been uninhabited for a long time. I thought Orsa would be a much better environment for you to grow up in."

"But, but didn't you read the newspaper? Didn't you feel sorry for the parents?" Sven looks questioningly at Ida.

"No, I didn't feel sorry for the parents. I was even so selfish that I cancelled the newspaper. I didn't want to know what was happening."

"And how did I react?"

"You were so sweet and nice. Not unhappy at all. You probably thought that it was all a thrilling adventure. And don't forget that you were so young. You immediately bonded with me. And I have, from the first moment I saw you, loved you so very much. And I have never repented having stolen you. I'll accept my punishment. It is worth a long punishment having had you as a son. And I'm probably old enough not to have to endure my whole sentence. Now I have nothing more to tell you for the moment. Just let me get ready before the police come to pick me up."

Sven does not know what his feelings are. He must first sort out his thoughts. What Mum has done is horrible. He should of course call the police immediately. But on the other hand... first he must get a chance to think.

"No, I´m not calling the police just yet. First I have to think. Don´t tell anybody about this for the time being. Even though I hate what you´ve done, it´s good that you´ve told me. I´m leaving now."

Without giving his mum any hug, Sven leaves the house. He is completely lost in his thoughts. He is just feeling a deep grief, except for the anger welling through him. He has always loved his mother. How on earth could she have done this completely inhuman thing? The act was so cruel. Is she a cruel and horrible person? Has she been hiding this cruelty from him during almost his entire life? There are so many questions. It is like a mess inside him. Sven sits in the car and drives to a protected opening in the forest outside Orsa. There his self control suddenly bursts. He starts crying. He cries for a long while. He cries over the parents he has lost. Maybe he has siblings? How could his mum do this? He is pondering and pondering, but then he starts to think also of his mother´s situation. On how loving she has always been. On what a happy childhood and youth he has had with her. And how brave she is having, for his sake, confessed her crime. That must have been so difficult for her!

Suddenly he feels tenderness for her. She must be enormously unhappy now. She is probably devastated. And quite alone thinking on how she has now lost his love. No, he must return to her. Explain how divergent his feelings are, but also that he still loves her. Because he does. He can feel that.

"Mum", he calls as soon as he has entered. He cannot hear any sound. Then he can distinguish sobs from his mother's bedroom. He goes there and sees her lying as a bundle on the bed. Completely absorbed by her grief. He sits on the bedside gently stroking her tear-wet hair. Bends down to give her a kiss on the cheek.

"Mum, regardless of what you've done, I love you. You have always been the best mother in the world."

Sven can feel his mother caressing his cheek.

"Mum, we'll wait involving the police. I'll do some tracing. Maybe I, myself, could find the family from which I come."

"But Sven, you could lose your employment if you don't report me."

"Let me handle that problem, Mum. For the moment you have to keep quiet about this. And so will I, but it is quite possible that I'll tell Jenny. She's such a good listener. And maybe she could give us some ideas on what to do. By the way, I want you to meet her soon but not as my girlfriend. Only as a very close friend. I'm sorry but I have to leave now. Do you think you'll be able to sleep tonight, Mum?"

"Yes, my boy. Your return to me a moment ago means so incredibly much. I'm exhausted and will sleep like a log. Good night, dear!"

Chapter 19

Mora, Sweden – 18 January 1974

Sven is feeling awfully depressed since he was told about his background. It is like being two different persons. One of them is feeling cheated out of his entire childhood. He finds it difficult to forgive his mother for the horrible things she has done. Has she never thought about his parents? How they must have been feeling? The other person loves his mother so incredibly much. He could never assist in putting her in jail.

He must find an understanding person with whom to discuss the problem. Somebody that can see both sides. Maybe help him see the problem in another light. Yes, he must talk to Jenny. He calls her in the evening after work. ”Hi Jenny, how are you?”

”Hi Sven. But how are you, actually? You sound so depressed and pitiful.”

”Could we meet tomorrow? I´m free then. I have so much overtime accumulated. Could we make an excursion? I´ll make us a packed lunch.”

”Of course. It would be nice but… What´s happened? You do sound very depressed”, says Jenny in a sympathetic voice. She can judge by his voice that something is totally wrong.

Sven picks Jenny up in the early morning. He has packed the car with sheepskins, thermos with hot chocolate and a pile of sandwiches with salami. ”I think we´ll go by car. I know a nice spot, where we´ll be comfortable."

It´s not very far, so within only a few minutes they have arrived. Sven parks the car beside a big snowpack. A little higher up, above the road, there is a beautiful cliff where the wind has swept away most of the snow. Sven spreads the sheepskins on the ground. They sit down and make themselves comfortable.

"Jenny, please forget for a while that I´m a policeman. I need you as a friend now. Do you think you could listen to me as such?"

"Dear Sven, I stopped regarding you as a policeman already long ago. To me you´re only a very close and dear friend. So get going!"

Sitting there, each of them holding a mug of hot chocolate, Sven starts to tell Jenny everything he has been told by his mother. The story is coming out disjointedly and stuttered when Sven´s feelings take over. At times Jenny gasps. Oh, what a sad story. Poor Sven!

Sven has at last finished his telling. While he has been talking he has cried a lot. Jenny has on several occasions hugged him and wiped his tears. It is visible that Sven is now feeling better, having eased his heart.

The two of them remain silent for a long while. Then Sven asks:"What do you think I should do? I´ve to see my parents and get to know them. But ... on the other hand, I can´t contribute to Mum´s going to jail."

"I think you should divide the problem into two steps instead of trying to solve it all at one time. Let us start by trying to find your parents. That should actually not be very difficult."

"What do you mean? How would I be able to do that?"

"Hello there, policeman! Use your head. There must have been a lot written about your disappearance in the newspapers. They have probably also mentioned your parents' names. Let's go to the local newspaper and ask them permission to look in their archives from Örebro."

"Jenny, you're a star. I would never have thought of that myself. And having found their names, we could start looking for them. I think you're right about doing that first. And later on we can start thinking about what we should do regarding Mum. By the way, thanks for sharing this with me!"

At a quick stop at Ida's house in Orsa, Sven is told the date of the kidnapping. Then they continue to the newspaper. Sven explains to the archivist that he needs to go through the newspapers after the date Mum has given him. They are shown into a room with a big table and, within a moment, they have a heap of Örebro newspapers in front of them. The archivist kindly asks them to respect the order in which the newspapers are piled.

Jenny and Sven roll up their sleeves and start searching. Already within some minutes they find big headlines on the newspaper's front page. There are detailed reports about Sven´s kidnapping. Also baby photos of him, even a photo of his birthmark. And another photo of a young couple – his parents. And yet another one of an elderly man, Anders, who must be his grandfather. He gets tearful as he looks at the pictures and reads the articles. He grabs a piece of paper and a pen from the penholder on the table and writes down the names of the couple. Now he is feeling quite hopeful. He will soon meet them. He relishes their names. David and Gunnel Torstensson. In that case his own name must be Sven Torstensson. What a strange feeling!

”Jenny, now we´ll have a coffee break. I have to digest this for a while.”

Jenny smothers. ”I´ve not wanted to tell you that my stomach has been aching for the past 30 minutes. Couldn´t we have a sandwich with the coffee?”

”A superb idea. Let´s go to my place and arrange that. Because afterwards we´ll have to sit down by the telephone and try to find my parents' address. This is so unbelievably thrilling, isn´t it?”

”Yes, and imagine with what speed we have reached this stage! And how easy it´s been. I hope it will continue like this.”

After a long conversation with Telephone Inquiries, Sven finally finds an address. Not in Örebro; they have obviously moved from there. The address is strangely enough, much closer. In Mora!

"It can´t be true. How ridiculous. It´s really hard to believe. Thus they live here in Mora. At least Anders and David." Sven laughs happily, but then he quickly swallows the laughter. "But now I´m starting getting nervous. It has suddenly become so close. What if they don´t want to know about me? I´m actually feeling afraid now."

"Are we not going there to call on the door tonight?" asks Jenny confused.

"No, no, not today. I can´t manage that. There are too many feelings inside me now. I´ll drive you home. Then I´ll continue to Orsa to spend the night at Mum´s house. I, after all, also have to tell her our findings."

Arriving in Orsa, he gives Ida long lasting hug. She looks at him questioningly but at the same time cautiously. She feels that something must have happened. She starts to tremble. "Have you told Jenny? How did she react? She´ll probably never want to meet me? I´m, after all, a child thief."

"Of course Jenny will want to meet you. But… I have to tell you. My parents´ names are David and Gunnel Torstensson and my grandfather´s is Anders. And… they live in Mora!"

Within a couple of seconds Sven can feel how Ida is fainting in his arms. Her face is a waxy white. Oh my God, what a thoughtless idiot he is. What has he done? He carefully carries her to the sofa. Puts her down and tucks her in. Ida is now starting to regain consciousness, but she is still terribly pale.

"Don´t be scared, my boy", she whispers. "This happens now and then and it´s nothing dangerous."

"How do you know that?" asks Sven. "Have you been to the doctor for a check-up?"

"No", she admits. "Maybe I should do that some day."

"No, now I´m the one making the decisions", mutters Sven. "I´ll drive you to the ER now, at once. And I´ll be staying with you until we know what´s wrong with you. You don't faint once in a while if you´re healthy. And now, please be quiet", protests Sven when his mother is trying to contradict him. "When I was a child I used to tell you to obey me, since I would be a policeman as a grown-up. And now I am." Nodding, Ida smiles faintly.

The examinations at the ER are thorough. They make lots of different tests and even an EKG. More than two hours have passed, when Doctor Larsson wants to speak to both of them.

"Well Ida and Sven, this doesn´t look so good. Ida, your EKG isn´t good at all. That means that your heart isn´t working as it should. That doesn´t necessarily mean that it´s dangerous, but we´ll have to do more tests. Furthermore, I can hear a rattle in your lungs and you´re running a fever. So you probably have pneumonia. Not even that should be dangerous. What´s worrying me is that the combination of these two problems could become dangerous. You´ll therefore stay here at the hospital for a few days so that we have time to check you thoroughly. And also get the results of the remaining test samples. Any questions?"

CHAPTER 20

Mora, Sweden – 28 January 1974

A few days later it is time for Ida to leave the hospital. Sven is looking forward to having her back home again.

"Oh, you're finally here, my boy", says Ida when Sven appears in the door opening to drive her home. "Oh, how I long to get out of here. It'll be so nice to be back home".

Once again at home in Orsa, Sven serves his mother a light but nice lunch.

"Well, how far have you reached in the search for your parents?" wonders Ida showing a face full of curiosity.

"As a matter of fact, we've not done anything about it. You've been ill, after all, and during that time I've not been able to think about them", answers Sven.

"Well, then we're lucky that I'm back home again, so that I can get you going. Have you been there yet? At Storgatan 12? If not, please pass there on your way back to the office. Enter and call the door. Don't hesitate. Just do as I tell you. The whole issue is automatically solved if someone opens. If nobody is at home, then you'll continue tomorrow. Do you promise?"

"Yes, stubborn Mum. I promise, but I'm to tell the truth a little nervous."

Sven returns to Mora. He calls the doorbell at Storgatan 12 and waits for a long time, but nobody opens. In a way, that feels nice. Because what would he actually say if someone opens? ”Hi Dad!” or ”Hi Granddad”.

Jenny is so slow in regaining her memory. Sven would like to help her in some way. Then he remembers his old idea and calls doctor Larsson.

”Good morning, Doctor Larsson. This is Sven, the friend of our Jenny. I have an idea on how we might help Jenny recover her memory, in a faster way. For safety´s sake, I wanted to check with you that it´s OK to try it.”

”Tell me what you want to do and I´ll give you an answer.”

Sven tells the doctor what he wants to achieve and how. After a few instructions from the doctor, Sven is allowed to go through with it. He is told he must be very careful and do it for a limited time, on each occasion. And immediately disrupt it in case Jenny becomes too upset.

”And please report any progress to me. It might not give the wanted results but it can hardly be dangerous for her. Good luck!”

Sven makes a list of questions. They are of very different kinds and without being sorted in any specific order. Finally he adds a column in which he will note Jenny´s reaction to the questions.

When Jenny and Sven, as usual, meet in the evening to have some supper together, Sven asks if he could try an experiment with Jenny in order to help her remember. "It´s nothing dangerous. And we´ll only do it for a maximum of 10 minutes the first time. Your doctor has approved of it. OK?"

"Of course, but what is it about?"

"I´ll ask you some questions. The most important thing is that you must answer at once, without thinking. I just want spontaneous answers. If you don´t know the answer, you should just hold up your hand. When you want to answer "Yes" you just nod or say yes. For "No" you just shake your head. Do you understand?"

"Yes, but what are the questions about?"

"Lots of different things. I´ve mixed them to make you more relaxed. Can we start?"

They sit down comfortably in the easy chairs in Sven´s living room. "Jenny, remember to answer at once. If you start thinking, I´ll immediately move to the next question. Now we start."

"Do you like oatmeal porridge?" - the hand is held up

"Do you know cycling?" – a nod

"Do you have a dog?" – shaking her head

"Do you have a cat?" – shaking her head

"Do you know your name?" – shaking her head

"Where do you live?" – "Mora"

"Do you know the name of any of your friends?" – "Peggy"

"Do you have a boyfriend?" – shaking her head

"How old are you?" – "Nineteen years"

"Do you live in an apartment" – shaking her head

"Do you like tea?" – a nod

"Do you have any neighbour you like?" – "Sonja"

"Do you know how to drive a car?" – the hand is held up

"Do you have a brother?" – first Jenny nods, then she shakes her head and starts crying.

Sven throws the questionnaire away and hurries over to Jenny to hug her. "I think we´d better stop this questioning for today", he says. "Do you want to go to the movies to see something fun?"

Having calmed down, Jenny agrees to go to the movies with Sven. During the evening neither of them mentions the question that has made Jenny cry.

When Sven has driven Jenny home after the cinema, he sits down with the questionnaire. He wants to see what he can get out from the spontaneous answers.

The answers indicate that Jenny is 19 years old, lives in Mora but not in a flat. That means she might be living in a terraced house or a villa. She has no boyfriend. Likes her neighbour Sonja and has a friend called Peggy. Jenny has neither a dog nor a cat. She does not know neither if she can drive a car nor if she likes oatmeal porridge. She knows how to bicycle and likes tea. She still does not remember her own name. Sven thinks that this far some useful information has been received.

The reaction on his last question worries him. At first Jenny answered yes but then rapidly changed her answer to no, whereafter the crying had started. That was probably a sign telling him that Jenny had lost her brother. Poor little one! This could be a really important piece of information.

Next morning Sven contacts the doctor once more. He tells what has happened during the questioning and which information he has received. Doctor Larsson asks Sven to continue the questioning, within a couple of days. He also says that Sven right now must avoid any questions related to Jenny's brother. She had better be left to think for herself, for a while, about her own reaction. Maybe that could help her remember a little more. And maybe she will herself bring up the subject with Sven.

Jenny is willing to continue the question experiment, at least a couple of times a week. She is very interested, hoping that something new regarding her background will be revealed.

Through the answers that Jenny so far has given, they now know that Jenny has been competing in cross-country skiing, is a good swimmer, loves fishing and everything else connected to outdoor life. She is, furthermore, very interested in gold and precious stones. Would love to go to Australia. She loves pickled herring with new potatoes but does not like blood pudding. And she does not even want to try "surströmming"- a type of fermented Baltic Sea herring.

A question that Sven is hesitant to ask is whether Jenny is married. And if she also has children. Jenny who, at this point, has understood that Sven is in love with her, one day asks him:"And when will you ask me if I´m married? You already know that I´ve not got a boyfriend."

Sven can feel how his face is turning all crimson. How very embarrassing. "Yes, if you want me to ask you that, then I´ll do it. Are you married?"

With a hearty laughter, Jenny cries:"No, no and no! Oh, you´re blushing so much!"

"Sorry, but I´ve to go to the bathroom for a moment. I´ll soon be back", says Sven running to the bathroom He locks the door and sits down on the WC. "Oh, my God, how embarrassing", he mutters. He washes his scarlet and sweaty face and flushes cold water onto his wrists. He takes a deep breath and then returns to the living room.

"Jenny", he says. "Do you like me a little? I mean, a little more than only as a close friend?"

Now Jenny is the one blushing. Suddenly she is feeling very shy. Does not quite know where to turn her eyes, but then she looks Sven in the eyes and with a lot of feeling she says:"Yes, very much!"

Sven jumps up from his seat and sits down beside Jenny. Puts his arms around her and kisses her tenderly on the lips. He gets an immediate response. There is no doubt that his feelings are answered.

"Let´s enjoy this wonderful thing for a moment. Can´t you wait for a couple of days with more questions? I´m so afraid that you´ll ask me something that would make me unhappy. I just want to be happy right now."

"OK, you´re right. Let´s just enjoy this. But I´ll never give up. I want to make you remember. It´s only if you, yourself, say that you don´t want to, that I´ll stop."

"Now I´m hungry. Can´t we go to the kiosk and order a really unhealthy hamburger plate each — with a lot of French fries? That would suit me very well now." Jenny can feel how she inside is bubbling with joy and happiness.

"Yes, my darling, let´s do that, but afterwards we have to pass Storgatan 12 again and call on the door. I´ve promised Mum to do that often. And I have, but so far nobody has opened."

At Storgatan it is crowded. It looks as if everyone in Mora is out shopping today. Sven and Jenny walk up the two stairs and call on the doorbell. They wait and wait, but nobody opens.

Suddenly the neighbour's door is opened and a friendly woman appears. "Can I help you? I've seen the two of you here before."

"No, thank you. We actually only wanted to talk to the family living here", answers Sven.

"The Torstensson family is away. They usually go away every year for six months a time, returning very sunburnt. They have now been gone for a long time so they'll probably return home soon."

"Do you know where they are?" wonders Jenny.

"No, as a matter of fact, I don't. They may have a house in for example Spain like so many others. Check at the Post Office."

"Thank you for your help", says Sven before they leave.

At the Post Office they meet one of Sven's friends. "Hi Sven, I've not seen you for quite some time. But that might have an explanation", he says, staring at Jenny. "I could never compete with her."

"Hello Bosse, no you surely can't. I'd like to ask you a question. Could I find out to which address mail is sent, if a person has made a temporary change of address?"

"No, that's confidential. It's absolutely forbidden. But you're a policeman and that could change the whole thing."

"No, no, Bosse. I´m here as a private person and not as a policeman."

Sven is suddenly afraid. If he acts like a policeman in this issue, which he has actually not reported as a police matter, he could be in real trouble.

"No, in such a case we´ll have to wait until the persons in question have returned home. Bye bye."

"We´ll have to continue sounding the doorbell until someone opens. They must return home sooner or later", he says to Jenny.

Once they are out in the street, Jenny grabs Sven by the hand. Satisfied and content, they walk on, chatting amicably.

CHAPTER 21

Orsa, Sweden – 4 February 1974

Last evening Sven found it difficult to leave Jenny to go home to Mum in Orsa. Sven however did not want to tell her by telephone what had happened between him and Jenny. He wanted Ida to see by herself how happy he was. Therefore he had, in spite of inner resistance, driven there. He arrived late and Ida was already asleep by then.

Sven rises very early in order to make breakfast for both of them. A delicious breakfast. Sven is working at the stove, making a lot of noise and clattering. He knows, within himself, that Mum is actually only waiting for her usual mug of coffee, but the doctor has said that she must have proper meals. Now she will certainly get one. After a while he puts down two plates on the already overloaded kitchen table.

Awakened by the noise, Mums enters the kitchen. ”What on earth are you serving me?” asks Ida in an almost frightened voice.

“American pancakes. But I forgot to buy maple syrup so there will be jam and cream instead. Jenny has taught me.”

”Oh dear, now I´m getting impressed. However, I´m not sure I can eat all that. By the way, where did Jenny learn that? Has she been to America?”

"I´ve no idea. I´ve forgotten to ask her that. That could actually be an important question, thinking about it. She might have been a kitchen assistant like you, learning it onboard a ship."

When both of them have eaten to the point of almost choking, Sven wipes his mouth with a napkin. "Now I´ve some news for you, Mum. Jenny and I are in love. And I´m so happy for that. You would not believe how happy I am."

"But how wonderful", interrupts Ida. "I´ve for a long time understood your feelings. The fact that they´re reciprocated is fantastic. I´m so happy for you."

"Be quiet so that I can tell you everything. We have planned that Jenny come here tonight to meet you for the first time. I´m sure you´ll love her. She is fantastic. Not only beautiful but also with such a nice disposition. You´ll understand when you meet her."

"It sounds wonderful but I´m still a little scared. Maybe she´ll find me horrible since I´ve kidnapped you."

"Don´t be afraid. She knows how much you mean to me. And she´s really looking forward to meeting you. Just be yourself, like you usually are, and everything will be a success. You´ll like each other, I promise."

With a tingling feeling in the stomach Sven, in the evening, helps Jenny out of the car outside his mother´s house. How will this end? Hopefully they will like each other.

As soon as Ida has opened the door, Jenny walks up to her giving her a hug. "Hello Aunt Ida, I´ve really wanted to meet you. Sven is always talking about you in such loving words. How wonderful to finally meet you."

At first Ida cannot say a word. Who is this wonderful creature? So sweet and nice. Then she realizes what Jenny just said, and she returns the warm hug. "I´ve heard so much about you too, Jenny. And I´ve understood, for quite some time now, that Sven is in love with you. Oh, I´m so happy to meet you, little one."

The three of them spend a couple of hours eating the tasteful supper Ida has prepared, talking animatedly. Sven can feel that Jenny and his Mum, without any doubt, truly like each other. What a relief! But, after all, he had never doubted that they would.

"Could I invite you two ladies to a dinner at Stadshotellet on Saturday?" asks Sven, just as he is going to drive Jenny back to Mora. "That way you´ll both have some time to make yourselves very beautiful. I mean: still more beautiful. Mum, tomorrow I´ll drive you to the shops in Mora so that you can buy something new and extra beautiful. And Jenny, you´re welcome to join us."

Both Jenny and Ida look delighted. Going to Statt is nothing you do very often. Imagine, spending a night out among other people and having a lovely dinner. And to be able to dress up. Both immediately accept the invitation.

But then Sven studies Jenny´s smiling face more closely. He is used to doing that during the questioning sessions they are having together. He can notice apparent traces of suppressed anxiety.

”But Jenny”, says he, ”you´re not afraid, are you? Everybody goes to the Statt, people like you and me.”

Without answering, Jenny makes a denying gesture with her hand, but deep inside she wants to scream:”That´s exactly what I´m afraid of – terrified, stupid Sven. Everyone is gathering there, probably also those that I wouldn´t like to meet. People who know me, although I can´t remember them. Maybe also those that would wish to harm me. And I can´t distinguish one from the other.

Sven drops the issue. Jenny is probably only tired.

CHAPTER 22

Erie, Pennsylvania – Boulder City, Colorado, USA– 1 February 1974

Maja has lived as if in Heaven since the receipt of Anders Torstensson's letter from Australia. To their great sorrow, Yngve and Maja have never had any children of their own, in spite of their long-term marriage. And now, suddenly, Maja is an aunt. Not only that, but a twofold aunt. A nephew and a niece. She fully understands that the children now would be in their teens. That they are no longer babies… But, she will spoil them so much! What are Yngve and she to do with all their money? They already have everything they need, but on the other hand her brother's children might need some help. A driver's licence or car or something like that. Now it is only a question of finding them. That is now priority number one. People cannot just disappear. They have to be somewhere. Maja is feeling confident that she is right in being optimistic.

Yngve tries to dampen Maja's expectations. "Dear Maja", says he, "you have to understand that nobody could guarantee that we'll ever find them. I, of course, also hope that we'll do it but… You would be so terribly disappointed… Try to dampen your zeal."

It is such a good feeling having been able to establish contact with Anders, a close friend of Maja's father Wally. But oh my God, how horrific for them to lose their little boy, not knowing whether he is alive or not. That must be horrible. And imagine that Anders and

David in spite of that are ready to help her and Yngve in their search for her family and that they are willing to take a detour via the USA in order to see them. How kind of them!

On February 1st, Maja and Yngve go to Pittsburgh Airport to pick up Anders and David. From the very first moment the four of them like each other. You can notice that in the atmosphere of the car. The conversation is relaxed. Sometimes they are even talking over each other.

They do a lot of sightseeing during Anders´ and David´s first three days in Erie. The evenings are spent in front of the fireplace in the living room. Anders tells about lots of the adventures Wally and he had during their adolescence in Australia. They had not only panned for gold and searched for opals but also travelled around quite a lot in the enormous country… There was, after all, so much to do. In their LandRover, they had crossed muddy rivers full of crocodiles in the rain forest up north in Kakadu National Park. They had climbed the beautiful ridge of Ayers Rock way out in the desert and after that decided to visit Alice Springs, centre for both the School on the Air and the Flying Doctors.

They had spent days on end driving on the Nullarbor Plain, from which they had the most wonderful view of the South Arctic Ocean, more than 100 metres below them, with all its whale colonies. Needless to say, they had also been snorkelling at the Great Barrier Reef among corals and sharks. And they had even found sapphires in the washing pan. The landscape was everywhere really worth seeing. The orange-yellow sand, strange mountain formations, high termite hills, jumping kangaroos, wild horses and wild camels... Everything seen against the mostly azure sky. It was overwhelmingly both big and beautiful. You got an enormous feeling of freedom!

Yngve tells them that years ago he had hired a private detective to search for Wally and Johan throughout the USA. He explains that there had not been any trace of them. And if they are now in Australia, then Anders would have found out. He has, after all his visits there, quite an enormous network of friends.

They of course also talk a lot about the disappearance of little Sven. The tears are running down David´s cheeks when he tells them about the horrible discovery that the son was gone. Anders succeeds in calming him down. He says that, as soon as they are back in Sweden, they will renew their search for the boy. Maybe try it from another angle than before.

Late one evening, Maja starts telling something, unknown even to Yngve. "Now I´ll tell you a secret. It might not matter in the search for Dad but I can feel that I have to tell you. In spite of the fact that I should probably not do it."

She pours some more beer for the men and a glass of wine for herself. Then she continues. "When I was rather small, maybe 10 years old, I started for fun spying on Dad. Sometimes, being bored, I followed him when he left our house in Boulder City. He used to be cycling, so I used to follow him on my own bike. I always kept quite a distance so that he wouldn't discover me. One Sunday, when I knew he was planning cycling away, I told my mother that I would be making an excursion with a friend. And that I wanted to bring some juice and buns."

"Imagine that. Maja you've always seemed so proper to me", smiles Yngve. "Please continue. I'm curious about the end of this story."

Maja continues:"Dad was cycling rather far into the forest on a forest path, at a certain distance from Boulder City. Then he hid his bicycle behind a tree. He started walking straight into the forest, along a small stream. I hid mine behind another tree. I pretended to be an Indian woman sneaking on a white man. Dad didn't hear me. He continued for about 30 minutes. Thereafter he climbed a cliff. He returned after a short while overloaded with things. Strange things. Things I'd never seen before. He continued down to the fast running brook. There he put something, similar to a kind of chute, just above the water line. Catching a spade he started digging in the sand close to the water edge. He poured the sand into the chute repeating that a few times. Then he filled buckets with water and let the water run down the drain."

Now Maja is interrupted by Anders, saying:"He was panning for gold, wasn't he?"

"Yes", answers Maja. "But I didn´t know that then. When almost everything in the chute had been swept away by the water, he started using a rather wide pan. He rinsed the chute so that the gravel and sand went down into the pan. Then he sat down at the stream, his feet in the water. And started moving the pan. At times he shook it, pouring away some gravel and adding more water. I was hiding rather far from him. Therefore I couldn´t see if the pan was completely empty when he stopped. He carefully rinsed the pan so that everything left in it gushed into a jar with a lid. Then he collected his things and climbed the cliff once more. He was obviously done for the day.

Once Dad was out of sight, I climbed the cliff. Furthest away, under an overhang was a small shed with a door. There was no lock, so I entered the small house. It was awfully small but rather cute. I looked around. On the uppermost box of a pile of boxes, I found a small purse. It was rather heavy, being so small."

"Maja, don´t tell me it was the purse Wally and I had, from Australia!"

"I don´t know, but inside it, there was a small package with beautiful stones shimmering in different colours. And was also something like a yellow powder. That might have been gold."

"Yes, Maja. That was gold and the stones were opals. How wonderful to hear!" Anders has a sentimental look in his face.

For a while they are thinking about Maja´s story. It has come as a complete surprise that Wally had been panning for gold in Colorado, USA.

"Maja", David is looking questioningly at Maja. "Would you be able to find that place again?"

"Yes, I think so. They could hardly, since then, have built new houses that far into the forest. And the cliff is just above the stream."

"I suggest we go for a couple of days to Boulder City, to try to find Wally´s little shack", says Yngve looking at the other three.

Said and done. The following day they take a flight from Pittsburgh, Pennsylvania, to Denver, Colorado. They drive a rented car to Boulder City, arriving there in the evening. A nice dinner is the finish of a tiresome day.

After an early and heavy hotel breakfast the following morning, they leave the hotel, packed with piles of sandwiches and thermoses. The weather is perfect. About five degrees below zero and brilliant sunshine. So far, there has not been very much snow this year in this part of Colorado. As a consequence there is no snow blocking the road. It gets a little worse when they have parked. Now it is time to walk on foot. They are dressed accordingly in thick boots and warm clothes, so it does not matter if, once in a while, they step into water. The stream can be distinguished through the rather thin layer of snow. They must concentrate on following it. A short walk and suddenly they are standing at their goal: the cliff.

David steps forward, saying in a, for him, unusually authoritative voice: "I´ll take the lead here. First I must check so that there isn´t a bear sitting up there waiting for us. As soon as I shout OK, you can follow. But be careful. It´s rather slippery."

David quickly disappears up the cliff, and then there is silence, a horrible silence. Then comes an "Ouch, what the …" and a small crash. David´s face is showing above the cliff edge. "I just slipped. It´s slippery like hell. There are however no bears to be seen. It´s OK. You can climb now."

Within a couple of minutes, all four of them are gathered on the cliff edge in front of the shed´s small wooden door. The cliff has an overhang forming a roof above the door. The cliff also contributes with the inner wall of the shed. The side walls and the front have been made of greyish wood full of moss. At some distance the shack is almost invisible. It looks like the tiny door to an elf´s cottage, leading straight into the cliff.

 The men make space for Maja to open the door and to be the first to enter. After all, the shed belongs to her father, Wally.

"It looks more or less the same as last time", says Maja astonished. "Strange, so many years have passed since then. But… wait a moment. Something´s changed. Yes, now I can see. There´s an envelope beside the purse up there on the uppermost box. That envelope wasn´t there when I was here."

Anders, being the tallest of them, stretches up to take both the purse and the envelope. He forwards the envelope to Maja.

"Anders, you take care of the purse. I have to open this envelope." She eagerly tears it open.

CHAPTER 23

Boulder City, Colorado, USA- 7 February 1974

Maja stares at the contents of the big envelope they have just found in Wally's shed. "Look, it contains two smaller envelopes. One is for me and the other one for you, Anders."

Anders and Maja carefully open their envelopes, finding inside them handwritten letters from Wally. They silently read them, noticeably moved. Maja sits down on the three legged stool. Putting her forehead in her hands, she silently cries. Anders wipes away some tears, rolling down his cheeks.

Anders clears his throat. "Now I can read my letter to the rest of you. But Maja, that doesn't mean you have to read yours for us. It might be too private."

He reads:

23 February 1970

"Dear Anders!

You are the best friend I have ever had. I, therefore, hope that your are present when this letter and the purse are found. I so much wanted to continue writing to you. But, unfortunately, I could not. Something horrible has happened in my life. Something that I, alas, am not allowed revealing, because it could mean dan-

ger to my other family members. Do not try to find me or the others. Officially, we no longer exist.

We spent wonderful years together, you and I. Think of all our adventures. And how fun it was. You left the purse in my hands to care for. Thank you for that confidence. I have added to the contents, since I´m panning quite a lot here in Colorado. I had intended to sign for a claim in your name. But then I realized that you too might now feel too old for that. You will have to settle with the thought that I would have done that, if the other issue had not arisen.

I would now like to ask you to do the following with the contents of the purse: Divide it into two equal parts. One is for you and the other is for me. Yes, it does not matter that I have added more gold. (You could call it interest on borrowed gold.) Then please divide my half in four equal parts. One is for my beloved daughter Maja, one for my beloved son Johan, one for my dear grandson and one for my lovely granddaughter. I hope there will be enough for them to make a piece of jewellery each.

Only you and Maja know my earlier surname. I beg you not to mention it to anyone else. However much I would love to, I cannot give you any more information. I hope you will have a wonderful life in the future.

Warm hugs,

Wally

P.S. I hope you remember that it was you naming me Wally. It was when I in vain tried to catch a small wallaby. I wanted to tame it and have it as a pet. Tell that story to Maja so that also she gets to know why I have been called Wally during my whole grown-up life. D.S."

Maja walks up to Anders and gives him a big hug. "I want to read you my letter to, even though it is personal. I would feel good sharing this moment with you."

She takes the letter out of the envelope, wipes her eyes and starts to read.

"23 February 1970

My dear beloved Maja, my wonderful girl.

I´m thinking so much of you and of all the years that we could not spend together. I ask you to forgive me that I perhaps was not a good father, prohibiting you to stay with the Amish people. I just wanted to do what I thought was best for you. Maybe I was wrong.

Like I have written to Anders, I hope that also you are present at this moment in my small shack. Maybe it was you showing him the location of it. Yes, you did not know that I noticed when you were following me. But I did. You were sneaking like an Indian but could not avoid the rustle of the leaves you were treading on. I thought it was fun. It was like having a secret together the two of us. When you had left home, I decided never to have any secrets for Johan. That is why I have also shown him my shack.

But there is one secret that I must keep to myself. Among other reasons, it is for your own safety. Something happened, after you had run away from home. Something terrible. I cannot tell you about it. The consequence was that I, Johan and Johan´s two small children – a girl and a boy – had to go underground. I can tell you neither where we are nor our names. I beg you not to search for us. Since only you and Anders know my earlier surname, I ask you to forget it. If you are not married, still carrying the same surname as I, then please do not tell anyone that we are related. I´m hurting so much not being able to see you. But it is for the safety of all of us (including your), I say that.

I will always love you, for my entire life. And miss you, dearest Maja. Thousands of hugs to my little darling.

Dad

P.S. You are probably wondering why I, writing my letters to both of you, suppose that you are in the shed together. It was actually just a feeling I had. That you would contact each other, sooner or later. I thought you might one day want a reunion between us. Then the most natural thing you would do would be to contact Anders. I hope I´m right.

D.S."

Again everyone´s eyes are wet. It has been so sad to hear these letters. Poor dear Wally. Poor dear Dad. Leaning on Yngve´s shoulder Maja is crying her heart out. It is as if the crying would never stop.

Quiet and pensive they return through the forest to the car. What could you possibly say having heard those two letters being read? Nothing. There are no words.

After yet another night at the hotel in Boulder City, Maja and Yngve decide to accompany Anders and David to their home in Mora, Sweden. They feel they need to leave the USA for a while. It would be nice spending some more time together. They have, after all, just shared a very upsetting experience. And Anders has promised to invite them to Stadshotellet in Mora, after their arrival. ”On Saturdays the whole town of Mora is meeting at Statt.”

CHAPTER 24

Mora, Sweden – 9 February 1974

When the beautiful trio, Ida, Jenny and Sven, arm in arm, on Saturday evening enter the festive restaurant of Stadshotellet, being by now almost totally crowded, there is a swish going through the room. Many of the guests smilingly wave at the newcomers. Mora is a small village in which it is difficult to remain anonymous. And who has ever before seen the village police assistant dressed up so well in a tuxedo.

Both ladies are enchanting in their new evening dresses. Sven has acted as an advisor during their respective shopping tours earlier in the week. The result is smashing. Ida, whom people has mostly seen in her school kitchen uniform, is dressed in a shimmering white-blue dress which brings out the white strands in her beautiful black hair. She has of course matching shoes and a beautiful necklace. Jenny's dress is in beige-apricot, harmonizing with her copper-red hair in a fantastic way. Also she has chosen her shoes with care. Ida, in her jewellery box, has found a beautiful pearl necklace that Jenny is now wearing.

The restaurant owner comes up to them, helping them to sit down. He waves Sven a little to the side. Whispering, they discuss something. Then Sven sits down again.

Within a short time, the head waiter comes up to the table, carrying a silver tray with three champagne glasses and a bottle of champagne in an ice bucket. Placing the tray carefully on the table, he shows Sven the bottle. Louis Roederer Cristal, a splendid vintage. Sven nods affirmatively and the bottle is expertly opened.

Sven clears his throat and lifts his glass in order to toast his ladies. "To a wonderful evening which I think will be memorable in many ways. We'll have a nice dinner together, and then the dancing will begin. I don't think I've danced for at least a hundred years, so you'll both have to forgive me for any steps on your toes."

Both Jenny and Ida giggle happily, but then Ida objects. "Sven, you'll have to do without me as a dancing partner tonight. I don't think the doctor would approve of me dancing."

The waiter is once again whispering something into Sven's ear, pointing at the clock. Sven rises. Walks around the table up to where Jenny is seated. He brings something out of his pocket, but then he kind of falls forward. When the guests see this, there is like a gasp through the restaurant. Mora's police assistant Sven is falling forward – down onto his knees. There is now complete silence at the tables around them.

"Dearest Jenny. Would you marry me?" Saying these words, he opens a jewellery box taking out a beautiful engagement ring.

Spellbound, Jenny stares at Sven. What did he say a moment ago? Did she get it right? With tears glittering in the corners of her eyes, she says in a soft voice:"Yes Sven, I do want to marry you. I love you so much." And then she holds out her finger to let Sven put the ring on it. Thereafter the newly engaged kiss each other.

A fanfare sounds from the stage and the restaurant guests are enthusiastically applauding. What a lovely proposal! Only a few occasional guests do not join in the applause. Two even look annoyed. Jenny might have been right in her anxiety about the visit. When everyone is gathering in the same place, you do not know who your friend is and whom you should avoid.

After some minutes of toasting and signs of joy, the delicious dinner is served. Both lobster, veal and a fabulous dessert. They have good wines with the food and for the dessert a glass of Madeira. An excellent dinner!

During dinner, dancing has started. A local folk festival orchestra is playing. And the audience enjoys them. When they start playing "Let's Twist Again", Jenny drags Sven up on the dance floor. It does not take long for him to dance as well as all the others, in spite of never having twisted before. The twist is succeeded by alternately rock'n roll and romantic music. Half an hour later Sven and Jenny leave the dance floor. Completely exhausted and sweaty.

"I'm sorry, but I'll have to visit the ladies' room to do some repair", smiles Jenny quite beaten.

"And I have to go to the men's room to do the same, but the only thing sufficing now would probably be a real shower, but I´ll use the basin for lack of that. See you."

As there is a queue in front of the mirrors in the ladies' room, Jenny goes into one of the cubicles, locking the door behind her. As she is sitting there, she can hear somebody entering the adjoining cubicle.

Through the wall a woman is saying in a low, almost intimate, voice: "So Mora´s own little newfound pet has now been engaged. Sweetheart… This could turn out dangerous for you, you bitch!"

The door to the adjoining cubicle is shut with a loud bang and the woman has disappeared. Jenny shudders, not primarily for the words but for the pitch of the voice. It had been like a mother or a kindergarten teacher correcting and warning a small child. Somebody with the power to punish.

In the men´s room, on the other side of the wall, a very sunburnt man is standing at one of the basins. He has obviously also been dancing because he is busy folding up his shirt sleeves.

When the man sees Sven entering, he says: "I really must congratulate you on your engagement. And what a lovely fiancée you´ve found!"

"Thank you so much! Yes, she´s really wonderful. The finest and best girl in the world, in addition to being beautiful. I´ve really been lucky."

"I saw you dancing. What energy! You´re also trying to cool off a little now, aren´t you?"

"Yes, as much as possible", says Sven. He takes the basin to the left of the man and starts folding up his shirt sleeves. Then he notices that the man suddenly is staring at Sven´s right arm.

"Oh, that´s really an unusual tattoo. A question mark."

"No, that´s not a tattoo at all. It´s a birth mark. A so called haemangioma - or fire mark or strawberry mark. It´s a little funny though that it looks just like a question mark." Sven continues washing himself in cold water.

"How strange", says the man, sitting down on the basin edge. "How very remarkable! My son used to have an exactly similar fire mark. At exactly the same place. A very strange coincidence, to say the least."

Now Sven´s brain starts working intensely. Could it be possible? Yes, maybe. The man is, after all, unusually sunburned. "Do you live at Storgatan 12?"

"Yes, I do. How do you know that?"

"I´ve been looking for you for several weeks. Have called on your door, lots and lots of times. But you have been abroad for a long time, I understand. At least judging by your sunburn."

Sven is holding his breath. Now the moment has arrived. The expected and almost feared moment.

The man silently keeps looking at Sven. Can it be true? Can it really be him? Then he lets out a deep trembling sigh. "It is …", then his voice cracks. He clears his throat and tries again. "It is you, isn´t it? If you knew how we´ve been looking for you. What´s your name now?"

"Sven."

"Come here Sven so that I can hug you. You can´t imagine how happy I´m now." Trembling, he holds out his arms so that Sven can walk up to his bosom. His grip around his son is almost cramped – as if fearing that his son would once again disappear out of his life. Tears are streaming down his cheeks but he does not care. Within only a matter of minutes, his life has changed. He is completely overwhelmed by emotions. Then he says: "We must hurry back into the restaurant to tell your grandfather that we´ve finally found each other. He´ll also be so happy. He´s never given up hope of finding you, something I actually had started to do."

Sven is feeling quite dizzy. What an evening! First he has been engaged to his beloved Jenny. And now he has suddenly also found both his father and his grandfather. It is almost too much to be true.

"No, I´m sorry but we can´t do that right now. There is a very – to me terribly important – reason for that. Couldn´t I, instead, come to Storgatan 12 later tonight, when my ladies have left? I promise to tell everything then. And then I´ll also be able to give Granddad a big hug." Sven, touched, is thinking that this is actually the first time in his life that he says the words Dad and Granddad.

"OK, I don't understand anything, but if it's that important, then we'll do as you say. Just give me another hug, my boy." They hug and Sven returns to his table.

"Now you're looking somewhat cooler, darling", says Jenny. "But has something happened? You're looking quite jumpy. Actually something scary just happened to me in the ladies 'room. Someone threatened me."

"That sounds unpleasant", says Sven without any further comments. He is too busy with his own thoughts about his father and grandfather.

"I'll tell you tomorrow morning", says Sven.

He wants to explain about Mum's situation to his father and grandfather. He must convince them that they, under no circumstances, are to contact the police. That would be horrible. It could kill his Mum.

Late at last, they leave the table. On their way out, Jenny whispers to Sven:"Do you see that woman over there in the corner? She has been staring at me the whole evening. Sometimes she even looks hateful. And it might be her threatening me in the ladies' room. Sometimes I've felt really uncomfortable."

Sven looks at the woman Jenny has been talking about. "Do you want me to go up to her and ask why she's been staring at you and threatened you?"

”No, never mind. To stare is, after all, not a crime. And I have absolutely no proof that it was her threatening me. Let´s leave it for the time being.”

Sven helps Ida and Jenny into the limousine, giving the driver the address. Jenny will stay the night in Orsa. He himself must start work early in the morning so he will sleep in his studio. That is quite a good arrangement tonight, since he will be paying a visit at Storgatan, to meet his father and grandfather.

CHAPTER 25

Mora, Sweden – 10 February 1974

When Mum and Jenny have disappeared in the limo, Sven wants to have some time to think things over before meeting his father and grandfather. He walks down to the quay in Mora and sits down on a bench. It is pinching cold outside, but his overcoat is rather thick. He exhales, feeling almost dizzy. The evening has been so full of experiences.

He smiles thinking of Jenny's happy face during his proposal. Oh, she is so beautiful. Sven has never looked for physical beauty earlier, when he has approached women. To him the most essential thing is that the woman he´d want to spend his life with has a good heart and a functioning brain. But… that Jenny also is beautiful is nothing negative. Yes, the two of them fit so well together. They will certainly be the happiest couple in the world. But, at the same time, he thinks that Jenny has some anxiety buried deep inside. It is almost as if she is trying to escape from something and that she is feeling persecuted. He is not sure that Jenny really was threatened in the ladies 'room. She must be mistaken.

Sven is thinking of what is awaiting him. The meeting with his father and grandfather. How will he be able to explain everything to them? The thought of contacting the police is out of question. He must make them understand that he is not going to abandon his mother. Yes, in the worst scenario, they will have to choose between putting mother in jail and having a relationship with him. Sven spends some minutes thinking about that. Finally, he understands that he can no longer postpone the meeting. Now it is time to go there.

A few minutes past midnight, Sven presses the doorbell to the Torstensson apartment at Storgatan 12. He has now braced himself and decided to let everything get solved spontaneously, in a natural way.

The door is opened by a sunburned elderly, handsome, man – Granddad. They silently look at each other. Then the man extends both his hands towards Sven. He grabs them, feeling a lump in his throat. He leans his head on the man´s shoulder, letting the tears loose. A moment later, he can also feel his father hugging him. They stay that way for quite some time, not saying a word.

"I think this moment requires one or several glasses of champagne, don´t you agree?" asks Granddad. He lets go of his son and grandson. "The owner of Stadshotellet was nice enough to give me a couple of bottles to bring home. You´ll have to catch a cab later."

"That sounds so good, Dad", says David, who up until now has not said a word. His eyes are quite shiny by the tears he is holding back. "We´ve so many years to catch up with my Sven… I don´t know how we´ll ever be able to do that." He is looking questioningly at Sven.

Having toasted in champagne and refilled their glasses, Sven starts talking. "I promised you, Dad, to tell you what's happened to me. And I want to keep that promise. I myself got to know about the kidnapping only as late as in the middle of January this year. Up till then, I didn't know anything other than being my Mum's happy son. Because I've been truly happy. My whole life has been so good being with her." He adds:"Since I still don't know you two, it feels a little strange for me to call you Dad and Granddad. Will you allow me to instead call you David and Anders to begin with?"

Both nod affirmatively.

Sven continues his story, with small interruptions. He remembers, quite well, the words Mum used, as she revealed the secret to him. Now he tries to use the same words. He tells about Ida's dead son. About her feelings seeing Sven. And, lastly, how the kidnapping had been done.

Dad's and Granddad's facial expressions show their different feelings throughout the story. When Sven is closing in on the end, their expressions are becoming more serious, almost hostile. Sven stops them from talking, holding up a rejecting hand. "To finish, I just want to tell you that I love Mum. She has a heart problem. She has, furthermore, just had pneumonia, which has weakened her even more."

Now Sven's denying hand is not enough any longer.

David almost rises from the chair, with a face now crimson by withhold anger. "But she's stolen my and my wife´s child. Stealing from us your entire childhood. And my wife, your mother, committed suicide because of her despair. You just can´t forgive something like that, Sven. That´s too much to ask, actually. No, Hell, it´s frankly quite impossible. Never!"

Hearing David´s words Sven turns quite pale. "Do you mean that my mother is dead? That my real mother is dead? Oh, how awful! I just saw the names of you two, not hers, on this address and thought that you might have divorced. I´ve been looking so much forward to meeting also my real mother. Oh Mum, what´ve you done?"

Sven is visibly chocked. He is trembling, feeling the tears running down his cheeks. He will never meet his real mother. The feeling of loss is unbearably heavy.

Granddad Anders sits down at Sven´s side. Putting his arms around him, he strokes Sven´s hair soothingly, speaking to him in a calm and reassuring voice.

David looks compassionately at Sven, but then he starts thinking of his beloved Gunnel. He sets his jaws in a firm and hard line, inhales and looks accusatory at his son. "Such a criminal act must be reported to the police. I guess you haven´t done that. Am I right?"

"I´ve not reported it. I actually didn´t know about this thing happening to my real mother. Maybe I would have acted in a different way, had I known. I must however defend Mum. She has, the whole time, been telling me to report her but I have refused to do that. It´s anyhow impossible to undo the things that have happened. And please remember that my childhood has been a very happy one. Nobody – not even you – could have made it happier.”

Now Anders starts to talk. ”Both David and I hear what you´re saying. But… If you let such an awful crime like this one, go unpunished, then where would we be heading? The Law is there to be followed. This could lead people to think that violating the law pays off.”

”But nobody knows about this, except the three of us, Jenny and Mum. If we keep quiet then…”

”Yes, but I still don´t know if that´s right. And you´re a police assistant, I´ve heard. How do you feel not having reported the kidnapping?” David looks questioningly at Sven.

”I´m ready to leave the police force – for the sake of Mum – if needed. And I´m also ready to accept any punishment. And I´m also ready – but with sadness in my heart – to be firm. To tell both of you that you´ll have to choose between reporting Mum and keeping me.”

Sven´s facial expression has hardened. He can feel how his heart is beating very quickly, out of nervousness. He really wants to keep his newfound father and grandfather, but he refuses to give Mum up. To let her suffer.

”I think that David and I have to think a little more about this”, says Anders. ”We promise not to contact the police until we´ve spoken with you, Sven. I understand that you care very much about your Mum. And I´m so happy that you´ve had a marvellous life with her, but as I said, we must get a chance to think this through, before deciding. OK Sven? OK David? ”

Both of them nod their consent.

”I only have to add”, interposes Sven, ”that Mum is ready to meet both of you face to face. And ask you for forgiveness. She is deeply aware of what a terrible crime she´s committed. Even though she still doesn´t know about my mother´s suicide. We´ve talked a lot about this lately, but I haven´t yet told her and Jenny that we met at Statt tonight. They understood that something had happened. I told them that I´ll explain tomorrow morning.”

Having said that, Sven unwillingly yawns. ”I´m sorry but I must go home now. There has been so much happening today and I must be at work on time. Could we meet again tomorrow afternoon?”

Giving each other a good-night hug, David wonders, in a soft voice: ”Couldn´t you bring Jenny tomorrow? She seems so lovely. And I would so much want to meet my son´s fiancée as soon as possible. She might even help us in our decision making.”

CHAPTER 26

Mora, Sweden – 11 February 1974

As Sven, exhausted, falters into the police station in the morning, he has not slept at all. He has had far too much to ponder.

The station is unusually quiet. Haven't his colleagues arrived yet? Strange. He takes off his overcoat, presses the coffee machine in order to get a cup of coffee and then enters his office. There he finds the explanation to the silence. All his colleagues are awaiting him inside the room. The writing desk has been set with a cake, coffee and flowers. An attempt to "Happy Birthday" is silenced by somebody. After all, it is not a birthday they are celebrating.

Hellström walks up front, in order to make a speech. He clears his throat, blows his nose, wipes his glasses and adjusts his tie.

"Dear Assistant Sven Martinsson, we would like to … Hell… Being formal doesn't suit me. So… Congratulations, Sven. You really caused a big sensation last night at Statt. You hadn't yet finished proposing before the whole village knew about it. And very well done, my boy, to claim the most beautiful and enigmatic girl of the village – Jenny."

The applause is strong. Hellström has probably not talked that much on end during the last ten years. When the cake and coffee are finished, Sven asks if he could take a couple of hours off. This is immediately granted and Sven hurries to the car. He has a scheduled meeting with Jenny and Mum.

On his way to Orsa he is pondering intensively. How is he going to tell about his mother Gunnel? That she has committed suicide. He hopes that Mum can cope hearing that. He does not want to lie or keep it a secret. It is much better to tell the truth. It will anyhow come out sooner or later.

Ida has set a table with coffee and freshly baked roll cake in the living room. She and Jenny are sitting there waiting for him. They are curious about what Sven is going to tell them.

Having given Jenny a tender kiss and Mum a warm hug, Sven sits down. He inhales. This is not going to be easy, but it has to be done.

"I met my father last night – in the men's room! When I was cooling down at the basin, he saw my birth mark. He immediately wanted me to meet my grandfather, who was still at the table. I asked him to postpone it. I promised to come to their apartment at Storgatan 12, later when both of you had left."

A trembling sigh is heard from Ida. She is, at the same time, looking both happy and worried. "Oh, Sven, how wonderful for you. I'm so happy for you." She hugs Sven. "I just wonder if they might have called the police yet?"

"No, not yet. Let me continue. I went to their flat rather late last night. We toasted in champagne for our engagement, Jenny. And also for the fact that we had finally met. Then we sat down. I told them what had happened when I was a small child. In the same way and using approximately the same words that you used, Mum, when you told me. I told them how happy I´ve been with you. That nobody else could be a better mother. They listened very attentively, but then David told me…" Sven makes a pause, looking at Ida. "Mum, how are you feeling? Are you OK? Can you bear hearing more?"

Ida nods, and Sven continues. "Yes, David told me something horrible. My mother, Gunnel, committed suicide a year later. She couldn´t bear it, any longer, being without me."

A painful scream is heard from Ida. Her whole body starts trembling. Jenny takes her into her arms, trying to calm her down. After a while, Ida succeeds in forcing a faint smile on her lips, while tears are running down her face. In a trembling voice, she says: "How horrible, how horrible. Oh, my God, what have I done?"

"Yes Mum, it´s really horrible! I think so too. I was completely devastated, hearing this, but I told them that nothing of all that´s happened, could be undone. My father and grandfather were, of course, very upset. They were of the opinion that we ought to report this to the police. Then I told them that they might be forced to choose. Reporting you might mean that they would lose me. Finally, they asked me for some time to ponder. They promised not to contact the police until they´ve talked to me again."

"Oh, the poor souls! Of course they must contact the police. At once!" exclaims Ida.

"No, Mum, it will be as I agreed with them. Time to think. And before I left, we agreed to meet again tonight, after working hours. And they want me to bring Jenny. They want to meet you, my beautiful fiancée. And they said that you, Jenny, might be able to contribute with something that could influence their decision."

Sven is now mentally exhausted. It has been so hard to tell poor Mum. Concerned, he looks at her, but apart from still being pale, she seems both quiet and nerveless. He hopes that she will not rush to the police, being alone.

Rising to go back to work, Sven pulls Jenny aside. Whispering, you co he asks her to stay with Mum during the whole day. And also to check that she is not calling the police in order to denounce herself.

CHAPTER 27

Mora, Sweden – 11 February 1974

When Sven in the afternoon reappears at Ida´s house in Orsa, she is still very pale. She gives him a feeble hug, but does not say much. It is as if all her strength has disappeared. Her steps are slow and heavy. Her look is lifeless. Sven can feel his heart contract in worry. Nothing bad must happen to her.

Jenny takes Sven aside. She informs him that Ida has mostly been resting all day. At first, she did not want any lunch, but after Jenny´s appealing she has finally eaten a little – like a bird, more or less. Neither has she said anything about the morning´s disclosures. Jenny is very worried about her. What will they do? Maybe Doctor Larsson could do something?

"Unfortunately, I don´t think the doctor could do very much", whispers Sven. "Now it´s more of a psychic than of a physical affliction. The main thing is that Mum must not lose her will to live. That she is mentally strong enough to fight the depression and overcome it. She is probably feeling, more or less, as a murderess. Oh, dear Mum! But, Jenny, if you think that Doctor Larsson could help her, then I´ll call him at once."

´"I think you´re quite right in what you´re saying, Sven, but how could we help her to want to live?"

"´For my part, I´d prefer to move back here. For a short term, of course. What do you think, Jenny?"

"The same as you. I´ll also move here. Preferably into your room, together with you, so that you could get a chance to know me a little better." Jenny is almost blushing, saying that. Sven looks as if he´d had a can of red colour thrown onto his face.

"But, if that is inappropriate, then I could fix that small extra room for me. If both of us stay here with your Mum for a while, it might cheer her up a little. And then we could, at the same time, keep an eye on her, making sure she´s eating."

Sven, having now recovered from his shyness, laughingly looks at his fiancée. "Why inappropriate? We´re actually engaged and the year is 1974. I´d love to have a bed companion." He gives Jenny a long kiss. "I´ll be back here tonight to pass the night. You could stay in Mora tonight. You could actually start packing the things you have there. I´m longing very much for you to move here with me. The sooner, the better."

Anders has reserved a table for them at a small quaint Italian restaurant. They have a really nice dinner together. Anders and David like Jenny from the very first moment and the atmosphere is open and hearty. Having finished their dessert, David suggests they return to Storgatan 12 to have a little chat in a calmer environment.

David, having served them a glass of nice red wine and put some snacks on the table, starts talking: "Yes, dear Jenny, I suppose that Sven has told you about the agreement we reached last evening. That Dad and I need some more time to contemplate which decision to make. Now you have your chance to tell your views, Jenny. As a matter of fact, you're now also a family member."

"Yes, I am and I'm happy about that. Quite spontaneously, I like both of you. I'm extremely happy that you and Sven have finally met and he is also so happy about that. But Ida has — even if it was done in the wrong way — up to now been Sven's only family member. They love each other so much. And, in my opinion, that's a love you mustn't kill. She herself knows what terrible consequences her crime has led to. Both Sven and I are deeply worried. She's changed so much since this morning, when she was told that your wife Gunnel had committed suicide." Jenny is tearful, saying this. "What I would like to suggest might be difficult for you to accept, but I think it would be both sensible and human. My suggestion is that you both decide a time limit, let's say a week. Within that week you ought to meet Ida a few times to get to know her as a person. To start with, at a couple of random meetings, that I could organize, and maybe one or a few meetings being a little longer. I don't think that Sven ought to participate, at least not to start with, but I will, however, be present the whole time. What are your feelings about that?"

Anders and Sven look hesitant. Jenny continues: "Don't forget that Ida, when she kidnapped Sven, had recently just lost her own son. She was beside herself of grief. Probably, she didn't quite know what she was doing."

Appealing, Jenny looks at them. "Give her a chance, dear! Don´t let her die of grief, like your Gunnel did." Jenny is looking appealingly at David...

"I find your suggestion both very human and nice", says David. Anders nods affirmatively. "I think we´ll go for it, Jenny."

Sven, who up till now has been silent, also nods. "I just want to tell you that Mum, when she heard about my mother Gunnel, thought you should immediately contact the police. She has, after all, more or less murdered my biological mother."

Anders opens his mouth as if to start talking, but David interrupts him. "Sven, what you don´t know is that Gunnel and I are not your biological parents. Gunnel was not able to get children, so we adopted you. Your biological mother was a girl in her early twenties. She worked as a domestic help in the home of some of our close friends in Örebro. Since we thought her a nice girl, we adopted you immediately you were born. We were in contact with your mother until sometime after your disappearance. About that time, we were informed that she´d been killed in an accident. She had no longer any relatives left in Sweden, since her twin sister had immigrated to the USA. I want you to know all this, even though it doesn´t in effect change anything in what we´re discussing. So, as said earlier, I and Dad accept Jenny´s suggestion."

After mutual hugs, Sven and Jenny leave. He drives her home and then continues to Orsa. He gives Mum a hug

and then he tells her that David and Anders need more
time, before making a decision.

CHAPTER 28

Mora, Sweden – 12 February 1974

In Orsa, calm rests at the breakfast table. Today, Ida has made an extra nice breakfast, inspired by the 'brunch' the high school pupils usually get before a sports days. Sven enjoys it. It is not every day he can eat bacon and eggs. It is really very nice. Ida herself does not want any, but after a while, tired of Sven´s admonitions, she gives up. She swallows one slice of bacon and half an egg.

Sven wipes his mouth. "Thanks a lot for a wonderful breakfast. It was really good. Now I´m going to give you some good news. Jenny and I are planning to move in together,"

"Oh, how nice to hear." Ida smiles happily. "In whose apartment will you live? Jenny is, after all, just staying temporarily at Doctor Larsson´s. It might be better for you to live in your small studio."

"No, Mum. We want to move in with you. My room Is big enough. And we would really like living here with you. You must, of course, tell us if you don´t want it yourself."

Sven is thinking about the only time, so far, that he and Mum had really disagreed. They had even quarrelled and been grim on each other for several days – something very unusual in their relationship. The disagreement had started, when Sven had graduated from the Police Academy and was going to start working at the police in Mora. Mum had then suggested that he move from home, getting a flat of his own in Mora. That way, he would be much closer to work and also learn to manage on his own. He had become so spoilt with a mum taking care of everything. Sven now ought to learn to cook, pay invoices and wash his clothes… Everything that a young man ought to know. Sven had been furious at the thought, believing that Mum no longer cared for him. That she wanted to get rid of him. It had taken them a lot of long discussions between the two of them, before he had finally agreed to move. And he was allowed to keep his old room at Mum´s house, to use when he was spending the night there.

Ida is overjoyed. She of course understands that the young ones want to keep an eye on her, making sure she is eating and taking care of herself. But that does not matter. To have company by the children is a wonderful thing. "If I go to jail, you could take care of the whole house."

"Take it easy. Let´s take each day as it comes. Now I must go to work. Jenny will call you later. I think she wants to visit an art opening in Mora and wants your company." Sven kisses Mum on the cheek before leaving.

An hour later Jenny calls, asking if Ida feels strong enough to accompany her to the art gallery.

"Put on something really beautiful. There is an opening today, and on such occasions lots of people usually turn up. I´ll invite you to a salad afterwards. Could you manage on your own, taking the bus to Mora?"

Jenny is waiting at the bus station. Ida gets a warm hug before they start their walk to the gallery where it is already rather crowded. The exhibition is about wood-carving, more or less in the same style that Döderhul-tarn used carving his creations, but less roughly hewn. Many things have been made locally. There are so many beautiful things to admire. They stroll around for a long while in the different rooms. A young woman is serving the guests juice and finger food.

An elderly man is waving at Jenny. "Oh, but Jenny, how nice to see you!"

Jenny introduces them to each other. "Aunt Ida, this is one of my friends: Anders Torstensson. And Anders, this is a very dear friend of mine: Ida Martinsson."

After a moment, Jenny adds:"Aunt Ida, I want to invite you for coffee and a cake with lots of calories. I think that would make you feel good. You, Anders, are wel-come to join us, so that the two of you get to know each other."

They walk to a small quiet tea room further down the street. Having sat down with their coffee and cake in front of them, the conversation starts a little haltingly, but when Anders begins to tell about his experiences and adventures in Australia it does not take long be-fore the three of them are talking in a very relaxed way. Anders is a good narrator. Everything he says becomes alive. Ida is feeling a lot of sympathy for Anders and is happy for the chat. She has not yet connected his name with Sven.

Jenny suddenly says: "What a coincidence. I've always wanted to go to Australia to pan for gold and find opals, and then I meet you, Anders, who's doing exactly that." Then she looks confused. "How do I know that I've **always** wanted to do that? Strange. But maybe it's another memory awakening?"

Ida is visibly happy hearing Jenny's disclosure. Anders, on the other hand, looks like a question mark. "Do you have a bad memory?"

"Hasn't Sven told you that I suffer from memory loss? Maybe my name isn't Jenny, but I believe it is. Yes, it's a long story that I'll have to tell at another time." Jenny is quickly finishing the sentence as she sees that Ida is on her way to say something.

"Anders, do you know Sven?" asks Ida in a muted voice. "Do you have a son called David?" She has suddenly understood why the name Anders Torstensson seemed so familiar. Now she is turning pale again.

"Yes Ida, I have. And my grandson is called Sven. Please don't look so afraid. We're not dangerous. Both Jenny and Sven have talked about you with such warmth. And I must admit that I think you're an adorable person." He smiles soothingly at Ida. "But now I think I'd better drive you Ida and you Jenny back to Orsa, so that you can have a rest."

During the drive all three of them are silent in the car. Ida has so much to think about. She likes Anders. He is a warm and sympathetic person. And Sven's father, David, is probably like him.

Ida thanks for the ride, before she and Jenny leave the car. "And thank you, dear Anders, for a lovely meeting. I would very much want to get to know both you and David. You're nice people, I've understood. I'm sorry that I, right now, don't have the strength to invite you into my home. It'll have to be on another occasion."

"Jenny, I think you'll have to pour me a small brandy. I think I'll need it. Oops, what a day! What experiences!"

Ida sinks down in her comfortable easy chair, sighing exhaustedly. She is relieved not to be alone any longer.

"Jenny, when I've recovered, perhaps you could help me organizing a dinner here, with Anders and David as guests. Let's plan it for the day after tomorrow. I believe Sven finishes his work early that day."

"I'd be happy to help you." Jenny laughs happily. She is, with all her heart, wishing that the serious question about the kidnapping be solved soon. Everybody is still so tense. Jenny has seen by herself that David is a caring and warm person. She thinks that the chances are good that he and Ida will like each other. Jenny has also noticed that Anders is already fond of her. Now it is all about David's decision.

They sit down at the kitchen table, equipped with paper, pen and cookbooks. Now they will put together a delicious menu. Not too extravagant but nice. Jenny is cheering inside as Ida finally seems to have regained her appetite. A lot is already won. According to the doctor it is very important that she eats.

"I think you should take a small rest after the food. We can continue planning later."

One thought strikes Jenny. "Aunt Ida, I´ve been thinking about something during the last few days. There is one thing missing here in Mora. Why have they removed that enormous and so nice Dala horse? And I can´t even find the place where it was standing."

Astonished Ida looks at Jenny. "What are you talking about? Which Dala horse? I can´t remember ever seeing an enormous Dala horse here in Mora."

Could this be yet another memory from Jenny´s subconscious? Ida must remember to tell Sven what Jenny just said.

CHAPTER 29

Orsa, Sweden – 14 February 1974

Ida is happy. She and Jenny have composed a nice menu. And Anders has, on behalf of himself and David, accepted the dinner invitation. Ida, however, understands that the evening with them might end in a tragic way. David might decide to contact the police. But Sven has, after all, found his family and he and Jenny will be happy together. She, herself, might be OK in prison. She will have to accept it as a "long term holiday".

Anders calls, a little later in the evening. He wonders if they might bring a couple of nice Swedish friends to the dinner the following evening. It is the couple they visited in Pennsylvania on their way home from Australia and with whom they thereafter have continued to Sweden. Their names are Maja and Yngve and they are more or less of the same age as David. Ida, loving having guests, immediately invites them too.

The dinner party is a success. Maja and Yngve prove to be a very nice couple and Ida, Sven and Jenny feel at ease with them.

Ida has placed David at her side so that they can talk a lot with each other. And they talk. They really do. About everything. Art, literature, values in life and upbringing, whatever comes into their minds. The others smile, seeing how engaged Ida and David are in their conversation.

Maja and Yngve have, before the dinner, decided not to mention, in any way, their own search for Maja´s brother Johan, his children and Maja´s father Wally. That has nothing to do with the lives of Sven, Jenny and Ida. That issue will have to wait until some other occasion. Right now focus is on Sven and his newfound family. And of course, also on his sweet fiancée Jenny.

David has, under a silence promise, told Maja and Yngve the story about Sven´s disappearance and life. He has also mentioned that he, tonight, must decide what to do with Ida. Whether he should involve the police or not.

Using his knife, David is making a clinking sound on his wine glass in order to get everybody´s attention. He rises to make a speech. ”Dear Ida, thank you for a wonderful and exquisite dinner with a fantastic atmosphere around the table. Tonight I have met a wonderful woman. You, Ida! You other two lovely ladies will have to excuse that I´m only talking about Ida. Ida, you´re both beautiful and intelligent. And you radiate such incredible warmth which I can´t resist. Anders has been telling me very good things about you and is already fond of you. I´m now, after only a couple of hours knowing you, joining the crowd of people worshipping you. I would like to meet you often from here on. Get to know you even better. Yes, I mean just that. I´ve made my decision: You´ve nothing to fear. I´ll not involve the police. What happened, happened long ago and isn´t important any longer. Forgotten! At the same time, I would also like to thank you for turning my son Sven into a nice and wonderful person. As Sven has said: Nobody else could have been a better mother. Thank you, sweet Ida."

There is absolute silence around the table. The first part of the speech almost sounded like a proposal. Then the ovations start. Jenny is crying, out of relief. Also Sven. Ida gives David a warm hug. Her eyes are shiny, because of withheld tears. It is as if Ida had added a decimetre to her height. Her demeanour is straight but relaxed. Her eyes glitter and there is like a shine around her.

CHAPTER 30

Torrevieja, Spain – 18 December 1973

Agnes Rojales is half lying on the chalk white chaise longue out on the terrace of her rather flashy Spanish villa in Torrevieja. She takes a big gulp of mojito from her glass. She is being irritated, and that is visible in her, usually, very beautiful face. She can feel how a small part of a mint leaf is getting stuck on one of her front teeth. She angrily spits it out. Then she puts her glass down on the small coffee table so heavily that half the contents flip out. Is everyone quite incompetent? Why can her servants not do a thing as simple as mixing a mojito without causing a mess?

She is bored, and she is tired of behaving well. She has spent ten years of her life, locked into a mental hospital, just because of an old man's accusation. Oh dang, she does not want to experience that again, but the alternative would have been prison and that would probably have been even worse. And, it is, of course, a nice feeling to have stopped taking drugs. Using drugs does not make anyone more beautiful, but being high on them had been so damned nice!

Yes, this thing about being beautiful is very important to Agnes. She knows that she, in spite of being already 42 years old, does not look a day older than 25. Sometimes, looking at a couple of photos of herself, she cannot see any big discrepancies, compared to how she is looking today. She is tall and slender and has a fantastic copper-red hair. It is now falling softly down her shoulders. Her eyes are green and her skin is flawless. Her nails are perfectly cut and beautifully painted. The shade of her makeup is exactly the right one. Yes, she can actually not find any defects on herself. Except… She gets furious when she thinks about the skin markings her two children have caused her at their births. The markings are maybe not that big, but she knows that they are there. Not to mention the horrible pain the child birth in itself had caused her. No wonder, she is feeling such strong hatred, when she is thinking of both her children.

The obstetricians, having seen her complete iciness towards the children, had explained that she was a true example of a woman suffering from child birth depression. It would pass. But it had never done that. Rather the opposite. Having to deal with pee and poop, getting her perfect nails destroyed by all the work with the children, had rather increased her hatred towards them.

No, she did not find it, at all, strange that she had tried to get rid of her tormentors. It was, however, a bloody nuisance that her father-in-law, Wally, at that time had lived with her and her husband. Wally always turned up at the wrong moment. As for example, when she was pushing a pillow over her daughter's face and, at the same time, another pillow over her son's face, when they were asleep. Had he turned up a few minutes later, she would have been free of the children.

Afterwards, there had, of course, been real chaos at home. Her husband did not want to believe what his father told him. He almost threw Wally out of the house. She had mediated between them. Had declared that she had only been taking care of the children, so peace was restored, but, unfortunately, she had not been able to curb her hatred for long. A few months later, she had assisted her daughter in climbing the balcony railing. She had been standing beside her, watching the girl's efforts, ready to throw also her son down. Once more, Wally had turned up at the very last moment hindering her.

This time nobody believed her. She was instead reported to the police for attempted murder of her children. Something she still does not understand, however, is that her husband managed to get her sentence changed from prison to closed psychiatric care, but he might have remembered how much he used to love her. Or felt sorry for her having started using drugs. But, oh my God, there had been absolutely nothing fun to do in the dump they were living in! Boulder City. Who had ever heard of that place? It was a small road intersection, filled with bearded gold panners? And her husband was such a diligent bore that it was embarrassing.

Agnes stretches indolently, inspecting her nails. Perfect! Then she hears a call on the door. A moment later, the butler turns up announcing that Agnes' friend Linda has arrived, bringing a mountain of boxes. Linda is Spanish and newly divorced from a rich Swede. She has, after the divorce, been able to get hold of a lot of valuable works of art, belonging to her ex-husband. Linda has asked Agnes if she can put the boxes with art at Agnes' place, waiting for things to calm down.

After a moment of intensive cheek kissing between the two friends, Linda, wide-eyed, exclaims: "But how lovely it all is. You were indeed very shrewd to catch Carlos. And to make him marry you. By the way, sorry about your loss – so sad that you've already become a widow, isn't it?

"Yes, Linda. Thinking of how expensive that car was, I think it ought to have had better brakes. Do you want a mojito?"

Agnes continues:"Oh, now I remember that there's something I haven't told you. When I recently was in the States for a short period, something happened that was a real pain in the ass. The car rental company, I normally use, wanted 2,000 US dollars to repair some small dents and scratches on the car. They looked at me in a funny way, saying that I would probably prefer not to have an investigation done by the insurance company."

"Oh, how nasty of them. You're a good driver. What happened?"

"I paid, of course, but now I'll change Rental Company."

"No, I mean: from where did the dents come? Did you back on something?"

"Stupid you, when you back on something the dents appear at the rear. Those dents were at the front. I just kind of saw a ghost of my first husband together with a boy on the pavement in front of the car. I, of course, stepped on the accelerator. But there were only small scratches, one dent and one stain. 2,000 dollars…!"

"Dear Agnes, ghosts do make neither dents nor scratches. It must have been some dust-bins."

When the butler has entered with Linda´s drink, Linda says:"Agnes, now I´m going to tell you something. You know that my ex-mother-in-law comes from Dalarna, don´t you? She helped my ex-husband to wrap some valuables, using newsprint, before putting them into the boxes. By some strange coincidence, the boxes have now come into my possession instead of my husband´s." She giggles. "As I checked a couple of boxes this morning I found a news story from Dalarna. It´s about a lost girl with a memory loss. There´s a photo of her in the story. Look."

Agnes receives the creasy newspaper page that Linda offers her. "Yes, and…?"

"But look at the photo. Whom does she resemble?"

"Well, in a way she looks familiar, but I can´t really say. What do you think?"

"She resembles you, Agnes. She is a copy of you, in those photos you´ve shown me from your youth."

Agnes stands up, walks into her bedroom and returns with a couple of photos. She compares the photo in the newspaper article with her own photos and then slowly says:"You might be right! But they say that every human has a look-alike – maybe she´s mine."

When Linda, a couple of hours later, leaves the house, Agnes sits down to think. It is really extremely odd how much the girl resembles Agnes. This is something she has to do some research on. This is almost as important as trying to locate father-in-law Wally to claim revenge. The revenge she has been brooding over ever since he reported her for attempted murder of the children. Agnes realizes that she is now starting on a dangerous road.

When time had finally arrived for her to be discharged from the Swiss hospital, the doctor had told her that he no longer thought his former diagnosis was correct: that she had some kind of antisocial personality disorder or perhaps borderline. When she had started telling him about her nightmares and hallucinations and the voices she frequently heard, he was more inclined to believe that she had schizophrenia. Therefore it was very important that she continue with the therapy treatment and that she take her mood stabilizing medicine. If she did not do that, she risked having even stronger mood swings. And that could be dangerous. Not only for her but also for other people. He also said that he therefore would have preferred to keep her at the hospital, but that she - since she now had stayed at the hospital for the whole sentence – was free to choose whether she wanted to leave. Agnes had listened to the doctor, had nodded and smiled but then had declared that she chose freedom. And then she had had her revenge for all those wasted ten years. What a wonderful feeling!

Agnes has lately also felt that something is happening to her. As long as she had obeyed the doctor´s orders she had felt more or less normal, but now she has, once again, also at very strange moments, started to feel hatred towards people. Like for example a while ago when she saw the newspaper photo of that young girl in Mora. Maybe she had better start taking her medicine again. She is so curious about that girl. She must try to meet her. And in order to succeed in that, she probably must start behaving normally. At least to begin with.

But how would she be able to meet Jane – as the girl is called in the news article? Yes, now she knows. Vasaloppet would take place at the beginning of March. She could then go to Mora and "happen" to bump into the girl. Mora cannot be very big. Agnes will probably be able to find the girl and teach her a lesson. Agnes certainly does not want any "Look-Alike". But Agnes intends to be cunning. Not booking anything in Sweden in her own name and only paying cash, when possible. She calls Linda and asks her if she could borrow one of Linda´s many credit cards. Linda´s rich ex-husband has, at the divorce, forgotten to demand back from Linda all the credit cards. He has not even blocked them. And he surely must have seen, by now, that Linda frequently is using them. Linda immediately answers 'yes' to Agnes´ question.

Now Agnes can use both Linda´s name and credit card number, when she books Stadshotellet in Mora and the car rental there. Perfect. She, furthermore, intends wearing a wig during her whole stay in Sweden. A brown wig and brown contact lenses. That way it will be much more difficult to trace her, if something should go wrong.

CHAPTER 31

Mora, Sweden – 16 February 1974

Agnes is pissed off. She is so angry that she is almost boiling inside. The world is really not fair. Why should others, far from being as beautiful as she, get all the attention? She is the one earning it.

She has now been in Sweden for some weeks. When she, in Torrevieja, finally decided to go up north to Mora in Dalarna in order to know more about the girl in the news story, it had been a quick move. She had, of course, made a detour to Madrid before departure. She had, after all, to get some more clothes. Agnes felt it was essential to follow the fashion season for skiing clothing. If not, people would stare at her in a funny way. And if you, on top of that, are staying at Stadshotellet in Mora, you certainly would need some modern evening dresses. The shopping tour to Madrid had cost a lot of money, but that did not matter. Carlos had left her millions, when he died. She can waste them in whatever way she wants. She giggles. After all, something good had come out of that dreary marriage. She is lucky that it did not last for very long.

Since Agnes had gone to Madrid and from there directly to Sweden, she forgot to buy more medicine. Out of habit, she always goes to Alicante to buy it. Under no circumstances whatsoever, people in Torrevieja are to know that she is a schizophrenic. And she has even forgotten to bring her prescription. To contact a doctor and tell him her secrets is absolutely out of the question.

And now she is sitting here in Mora, feeling in an even worse mood than before. She finds it difficult to control herself. She has even been close to beating up the cleaning girl, when she one morning entered the room believing that Agnes was not there. Agnes was asleep in bed and was abruptly awakened by the cleaning girl's entrance. When the girl told her that Agnes should have put up the sign "Do not disturb", Agnes was very close to hitting her.

Her stay in Mora has been a catastrophe, already from start. The evening of arrival, she dressed up for the Saturday dance. The brown colour of her wig fitted her new evening dress so well. And using her brown contact lenses, she found herself incredibly beautiful. Since she had not reserved a table in the restaurant, she was shown to a corner table. The absolutely worst table. And the service was almost non-existent. Not to mention the abominable food.

Sitting there alone, sipping a glass of champagne – actually horrible that too – a young man in tuxedo entered. He was holding a lady under each arm. A young girl and an older woman. Agnes was almost choking, having still champagne in her mouth. The girl was the same one as in the news story - the girl that Agnes had come to check on and the girl she, hopefully, would teach a lesson.

On top of it all, that asshole after a while went down on his knees, proposing to the girl. And they had gotten fanfares. And lots of people congratulated them. All this while she was sitting all alone in her corner. Unfair. So unfair. To get some revenge she had disdainfully been staring at the girl the whole evening. And the girl had probably noticed that, since she whispered something to her fiancé as they were leaving. But before that, Agnes had followed the girl into the ladies' room, saying some words of truth through the cubicle wall. Well done, Agnes! Agnes is really hoping that she has destroyed the evening for the brat.

She had been so furious that evening that she, the following morning, had left for Stockholm. She had expected the Stockholm people to be better in showing appreciation for beautiful persons. But, oh no. Nobody even seemed to care about her in the first-class restaurants she visited during her four days in the capital. And, at her return to Mora, the hotel owner was upset with her. He pointed out that she should have informed him about her absence. Nobody had known where she was. Or if she had absconded, not wanting to pay her bill. This did not put her in any better mood.

Agnes sighs heavily. As a matter of fact, she cannot go on like this. She must concentrate on her main task during this trip. Putting the hook on 'wannabes' is, however, a work she finds meaningful. Doing that, she gets rid of competition as being the most beautiful woman. But her main purpose is, after all, to find father-in-law Wally, and to give him a matchless revenge for her ten years locked up in a psychiatric hospital.

Many years ago, Wally – the name means dimwit - was obsessed by Vasaloppet and that obsession would hardly have passed. And Wally always was at the centre of things, being such a chauvinist. He had even witnessed against her, during the trial, saying that she had acted in a strange way.

During her pondering, Agnes suddenly finds a strategy on how to locate Wally. It is an easy strategy. The hipster from Statt is, as it looks, everybody´s goal of attention. Therefore Wally will, undoubtedly, approach her. Maybe he has not yet come to town. She only has to point mark the girl and wait for Wally to turn up. Then she will get her revenge, and she will be famous doing that. People will understand her.

Earlier in life, when Agnes lived in Colorado with her husband and children, she was quite a good skier. Cross-country skiing suited her best. And doing that, she need not be afraid of hurting herself. Maybe getting life-long scars. No, slalom was too dangerous. So she went for cross-country skiing. She actually became quite good at it, according to their friends of that time. And now, having bought the most expensive and modern skiing clothes, she ought to start using them. To get out into the ski trails, to shine before the others. Being able both to show her beauty and her skill. Just imagine how jealous they would be. And that hipster would be reduced into a nothing in the eyes of everybody.

Yes, waiting for Wally, Agnes will continue intimidating the girl. Make her feel ridiculous, stupid and ugly. By the way, did she not hear that awful evening at Statt, that someone had called the girl Jenny? Yes, that was it. Her name is apparently Jenny. Or maybe not. Perhaps they just call her that. According to the news story, she has lost her memory.

To begin with, Agnes must find out where Jenny lives. She has seen Jenny, around 10 a.m. stepping out of a beige-coloured Volvo Amazon. Collecting her skis and poles from the car roof. After that she usually waves at the driver, who moves on. Thus it seems that someone normally gives her a ride. Jenny might not even live in Mora itself, as Agnes had earlier thought. But she will have to keep a lookout this afternoon. Jenny might be picked up then. Probably by the same guy or by her fiancé. Agnes has a car so the only thing she has to do is to follow that one.

Agnes is lucky. At 4 p.m. Jenny comes walking with her equipment on her shoulder. She stops at the street corner, close to Statt. The beige car stops and Jenny and her odds and ends are loaded into it. Then the car moves on. Agnes follows it, keeping a certain distance. She does not want to be discovered.

The girl leaves the car in Orsa, outside a red two-storey timber house. The door is opened. A woman steps outside, giving Jenny a welcoming hug. What? That is the old woman, sitting at the same table as Jenny the other night. Do they live together?

Agnes stays in the dark for an hour to see if also the fiancé will turn up. Yes, he suddenly appears, at a good speed, in his old rusty car. Why can people not get themselves beautiful cars? Those rusty things disturb Agnes´ sense of beauty.

Now Agnes knows how to proceed with her plans. The following morning, she dresses in her most beautiful ski dress. She puts on her brown wig and her brown contact lenses. Then she drives to the ski trail. Her skis have been put into the rental car. There she stands at the beginning of the trail, pretending to be busy with her skis, waiting for Jenny to turn up. When Agnes sees her striding along, she puts on her skis and rushes to catch up with her.

"Hi, there! Could you stop for a moment?"

Confused, Jenny stops. She recognizes the woman as the one having stared at her in such a strange way at Statt. "Yes, what do you want?"

"I saw you the other night, when you were getting engaged. Congratulations! But I couldn´t help noticing that the person dying your hair is not good at it. It really looks homemade. I wanted to help you, by letting you know that. So that you know. And, by the way… Your skin is looking awfully washed-out. You should probably go to someone who can help you with that. Look at my skin, it´s really perfect!"

Jenny just stares. She is so astonished by the rudeness that she cannot even bring herself to interrupt the woman. What kind of person is this? You do not act like this; do you – at least not to strangers?

"Do you want me to ski in front of you, showing how to do it?" asks Agnes in a superior way.

"No thank you, I can manage on my own", says Jenny, as politely as she can manage. Anger is boiling inside her. She skis on, at top speed, but she can feel that her ski tour has been destroyed. Her mood is now at zero. She stops, turning around. She is going to interrupt today´s skiing. It is not fun any longer, after what has happened. Suddenly she feels a violent push and falls laterally in the trail. Agnes swishes past her in the other trail, happily waving at her. She has apparently taken the opportunity to push Jenny, when she was alongside her.

"Hello, how are you?" A voice is heard from some distance. It is Nisse Nilsson on his way to today´s skiing. "Oh, but look, isn´t it Mora's Jenny lying here. Come and I´ll help you get up. What happened? Why did she do that? Who is she, after all? Do you know each other?"

Jenny sorts out the mess of skis and poles. With the help of Nisse she is soon standing up again. Brushing away the snow, she thanks for the help. She explains that she does not understand anything. She does not know the person. Cannot understand why she seems angry at her. Does not at all know who she is. When Jenny has explained to Nisse what has happened, she suddenly says. "I actually don´t understand why I´m feeling that you and I know each other. I´ve a feeling that I usually call you Uncle Nisse. Do you know why?”

”No, I actually don´t.” Nisse drags on the answer. ”But in a way, I think you´re right. I wonder if we haven´t met somewhere sometime. You seem familiar to me!” He is brooding for a short while. ”Listen Jenny, I heard a small bird whispering – we might call the bird Sven – that you´ll, disguised, run the Vasaloppet race. Sven is my friend, and he´s told me confidentially.”

”Yes, I will”, answers Jenny. ”For some reason, I feel that I have to do it. I, actually, don´t understand it my-self. But I have to do it.”

”I was thinking that I, as the old skier I am, maybe could help you with something. Do you think you´re good at waxing the skis? If not, I could maybe help you explaining how it works? I haven´t run the race in rather many years and I´m not planning on participat-ing in it this year either. Therefore I´ve enough time to help you.”

”Oh, that would be wonderful”, exclaims Jenny with a smile. ”I, actually, don´t know much at all about the waxing. And I know that it´s so important. Do you really want to help me – Uncle Nisse?” asks she with a smile. She is suddenly in a radiant mood.

”Yes, I think we should start tomorrow morning. Around this time and here. I´ll bring some different waxes. Then you´ll have to ski for one day to test it. Then we´ll try another wax. They say that the weather will change quite a bit during the next few days. That´ll be good when you test different ways of handling the skis. Is that OK with you?”

”Fantastic! Lovely! Thank you ever so much!” Jenny is rejoicing with joy. Oh, how wonderful it is to meet a lovely and kind person, having met that awful woman.

CHAPTER 32

Mora, Sweden – 18 February 1974

Two mornings later, Agnes decides to ski a bit in the trail, before confronting Jenny again. When she sees Jenny, at some distance behind her, she leaves the trail to hide behind some trees. Jenny is swishing by. Agnes follows her in the distance. Jenny is slowing down. Finally she stops. She seems to be looking for a place to rest. After a while, she takes off her skis and walks up to a big boulder near the edge with a view over the valley. She brushes it and sits down, taking out her water bottle. It looks so idyllic.

There comes Agnes. At top speed, she skis towards the boulder. Makes a turnabout in order to get a quick stop. Throws herself towards Jenny, not caring that she still has her skis on. Now she has, once again, become infuriated at the sight of the girl. She absolutely has to do what she has wanted to do for such a long time. With both her hands, she pushes Jenny´s lower back. She does it with such a force that Jenny is almost flying off the boulder. She is hanging in the air for a quick moment before starting to slide down the steep hill. Jenny is turning her alarmed and flabbergasted face upwards. It is not until then that she discovers Agnes. Jenny´s face is distorted in death anxiety as she is trying to gain a foothold.

But then Jenny´s feet finally find a ledge she can use as support. Jenny is now once again in balance. Her hands have found things to grab hold of. She manages to stay on. A few millimetres at a time and with big difficulties she succeeds to climb. Agnes is blown away.

Next morning Jenny is still chocked by the incident. When she tells uncle Nisse about it, he is very upset. "From now on, the two of us will train together, Jenny", says he. "That woman seems dangerous. I wonder why she´s going for you. It seems as if she really hates you. Are you sure that you don´t know who she is?"

During the following days, Jenny and Nisse keep company in the trail. When Nisse wants to ski at his own pace, he does it when Jenny is not there. At such moments he asks her to either be at home with Ida or in Mora town with lots of people around her. On several occasions, he also speaks with Sven, pointing out that the police must try to find out who that woman is. If they know that, then it might be easier to understand why she is chasing Jenny and nobody else. They are thinking of bringing her to the police station for questionin, but it is very difficult to prove that it was not an accident. It is a matter of word against word. Might this have something to do with Jenny´s earlier life, before her memory loss?

CHAPTER 33

Mora, Sweden – 25 February 1974

During the last few days, Agnes has found it difficult to approach Jenny. There are always people around her. And nowadays, Jenny always is in the company of an older man when she is in the skiing trail. Could that man maybe be Wally?

But there are other ways to irritate Jenny. To make her feel embarrassed. It does not always have to be with violence, even though violence is always close for Agnes. She could also try to make Jenny look ridiculous in front of other people. Make them stare at her in a strange way.

It is not very difficult to find such opportunities. Like for example, when Agnes is standing behind Jenny in the cash register queue in the supermarket, she frowns and exclaims:"Yuk, it´s smelling so bad here. It´s uncivilized to fart in a supermarket!" It does not smell bad at all, but the people in the queue look at Jenny in an accusatory way. Oops, how embarrassed Jenny is then. Her face becomes blossoming red.

In the bookstore Agnes exclaims:"But hi there! Are you really putting books into your handbag?" Once again, accusatory glances at Jenny, although she has not done anything.

In this way, Agnes continues to taunt Jenny. Each day, Jenny is feeling less and less inclined to go to Mora for shopping. There is always something nasty happening,

caused by that awful woman. Jenny does not understand what wrong she has done to the woman. They
do not even know each other.

Jenny speaks to Sven, telling him about those incidents. Downhearted, he says that the police cannot
intervene as long as the woman makes the accusations
so general. She could defend herself saying that they
were not aimed at Jenny. No, the woman must, in a
direct way, turn to Jenny accusing her. And there must
be witnesses.

Only a couple of days before the Vasaloppet race,
when no one else is close, Agnes says in a threatening
voice:"Jenny, I know that you´ll participate in the race.
If you, at all, can keep your skis on and come as far as
Oxberg, I can guarantee you that you´ll not come any
further. I´ll make sure of that. It´ll be wonderful to see
your face, when it dawns on you that you´ll not be able
to complete the race." Smiling scornfully, Agnes walks
away.

Was that not a threat? In the evening, Jenny tells
about this during dinner. Ida gets scared. Also Sven
looks upset. "Sorry Jenny, but there was, according to
you, no witness. But I´ll talk with my colleagues and
also with Nisse. Somebody will have to keep close to
that hag, during the race. Maybe one of the race
guards. That woman has gone too far now. She´ll get
caught and be forced to leave."

CHAPTER 34

Mora, Minnesota, USA – 1 March 1974

"Finally! Something is finally happening", says Mikael in a happy voice, as he is putting down the receiver.

Sonja hurries into the living room. She does not care if the food on the stove gets burnt. She has heard the joy in Mikael's voice. Understands that it must be about Jenny. She is trembling with anticipation.

"No, my darling. Go into the kitchen and turn off the hotplate first. I certainly don't want burnt food", says her husband, frowning.

"Yes, yes. I'll soon be back." And she really is. How she could, in such a quick moment, go to the kitchen and return, transcends Mikael's understanding. "Yes, who was it? And what's happened?"

"It was the lawyer, Nicklas Burger. He has spoken to his contact within the state police, a moment ago. Now they have checked all the answers from the shipping companies. And they had nothing to tell."

"Nooo," Sonja is disappointed. She had really hoped that they would be successful that way.

"Calm down, honey. After that Nicklas clarified his answer. No shipping company has hired anyone that could be Jenny. But one company has had a passenger, who fits in really well with her. Long, copper-red hair and green eyes. In the right size and of the right age."

"Oh my lord, where is she? Where is my little girl? Tell me!"

"If you can keep your mouth shut for a moment, you´ll know. Well, it was Tor Line, a company on the route between Felixstowe in England and Gothenburg in Sweden. One of the girls at the reception, who has been away on a long leave, now remembers her."

"But how can she remember Jenny? A long time must have passed since she travelled on the boat?"

Already before Sonja has finished talking, Mikael continues: "She noticed Jenny when Jenny got her cabin key, at the departure in England. She found Jenny very sweet, but she reacted when she noticed how terribly sad she seemed. Jenny had asked how she could get to Dalarna. She then got a map from the receptionist. And then… Don´t interrupt me all the time, Sonja." Mikael almost shouts at his wife, who looks scared. Mikael hardly ever raises his voice.

"Go on, Mikael."

"Yes, and then Jenny returned crying to the reception. Someone had stolen her duffel bag with all her belongings. Also the passports were in it. The receptionist reported it, in accordance with the company rules, but the bag was not found onboard. Then Jenny disembarked in Gothenburg." Mikael is silent. He has nothing more to add.

"Poor Jenny, to lose everything. As if she hadn´t had enough already. Do you mean, Mikael, that she´s in Sweden?"

"Absolutely. That is if she hasn´t continued. But I don´t think she has. Don´t forget that she´s also Swedish."

"I suggest we invite Monica and Peggy and their parents for dinner the day after tomorrow. Then we could, together, discuss what Jenny has said about Sweden. She might have told someone that there is a certain place she´d like to visit. Johan and his father have always been so secretive about their past."

"Good, Sonja. What a brilliant idea."

Sonja calls both families, inviting them to dinner. At the same time, she explains why they should meet and that it would be good if everyone could start thinking about their contacts with Jenny, already before the dinner. In that way, they might gain some valuable time.

As always at Sonja´s and Mikael´s home, the dinner is joyful, excellent and agreeable. As expected, it is Monica and Peggy who can contribute most about Jenny. Being best friends, they could have heard things the grown-ups have not heard. And they have.

When the grown-ups have contributed with the little they know, Monica starts talking. "Look, Jenny gave me this photo once. It´s from Lake Siljan, a lake in Dalarna.

She thinks it´s the most beautiful lake in the world, but I didn´t agree. I think our lakes here are at least as beautiful."

Now Peggy starts. "Once, when Jenny was angry at her grandfather, she came to me. She said that it was so silly that she and Anton were forbidden to tell anything about the family´s background in Sweden. As if they were thieves or something. She had indeed, on one occasion, been eavesdropping. She had heard her father saying that it was a little strange that out of the three places in which they had been living, two had the same name."

"And imagine, both those places have more or less a similar skiing race", adds Peggy.

"But girls, you´ve just solved our problem. You´re wonderful. Let me hug both of you!" exclaims Mikael jubilant. "I knew it; I knew that there had to be a natural link. You just found it."

He pulls Sonja up from the chair and starts a wild polka through the living room with her, only without music.

The others questioningly stare at Mikael. What has happened to the man?

"And I can, indeed, add something to that", says Mikael proudly, having finished the dancing. "Our Mora was declared sister city to the other town with the same name. As late as in 1972. Only just a couple of years ago."

"Do you mean that you´re talking about Mora in Dalarna, in Sweden?" asks Monica´s father, who knows a lot about the story of Mora.

"Yep, exactly. Mora at Lake Siljan in the county of Dalarna in the kingdom of Sweden. That is exactly where our Jenny ought to be now. That´s where we´re going to search!"

"Yes, so many coincidences. It simply has to be as you say", agrees Peggy´s mother. "What should we do now? How should we proceed?"

While the others are talking, Sonja is sitting silent on a chair. Her tears are running, but she does not wipe them off. All the time, new ones are coming. Will she, finally, soon be seeing Jenny again? She is longing so much to be able to comfort and help poor Jenny. After all, the young girl has no family left. Then, suddenly, she toughens up. "We´re going there, you and I, Mikael. We´ll leave already tomorrow morning. Even if I have to knock on every door in the town in order to find Jenny, I´ll do that. Mikael, we must find our best photos of her to bring with us."

Mikael tenderly kisses his dear Sonja. "Yes, my love, we´ll leave immediately. But first I´ve to call Nicklas Burger. I´ll test his home number. He´s said that we can use it, if it´s urgent. And now it is."

Mikael sits down at the desk in the study and dials the emergency number Nicklas has given him. The wife answers, somewhat grouchy, but when Mikael explains that the call is urgent, she brings her husband to the phone. Mikael tells the whole story about how they have tried to find out where Jenny might be. And how they had arrived at their conclusion.

"Quite wonderful, Mikael. I think you´re right in your guess. Mora and Mora. It must, obviously, be like that." Mikael can judge by Nicklas´ voice how relieved he is. The destiny of the poor young girl must have affected him seriously. Now it can probably be solved, he hopes. "I´ll be booking a flight for you and Sonja and me for tomorrow with Pan Am. Do you think you´ll have enough time to get ready?"

Mikael cautiously asks:"Do you think your law firm could pay our tickets, for the time being?"

"Don´t worry. The estate will take care of costs like that. Just make sure that you´ll be at the Minneapolis airport very early tomorrow morning. Let´s say at 7.00 a.m. I´ll also be there at that time. If we need to be there earlier, I´ll call you as soon as I´ve spoken with the airline."

"Oh, it´s such a good feeling that you´re helping us, Nicklas. Thank you so much for your help. Should we bring any special documents? In that case, we could check for them in Jenny´s house."

"No, I´ll bring the papers we might need. See you early tomorrow morning. And I wish you a tight sleep, at last."

"Thank you and likewise", says Mikael, finishing the call.

Jubilant the party now splits up, wishing each other good night. They understand that their host and hostess have a lot to take care of. And that they will have to rise very early in order to catch the flight.

At Nicklas Burger's home there is a phone call at 3.00 a.m. It's George, his dad, who wants to chat. He explains, in a very detailed way, how very nice the new 70-year old female guest from the adjoining corridor is. Nicklas sighs. He could really have needed some more sleep before the departure for the airport. Nicklas, absent-minded, listens to George's continued story about how he has just cleaned his wardrobe in his room at the retirement home. Then, suddenly, Nicklas sharpens his ears and, at once, becomes wide awake.

"And, listen Nicklas, I just found my documents — the ones that were lost. Do you remember me telling you that I still had a set of documents regarding Wally, in which I hadn't erased anything? Well, they were in my wardrobe. I wonder how they got there."

"But, oh my God. Dad, I need them at once."

"No, impossible. You'll have to fetch them some time tomorrow. Now everybody is asleep."

"But I'm catching a flight for Sweden within a few hours. I must have them now. At once!"

"OK, Nicklas, are you maybe be going to Mora in Sweden, Wally's old birthplace?"

"Dad, have you known about Mora the whole time? Why haven´t you told me about it earlier?"

"Well, maybe you didn´t ask me. You should know that I´m, actually, not always senile. So how do we solve this? There´s nobody opening the door at this time. Could you come to my window so that I can give you the whole pile of documents through the window?"

"Wonderful, Dad. I´ll come at once. Thank you so much, dear Dad!"

After really quick packing, a dangerous drive at high speed to George´s retirement home and a lot of hush-hush from other sleepy guests, being disturbed by Nicklas´ window knockings, Nicklas finally has a whole dossier of the awaited important documents. He puts them into his briefcase. Now it is important that he reach the airport on time. And he does. Only five minutes before the appointed meeting time, he arrives, sweaty and starving but in a good mood, to his appointment with Sonja and Mikael.

CHAPTER 35

Minneapolis, Minnesota, USA – Mora, Sweden – 2 March 1974

The three happy travellers meet outside the Departure Terminal in the morning. Nicklas does not tell the others about the busy night he has had in order to arrive on time. He does not want to wake up any hopes until he himself has had a possibility to study the newfound documents.

The flight goes smoothly. Nicklas is sleeping during the whole trip, so there is no time left to read the documents. Sonja and Mikael are sitting, holding hands, whispering to each other. They are wondering about the outcome of the trip. Will they find Jenny?

At their arrival at Arlanda airport, outside Stockholm, the rental car Nicklas has booked is waiting. Nicklas tells them that he has also booked hotel rooms for them at Stadshotellet in Mora. That had not been easy since there were obviously many tourists in Mora at this time of year, but he had finally succeeded in persuading the desk clerk to give them two rooms.

During the drive, Sonja asks something that has been on her mind for a long time. "Why hasn´t Jenny contacted us? She knows that we love her. Why?"

"Well, that´s a good question. But maybe something happened to her. We´ll have to ask her when we see her."

Nicklas and Mikael take turns at the wheel during the long drive to Mora. Fatigue has now caught up with them all. The day has really been long and eventful.

"How lucky that Sweden changed to right-hand traffic some years ago. I don´t know if I would have had the courage to drive on this wintry state of the road otherwise!" says Mikael suddenly.

"I completely agree. And what heavy traffic. It´s really strange. Is there anything special happening?" Nicklas sighs and flips the car window in order to get some fresh air.

"Yes, don´t you know that the Vasaloppet race is tomorrow? People from all over the world will be participating. On the flight, I read that they estimate there will be approximately 8,000 participants", interposes Sonja from the rear seat. "Will we soon be there?"

"Yes, within a few minutes, we´ll start looking for signs with 'Stadshotellet' on. We´re already in the outskirts of Mora."

Relieved, Mikael sighs. He is thinking of tomorrow, when they will start looking for Jenny in a mess of thousands and thousands of people. It will take time. He hopes they will find her. Alive.

The hotel is easy to find. They park the car on the yard. A moment later they are standing in front of the receptionist.

"How lucky for you that you´ve arrived now!" says he. "I have probably fifty persons standing here, hoping that you would be a no-show. They would all have wanted to take over your reservation. Welcome!"

They are quickly registered and receive their keys. Suddenly Sonja looks hesitant, but then she decides. Poking around in her handbag, she finds the envelope with photos of Jenny. Mikael shakes his head but agrees. He knows how headstrong she is, once she has made up her mind about something.

Sonja passes on a couple of photos to the receptionist, asking in a cautious voice: "Do you recognize this girl?"

The receptionist, whose name is Carl according to the name tag on the jacket, happily answers:"Of course! That is Jane. Mora´s little Jane. She actually got engaged here at Statt some time ago."

Now Nicklas takes over. "But the girl´s name is Jenny and not Jane. We know that, for sure!"

"That might be right", says Carl. "Since she is suffering from memory loss, the police started calling her Jane. You know, like Jane Doe, in the thrillers. But later I heard somebody say that she wanted to be called Jenny."

"Where does she live?" asks Sonja eagerly.

"I don´t know. Tomorrow you could ask at the police station. Although… I don´t know if it´ll be manned then. Most of the policemen will be out in town and at the trail. It´s, after all, the Vasaloppet Sunday. But look for police assistant Sven. He´s Jenny´s fiancé.”

Almost intoxicated by joy and tremendously tired, the trio totters up the stairs to their rooms. Before parting, Nicklas invites them for a nightcap, some whisky, to celebrate their success.

CHAPTER 36

Vasaloppet, Mora, Sweden – 3 March 1974

It is a fête-day in Mora, the crown of Dalarna. Now it is time to win the Vasaloppet race! A murmur of foreign, non-residential languages is heard above the rooftops: Japanese, English, Russian, and Stockholmish. In the street below Statt, something as unusual as a traffic jam is formed once in a while, when people leave in their cars to be on time for takeoff at Sälen, about 100 kilometres away. Everywhere skis, skis and skis as the TV-reporters on Sports TV use to say in their commentaries.

Sven and uncle Nisse are carrying Jenny's skiing equipment from the nearest parking lot to the takeoff area in the hamlet of Berga, in the outskirts of Sälen. From here, 7,000-8,000 skiers will be let off into the Vasaloppet trail where they will be skiing all the ninety kilometres down to Mora. Uncle Nisse is taking care of Jenny's trainer's chores. He is, among other things, checking the skis and the waxing. He hopes the weather will not change during the race for safety's sake uncle Nisse puts a couple of other waxes into one of Jenny's pockets.

After a big porridge breakfast —ordered by uncle Nisse – Jenny is now softening up her joints. She hopes that she is not dressed in too warm clothes. There is nothing worse than sweating when you have to ski really fast. No, she thinks she is properly dressed, layer on layer. That way she can quickly throw off garment after garment, should it be necessary.

This is an important day. She does not yet know why. Sven believes that Jenny will regain her memory during the race. She herself is pessimistic. But it will, anyway, be a memorable day. She is aware that she is running out of competition. She is disqualified already from the start because of being a woman. Only men are allowed to compete in Vasaloppet. That in itself is a challenge: to find out how skilled she is in comparison with men. If she can only beat some men to the goal, she is happy.

What Jenny does not know is that Agnes has left her hotel room in Mora already in the morning, now being on her way by car to one of the depots along the skiing trail.

Uncle Nisse gives Jenny some final instructions. ”Don´t spend yourself already at the start, Jenny. The trail is long. And there are ascents, as I´ve shown you. So keep the right pace from the start. Stay as far ahead as you can manage, but don´t, under any circumstances, spend yourself, because then you´ll not have enough strength to sprint, when you need to. Don´t forget to drink. And remember that even being the second last is a good result. Off you go to the start. But first, please give Sven and me a hug each. See you in Mora!”

Having received the obligatory kick in the ass, Jenny skis away. The boy cap is firmly pressed onto her head to conceal the copper-red hair. Sven has painted her jaw, using a burnt cork, in order to make it look like bristles. But it is still obvious that Jenny is not a man. She is competing under the name of John Doe for the imaginary club The Skiing Fans IF.

Jenny is standing far back among all the thousands of participants in the start area. Therefore, she does not see when the race starts. When the group in front of her is dissolved, she understands that the race is on. So Jenny hangs on. Oops, what a mess with all the skis and poles in the throng before the first ascent. The height difference is 150 metres. And it is as long as two kilometres. What a start! It takes a long while to get free of the mess and begin moving upwards. And then, suddenly, all problems are solved. Everyone has found a place in the trail. Soon you can see a long, rather wide, snake-like mass of skiers starting to move at an increasing pace.

Jenny advances in a methodical way. She intends to obey her trainer's advice of not running too fast from the start. She has, after all, ninety kilometres to ski. She must do it in a clever way. Through tough and purposeful skiing she intends to gradually leave a lot of other skiers behind. It is, according to what she has heard, just a question of setting part-goals. And then to fulfil them, one at a time.

The waxing is perfect. The skis are softly sliding on the snow. Now she is going rather fast, but sometimes she has to reduce speed in order to be able to pass others. You should not disturb them in their skiing. Jenny has her first part-goal in Smågan. It is only eleven kilometres away. There she will drink water.

Happily skiing, Jenny's thoughts start moving freely. Oh, how fun it would be to make this race together with Monica and Peggy. Make it like a competition between the three of them. Her friends and she are more or less of the same calibre, when it comes to skiing. It could really be very thrilling. Hello, Jesus! She has not thought of Monica and Peggy for a long time. She is amazed at the thoughts she just had. It strikes her that she has suddenly remembered two friends from her earlier life. She even remembers what they look like. Hurray! Jenny is rejoicing. Warm in her heart by joy, Jenny is reducing speed in Smågan while she is gulping down the water. She has two wonderful friends. She had completely forgotten about them.

Now she has gained speed and is on her way to Mångsbodarna, next part-goal. It is only thirteen kilometres way. And she knows that she can get a bun and some blueberry soup there. It is a tempting thought.

Jenny is, once more, passing a lot of men who have earlier been in front of her. They seem to be socializing in the trail, more than actually skiing. They laugh and talk with each other. And they are probably participating in the race more to be able to check off this on the"Been there, seen that, done that"-list than to actually set a new record. She laughs and waves as she passes them. As an answer from them she hears a lot of whooping.

She is really in a fantastic mood. She notices that she is humming as she is staking her way. And suddenly she feels how words from her insides are just pouring out of her mouth. "Dad, Granddad and Anton, I´m doing this for you. I hope you´re cheering on me! I´ll make the whole race. I promise you." And then, suddenly, she remembers what they look like, their names and what food they like. What a wonderful feeling! She has her own family! Or… does she not? Jenny hesitates, but then discards the doubtfulness. Of course she has a family like everybody else!

At Mångsbodarna Jenny finishes both the bun and the blueberry soup in an instant. There is no time to lose. Now she will do some real skiing!

The next depot is at Risberg, thirty-five kilometres from the start. On her way there, she must use a lot of strength to climb a long ascent. It is actually quite tough, but the thought of the following descent is comforting. She descends at a high speed. She can see a lot of men, who have fallen. They form a moving heap at the side of the trail. Adroitly she avoids joining this mess.

Next part-goal is at Evertsberg, forty-seven kilometres from the start. That means a little more than half-way. It was there Peter left her on her way up to Mora. So much has happened since that day. Once again, Jenny lets her thoughts wander haphazardly. It is thrilling. Oh yes, now she remembers even more… How could she have forgotten dear wonderful Aunt Sonja and Uncle Mikael? They are like extra parents for her and Anton. They are so nice and understanding. Oh, how she misses them. But, by the way, they must be awfully worried about her? She must try to call them as soon as possible. They must believe she is dead…

Without herself noticing it, Jenny has changed into an overdrive. Now she is skiing really fast. When she is approaching, lots of other skiers leave the trail so that she can pass. The cap has come off long ago. The long copper-red hair is fluttering in the airspeed. Appreciative looks and wolf whistles follow her. People from Mora, standing at the side of the trail are cheering: "Come on, Jane. Come on!" Others, who have heard that Jane now wants to be called Jenny, are calling out:"Come on, Jenny. Yippee Jenny!"

The last bit to the depot at Eversberg suddenly becomes tough. But, oh my God, she has, after all, already been skiing for more than forty-five kilometres. No wonder her legs feel so heavy.

What Jenny puts into her stomach at the depot, alleviates her a lot. She immediately feels better. Each step is easier to take. Most probably, her great happiness over her memories makes her move much smoother now. She is met by many smiles and kind comments. When you see her smile you instinctively answer with one.

Jenny is looking forward to the quite long descent, coming after Evertsberg. There she will be able to rest her legs for a rather long while, actually during several kilometres. Jenny bends her knees, so much that she is almost sitting down, in the long descent. The smaller she can make herself, the lesser will be the resistance of the wind. And the higher will be the speed. She wants to use the inclination to a maximum to be able to reach far as quickly as possible.

Now that Jenny does not have to concentrate on how to use her ski sticks, her thoughts are once again moving in her mind. What is her real name? Oh yes, it is really Jenny – Jenny Johnson – and she lives, as she has insisted in telling Sven, in Mora. But… her Mora lies in Minnesota, USA. No wonder that she sometimes, in the eyes of other people, might have seemed a little unhinged. Like for example the other day, when she asked why Mora had had the giant Dala horse destroyed. It actually sits in Mora, USA. And it is the biggest Dala horse in the world.

No, now she really has to concentrate on the skiing. Only let the memories out at intervals. During the descent, Jenny passes lots of other skiers. When she casts a glance backwards, she sees a swarm of people. Many are afraid of the descent and therefore take it very slowly and carefully. Some people actually even walk beside the trail.

She will soon arrive at the famous and strenuous ascents before Oxberg. She must be careful here, according to Uncle Nisse. She must not, under any circumstances, spend herself during the rise. She must vanquish them in a soft way. Must not lose too much strength during the climb. She still has tens of kilometres left to ski. Jenny peels off a sweater in order not to sweat.

At the Oxberg depot, a quarrel is starting. A female spectator is forcing herself through the mass of onlookers, halting at the very front. She menaces those who protest with a ski stick, the tip of which has been sharpened.

This ascent is extremely tough! Jenny can see the Oxberg depot at a distance. And a lot of onlookers along the trail. Jenny skis towards the depot, at the right side of the trail. Her stomach is tying up. She feels danger. Remembers that nasty woman in Mora and her threats. She hopes there is a guard in the proximity of the woman, if at all she is there. Very tense and wary, Jenny scouts ahead along the side of the trail. Then Jenny sees the woman, approximately five metres further ahead. Sees her hateful face and how the woman gets ready to throw something.

CHAPTER 37

Vasaloppet, Mora, Sweden – 3 March 1974

Through the loudspeakers you can hear the radio sports commentator change the pitch of his voice. "And now, we quickly tune in Oxberg. There is, obviously, something happening there."

The voice of an excited reporter from Oxberg cries out. "This is the worst I've ever seen. Yes, it's happening right now. A woman from the row of onlookers is pushing her way forward, up to the trail. Oops, she throws a ski stick. Right in front of the passing cluster of skiers. She seems to be aiming at a specific skier. It's a girl."

You can hear an angry hoot from the spectators.

"How good! There is apparently no problem. A skier, number 2332, who has just left the trail and taken off his right ski, swings this ski through the air, like you do with a long baseball bat. The ski hits the thrown ski stick and it shatters. The pieces bounce back on the woman who has thrown the stick ripping up big holes in her trousers, but I can't see any blood. There must have been real force in that hit!"

Now you can here the spectators cheering.

"Well, God obviously punishes some people at once. You should see what I see now. The woman falls backwards, right down into a snow-filled trench. Only her legs are visible. What a delightful sight!"

Laughter is echoing on the radio. Suddenly the hoot is back.

The reporter speaks again. "I´ve to see what´s happening. The woman now standing up, yelling. She seems furious. And she is wildly tearing her hair. Oh, now I can see. She is, obviously, wearing a brown wig that has come askew. How very embarrassing for her! Wait a moment. I´ll soon be close to her."

Yes, you can easily hear on the radio that the woman is really furious. She yells that she intends to sue the community of Mora, the man throwing back the stick at her and the girl in the trail. There is no way of stopping the woman. She does not seem hurt, but it bothers her very much that the skiing dress is ruined. She seems not to care at all about the fact that everything she says is heard on the radio.

A safety guard with a determined look finally leads the woman away. All this is mockingly commented by the onlookers.

Jenny saw the stick flying through the air towards her. Had that man not stopped it with his ski, making it bounce back, there would surely have been a terrible accident. Did the hag not understand what terrible injuries she could have caused? Not only to Jenny but also for lots of skiers? Or did she not care? Thank God that everybody has managed without harm!

Jenny quickly passes the place of the atrocity, leaving it behind. She cannot stop herself from demonstratively showing the forbidden finger in the air, for the woman to see. She feels malice. Hopes that the woman is now ashamed. She has at least made a fool of herself.

Oh, how wonderful to hear the people along the trail edge calling "Go for it, Jenny" so intensely that it is echoing. It really comforts her.

Next part-goal is at Hökberg, only nine kilometres from Oxberg. That is a nice feeling. The day has been long and tough. It would have been nice to reach Mora soon! But... she has to cope and continue to fight. She will not give up this late in the race. Under no circumstances. Jenny knows that she is doing quite well today. She is curious whether she will be among the best 3,500 – thus among the better half.

She allows herself time to swallow a few gulps of hot coffee at Eldris, before taking off towards the goal. "Mora, here I come!" says she, in such a high voice that the boys in her cluster start laughing. Everybody seems to like her. They voluntarily move to the side when she wants to pass. And when she leaves them behind, she can hear them calling out:"Go for it, Jenny! Best of luck, sweetheart!"

Now only nine kilometres left. Rather flat terrain. Oh, maybe she ought to have bettered the waxing in Eldris. But... It is a little slippery but she thinks she will make it anyhow. She will cope all the way to Mora. Even if she has to crawl the last few metres. She hopes that the guards have not driven the woman down to Mora, releasing her there. In such a case, she might now be standing, waiting for Jenny, at the goal...

Imagine how happy her friends will be when they hear that her memory is returning. And how wonderful that David has decided to forgive Aunt Ida!

During the last kilometres to Mora, Jenny is skiing, absent-minded but quick. The thoughts have once more begun to flutter in her head. One thought, in particular. She has tried to avoid that one, but now she can no longer keep it stacked away. She remembers that Granddad Wally had died of myocardial infarction, having participated in the Vasaloppet in Mora, USA. That was now exactly a year ago. But, but... Where are Dad and Anton? Will they be waiting for her at the goal? Nooo, she would have known in such a case. She can feel how anxiety is spreading through her body. And then she can hear Aunt Sonja's voice in her head: "Oh, my sweet little darling... Something so terrible has happened... An accident. Your Dad and your darling brother Anton... They were both hit by a car, and they're both dead. Dearest darling Jenny, I'm so very sorry!"

Jenny's heart cracks by despair. Tears run like rivers down her cheeks. She is not able to wipe them away. Has no time for it. She absolutely **has** to reach the goal line first. She has, after all, promised Dad, Anton and Granddad that and she will show them that she keeps her word, whatever her name might be.

Sven has been pacing up and down at the goal line for several hours. Quite insane of him. He knows that Jenny is to be expected – if at all – not until close to the end of the race. Still there is no peace in his mind. He has to be there when his darling Jenny arrives.

The commentator´s voice is echoing in the goal area in Mora:"And wait… Here comes… Who else but Mora´s own Jenny Doe! She is number 1699 and has completed the ninety kilometres of the race in unbelievable six hours and approximately fifty-six minutes. Of course out of competition but still… What an admirable achievement!"

Hearing the audience´s ovations and applause, Jenny, stumbling, stakes across the goal line and falls down into a heap on the ground.

CHAPTER 38

Mora, Sweden – 3 March 1974

As Sven sees Jenny pass the goal line, falling in a heap, he runs up to her as swift as lightning. Takes her into his arms and strokes her hair. He can also see her tear-wet face. Then he understands. "You´ve regained your memory, haven´t you?" he whispers in a tender voice.

Jenny is not able to answer. Her heaving sobs almost choke her. She is feeling dizzy. Has a dry throat. Wet in the face. Happy but at the same time also sad. There is too much to cope with now. It is a nice feeling having Sven´s safe arms around her. A moment later, she is hugged by yet another pair of hefty arms. Uncle Nisse has hastened up to the goal line as the speaker had announced Jenny´s arrival. Supported by both men, she manages to stand up and reach a bench.

"Congratulations, little one. You managed all the way to the goal. Actually, I didn´t believe you would. A fantastic accomplishment, Jenny!" Uncle Nisse gives her a bottle of water, encouraging her to drink.

"You´ve got your memory back, haven´t you?" Sven tenderly repeats.

Jenny nods affirmatively, but she can still not speak. There is, after all, so much to remember. Both terrible and nice things. Before she can share them, she must first sort out her thoughts herself. And imagine how much she had wanted to get her memory back! She had not expected it to be as painful and horrible as it has resulted.

"Oh, I´m so happy", says Uncle Nisse. "It´s much better that you remember on your own than if somebody tells you who you are. I actually found out who you are this morning, before the start. And where we´ve met. But enough of that now. You´ll certainly tell, when you´re ready for it."

Sven can feel a lump in his throat. He is so happy. Now everything will be solved. The only thing missing to make their happiness complete had after all been Jenny getting her memory back.

Jenny, suddenly, stiffens where she is sitting on the bench. She is staring for a while at the mass of onlookers. What she sees makes her regain her strength. With a jump, she gets off the bench. Runs towards the throng of people and throws herself around the neck of an old woman.

"Aunt Sonja!" she exclaims. "Aunt Sonja and Uncle Mikael, are you here? Is it true that you´re here? You can´t imagine how much I need you now."

"Dear child. We flew here together with Nicklas Burger, your lawyer, to look for you. Finally we understood that it was here that you might be. We´ve been so worried about you."

Sonja and Mikael almost end up fighting in order to be able to hug Jenny one time after the other. They both have tears in their eyes and are very emotional.

"Come on, you have to meet Sven, my fiancé, and also Nisse Nilsson. He´s helped me so much." Jenny sees how also Anders and David are approaching. "And over there you can see more friends of mine."

Jenny can now feel how exhausted she is. Barely capable of standing on her feet. As in a haze, she can hear Anders saying:"Let´s move outside the goal area. Jenny needs to rest for a while. Ida has prepared some food for Jenny at David´s and my apartment. The girl needs food and drink. Then she has to sleep for some hours." Anders continues:"If I know Ida, she´s probably made enough food for us all, if we want. We could sit talking in the living room while Jenny is asleep. And I´ve also reserved a big table for all of us for tonight at Statt. So, see you in a while at Storgatan 12. Nisse, you´re of course also very welcome."

"Sorry, but I don´t have the time in the afternoon. I have so many skiers to celebrate, but I´ll try to come to Statt tonight."

Sonja and Mikael, now finally knowing that Jenny is alive, retire to rest for a few hours after the flight, but they will of course come to Statt. And they will come, accompanied by Jenny´s lawyer Nicklas Burger.

In the living room at Storgatan 12 Anders, David and Sven are sitting, nibbling some food. Ida is running back and forth. Sometimes, she sits down for a short while and sighs a little. Then she rises again. What will happen now that Jenny has regained her memory? No, they should not be speculating. The best thing is to hear it from Jenny herself, when she wakens up. Maybe she will tell during the evening? If not, they will have to wait until she is ready to do it.

CHAPTER 39

Mora, Sweden – 3 March 1974

Having forced her way up through the deep snowpack, into which she has fallen head downwards, Agnes feels embarrassed. Yuk, people are really hissing at her! Or might it be at the girl in the trail? Or at the safety guard? No, alas, she must confess that she has made a spectacle of herself. It stings her ego to admit that. And that feeling is not easier when she discovers that her wig has come askew. She hopes that nobody has seen that her natural hair colour is copper-red. But her hood, which has fallen down over her head when she was turned upside down in the fall, might have hidden her real hair. She cautiously moves her hands to adjust the wig, making it sit in the proper way.

But now she has to pull herself together and focus on her revenge on Wally, who should actually be in the neighbourhood.

"Are you quite out of your mind, old hag? The skiers could have been severely hurt. Not to think of their reaction if they'd had to interrupt the race. Explain yourself!" The security guard is furious at the woman. "And, by the way, why did you aim at Jenny from Mora and nobody else? She hasn't done anything to you, has she?"

Agnes is boiling inside but changes to a plaintive voice. "There was someone behind me hitting me at the back.

I lost the balance and then my ski stick flew away. It was really not my fault." That must have sounded credible, she thinks.

The guard looks at her. "Well, I actually don´t believe that. Don´t forget that I was quite close to you. And that I had actually been told to keep an eye on you."

That was the worst Agnes had ever heard. Keep an eye on her? It was, actually, her that everybody was going for. That is a constant feeling she has. That everyone wants to hurt her. Be evil to her or make her appear ridiculous. Now Agnes looses all self-control. Starts to yell. Tries to break loose but then she controls herself. This is actually exactly how people want her to behave. She must try a softer approach again.

At that moment a police car is heard. It is honking and driven slowly, in order not to hurt any of all the onlookers pacing around in the depot. When Sven has heard, on the sports radio, about the incident at Oxberg he has quickly called the police station, asking his colleague Jonas to go up there.

Seeing the police car halting, Agnes says to the guard: "I have to go to the ladies´ room. I´ll hurry!" Agnes stands with her legs crossed, looking in need to take a leak.

"No, I don´t trust you. You´ll have to wait until the police station."

"Blame yourself! But you´ll be responsible if I pee all over the police car."

Since the guard does not like the idea of Agnes doing exactly that, he allows her to go to the ladies´ room. He stares at her to check that she is indeed going there. Police assistant Jonas calls him, with a wink. He explains that he himself is now taking over responsibility for Agnes. The guard is now freed from it and can go on checking that everything else is in order.

When Agnes reappears, she can, to her disappointment, see that the police car has been parked just outside the toilet. There is thus no way to escape, but using some female cunning there might be a chance after all. She walks up to the car. Jonas makes a sign that she should sit down in the rear. She pretends not to understand and remains standing. Jonas then leaves the car and walks up to her. At that moment, Agnes pretends to be tripping and drops her waist bag in such a way that it falls under the car. The blockhead automatically bends down and tries to ease it out. Agnes sees her opportunity. She puts all her force into the kick she gives Jonas in the crotch. A funny gurgling sound is heard from the ground. There was obviously strength in that kick. Wonderful! He has really deserved to be in pain. He has, after all, intended to bring her to the police station.

Right then Agnes feels an immeasurable pain in her right ankle, as Jonas, from below the car, hits her with his truncheon right on top of the wounds from the ski stick. Agnes falls at full length on her stomach with the face in the snow. She is so giddy and in such pain that she hardly notices how Jonas connects both her arms with handcuffs behind her back and then drags her into the car´s rear seat.

When Agnes comes around, the police car is going at high speed on its way to Mora. Agnes watches, through the gap between the front seats, which buttons Jonas presses when he puts on the siren and the blue lights. Agnes gets an idea. This car is perfect for her plan. She will drive it.

Agnes starts sobbing. Jonas casts a glance backwards and then starts humming an old hit:"

" *(Dee doody doom doom, dee doody doom doom)*
(Dee doody doom doom, DOOM)

Seven little girls sittin' in the back seat
Huggin and a'kissin with Fred
I said "why don't one of you come up and sit beside me?"
And this is what the seven girls said

CHORUS
(All together now, one, two, three)
(Keep you mind on your drivin')
(Keep you hands on the wheel)
(Keep your snoopy eyes on the road ahead)
(We're havin' fun sittin' in the back seat kissin' and a'huggin with Fred)
(Dee doody doom doom, dee doody doom doom)
(Dee doody doom doom, DOOM)..."

"You´ve broken my rib, you bastard. I can´t breathe. I can´t get air. I have to go to the hospital."

"What a good idea, nutcase. Then I´ll be able to have a check on my crushed balls. Without hesitation, you´ll get arrested for Assault against Officer."

Jonas puts on the police radio. "Jonas here. I´m on my way to town with the woman. But we´ll pass by the hospital. She´s complaining of respiratory distress. Could you also make an addition to the offense? Add Assault against Officer. And please call Gertrud at the Emergency Room and warn her so that she will meet us with a stretcher and some strong men to hold my little lioness. Tell them to also bring a tensioning belt. The bitch is probably used to them."

Agnes is lying silent. This will work, she thinks. Unless they make a body-search at the hospital. Two pill strips that she bought at Plattan in Stockholm are safely hidden in her panties. Taking the opportunity, she has then also bought quite a lot of this and that. Pills that could be useful in case she needs poppers. Those are now hidden in the car, which she has parked on a forest road at Oxberg. She has however not been able to find the medicine she needs most – the mood damping one. And she knows that it is that one she is in urgent need of.

Gertrud is awaiting them at the ambulance entrance with a stretcher and two caretakers. She looks through the side window. "Oh, so it´s you Jonas? I was hoping that Sven would come. He is stylish and well-behaved. Not a forest bum, like you."

"Extremely nice to meet you too, Gertrud. Next time we meet, I´ll pick you up for Miss-establishment of an Official. I know my paragraphs, you see. But Sven will spend the evening celebrating at Statt with his fiancée Jenny and a lot of distinguished guests from the US and Australia, you see. Gold panners, among other things, so from him you can´t expect anything more. So follow my advice: forget him. "

Agnes hears everything from the rear of the police car. What was he saying? USA and Australia! That must mean that her father-in-law Wally has arrived and is a Statt. He has always been crazy about gold. Now revenge is near!

While Jonas is talking, Gertrud opens the back door of the police car. There lies Agnes. She is now starting to cry. "Help me, please! Please! Please! He beat me on my way here. He hit me. I can´t breathe properly. It hurts so much."

Gertrud looks harshly at Jonas: "What have you done, Jonas? Doctor Larsson has to look at this, when he comes in from the ski track. He's on his way. We may have to report this to your superiors as well. Take away those crazy handcuffs immediately! "

"But she´s under arrest…"

"She is a patient at the hospital and, at the moment, nothing else. You´re on the hospital´s territory. My assessment is that she´ll be admitted, pending investigation and examination. Here I´m in command until the doctor arrives. "

"But…"

"No buts! You can guard her. Nothing else."

"Please, don´t let him come close to me", cries Agnes desperately.

"No, dear," replies Gertrud. "Jonas, you can sit on a chair outside the door. You have no authority to enter the patient's room. Have all of you heard that? If you see Jonas go to the patient, you should report it to me without delay. "

"This is embarrassing", says Jonas in a low voice.

"Yes, you should have thought about that before beating her," answers Gertrud.

"Dracula!"

"Bum!"

Agnes enters the room together with the hospital assistant. "Look, I'm so terribly thirsty. Do you think I could get a big jug of tea?" asks she.

"Yes, of course", replies the assistant. "Do you want milk and/or lemon with it? I´ll arrange it."

When Agnes is alone in the room, she pulls out the two slips of sleeping pills from her panties, takes out twelve tablets, puts them in her pocket and hides the rest under a chair pad. When the tea arrives, she pours a cup of tea, crumbs four pills and puts the powder into the cup. After a while she presses the nurse button again.

When the assistant returns, Agnes says: "Thanks for the tea. It was delicious, but there was too much, so I thought you could carry a cup to the constable in the corridor as well. He must also be thirsty. I have rinsed the cup and replenished it with tea from the jar.

"That was kind of you," says the assistant, takes the tea and goes out to Jonas, who gratefully receives the cup.

A moment later, Agnes peers through the door window. She can see that Jonas is just falling asleep, where he is sitting on the chair. Agnes hurries out to him through the door.

"But Jonas, you can't sit here sleeping. You can rest on my bed for a while. It's much more comfortable. "

Supported on Agnes' shoulder, Jonas walks like a sleepwalker into the room and collapses on the bed. Agnes picks him mildly on the cheek. "Now I'll just take your service weapons too, so you'll sleep better, imbecile."

Jonas lazily nods and falls into deep sleep.

Having has freed Jonas from the service weapons, the car keys, the cell phone and his police ID, Agnes calls the assistant. Agnes meets her in the door to prevent her from looking into the room.

"Could you get the ER nurse for me? It´s important."

"Yes, I will. But where is the policeman?"

"He is ´s gone to pee. The poor thing has such a small bladder. "

"Doctor Larsson has arrived. Should I get him too?"

"Yes, how kind of you. After that, you can leave. I don´t need your help anymore. Here you have a 500-note for your help. Go into town, buy something really good and have a nice evening. You´re worth it. I´ve cleared this with the surgeon. It's OK. "

Agnes is hiding behind the door when Doctor Larsson and Gertrud come. She has heard Gertrud comment that Jonas is not in his place outside the door and now the two can see Jonas, sleeping deeply on Agnes´ bed.

"I should have understood that," exclaims Gertrud. "He couldn´t stay away. This has to be reported. "

"But where is the woman? That´s the most important issue right now", replies Doctor Larsson.

"The woman is here," says Agnes with a grin, as she steps out of her hideout behind the door with Jonas' gun sharply aimed at the two.

"Now you'll be quiet and listen to me. I don´t intend to hurt you, if you obey. Otherwise, I'll shoot. I've lived in America so I can shoot. "

"I´ll call the police," exclaims Gertrud, but she gets silent when Doctor Larsson puts his calming hand on her forearm.

Agnes laughs a little mockingly. "The only police officer on duty in Mora right now, is straight in front of you on my bed."

"This is how it is. You see the two mugs with water on the bedside table. They contain a harmless but strong sleeping pill. Drink a mug each and sit down on a chair. I'm waiting while you fall asleep. When you wake up, I'm far away. Before you fall asleep, put your keyboards and mobile phones on the floor in front of you. If you don´t do it, I'm forced to shoot you in your neck. I'm not a beginner, and I think it is great fun shooting people. "

A thought strikes Agnes. "Where do I find medications? Where is the infirmary store? Quick, answer! I have no time at all to waste on you. "

"What kind of medication do you need?" asks Doctor Larsson.

"A mood dampening one. I can´t remember the name."

"I'm sorry, but we don´t have that kind in the infirmary. We always have to request from the hospital pharmacy. And we can´t get in there," replies Dr. Larsson, who realizes that the woman is really in need of such medicine.

Disappointed with the answer, Agnes returns to her plans. Twenty minutes later she leaves the hospital building to pick up the police car. The three are in deep sleep in the carefully locked hospital room. The healthcare assistant is eating punch ice-cream at a pub a few blocks away.

CHAPTER 40

Mora, Sweden – 3 March 1974

At 6 o'clock in the afternoon, Jenny starts moving in bed. She stretches but moans at the same time. Ida, who has been peering into the bedroom once in a while, enters and gives her a hug."Anders has good advice to give you. You´ll have pain in your entire body after the race. Therefore, he recommends a long and nice shower. Then Sven can come in and massage you with a special oil Anders has. That sounds nice, doesn´t it? "

"Wonderful," Jenny moans. "But first a cup of coffee, right?"

"It won´t take a minute," smiles Ida. And in a very short time, she returns to Jenny with a cup of hot coffee with milk. Jenny thoroughly enjoys it. She is now feeling so relaxed and rested. Life is really beautiful! And she has at last completed Vasaloppet and done well. Much better than most male skiers. Sooo nice!

After a long and nice shower, Sven comes in to give Jenny a massage. She can feel how the muscles are gradually softening. Everything feels nice. After a while, Jenny sends him out of the room. She has to get ready for the evening. She worries a little at the thought of it. She must probably tell the others what she remembers from her previous life. But the strange thing is that she really likes the life she has here and now so much, that she almost is afraid of talking about her past. No, she actually must be honest to them. And she knows that she neither used to have a boyfriend nor a husband or child, so there's nothing that could worry Sven.

There is almost shuttle service between the bedrooms, when everyone is getting dressed for dinner. Ida and Sven have brought the clothes of both Jenny and themselves to Storgatan, because no one had wanted to go all the way to Orsa just to change before dinner. And they are now like a single family, all five of them.

The table at Statt is booked from eight o'clock in the evening. The whole company - except for Sven and Jenny - meet in the foyer. There Anders introduces everyone to each other, as well as he can manage not knowing everybody. Coming to Sonja and Mikael he looks a bit confused.

"And how do you know Jenny? Can we agree to call her Jenny for the time being? And not to reveal where she comes from? It is better that she tells us that herself. "

"Yes, we´re Jenny´s neighbours. I have been her day-time caretaker, since she was very small. She is, to me, as if she were my own daughter," says Sonja. Yngve, agreeing, nods.

Anders then turns to Nicklas Burger. "Tell me about your relationship with Jenny."

"Well, there´s not much I can tell you at the moment. I've been in contact with Sonja and Mikael ever since Jenny disappeared. Have tried to help them find her.

I´ve some contacts within the police that I´ve also used. Maybe I´ll be able to tell you later this evening."

Then Anders introduces Maja and Yngve as a couple of good friends. He explains that he and David have visited them in the United States and then travelled with them to Sweden.

Jenny and Sven are now entering the hotel lobby, joining the rest of the dinner party. Jenny looks fresh and healthy. It is impossible to see that she has been skiing all the ninety kilometres of Vasaloppet earlier in the day.

Anders has reserved a table in a more secluded part of the large dining room. He is aware that important and delicate subjects may be addressed during the evening. Then it would be nice not to sit in the middle of all the guests.

The head-waiter comes out to the lobby and discreetly winks Anders aside. The table is now ready to receive the party. When the door to the full dining room opens and the party enters, they are met with standing ovations. Jenny is met by "Hey, Jenny!" and "Well done!" When you look at the rather robust men sitting there, many of them skiers, and then compare them to tiny Jenny, it's hard to imagine that she has competed against them. And even won over a large part of them. Blushing, Jenny waves at the guests and hurries to the table.

When they are seated at the table, having received a glass of Louis Roederer, Anders, with the elder´s right, starts speaking.

"Dear Friends, welcome here tonight. We have a lot to celebrate together, but at first, I think we´ll toast for the Vasaloppet skier Jenny. You´ve done a great job today. It will certainly be remembered for a very long time here in Mora. And that this memory will never die with us, your friends, I can guarantee. Cheers to Jenny!"

As usual, Anders, in consultation with the restaurateur, has put together an outstandingly good menu. Everyone is delighted by the appetizer and the conversation is soon in full swing around the table. It is quite obvious that everyone is enjoying themselves.

Having all of them put down the cutlery after the appetizer, Jenny makes a speech. Having toasted with her friends and thanked them for all the nice words, it's time for her to speak.

"It feels safe to be here with you all around me. Today I´ve been involved in something very upsetting and partly horrible. And I don´t mean the Vasaloppet." She takes a gulp of wine and starts again. "What happened to me was that, in the middle of Vasaloppet, I got my memory back. I know who I am and from where I come from. I remember you both, lovely Aunt Sonja and Uncle Mikael. I remember you, dear Nicklas Burger. I also remember my best friends and my classmates and other friends from home. And," she says as the tears rise in her eyes, "I remember what happened to my dear father and my beloved little brother. And what happened to my dear grandfather about a year ago. "

Sven offers her a handkerchief to wipe the tears. Sonja and Mikael stand up, go to Jenny and hug her.

When Jenny has calmed down, she continues. "My name is actually Jenny Johnson and I come from the small town of Mora in Kanabec County, Minnesota. My grandfather died in a heart attack after completing the American Vasaloppet. He actually came in fifth place. My father Johan and my brother Anton died in a horrible accident on June 20 last year. Actually on their way to a tennis match, where Anton was to play tennis for a talent scout. I was just about to go a disco, with my best friends Peggy and Monica, when I was told. In a single moment, my family disappeared. Had not Aunt Sonja been there then, I don´t know what I would have done. Yes, if you wonder if I have a mother, I of course did. Her name was Agnes, but she is no longer there. She died when I was little. Unfortunately, I don´t have any memories of her. Not only now, but never. Those memories are quite dead! So I'm completely without a family."

She takes a new gulp of wine and sighs. As she looks at her friends, she can see how David is wiping away Ida's tears and then gives her a light kiss on her lips. Ah, she thinks, that's why she has been singing a lot during the last few days.

"But ... But I've had a new family, during my memory loss, and I'm very happy about that. Sven, my beloved fiancé, Aunt Ida and Sven´s father David and Grandfather Anders, you have really made me happy and you´ll continue to do that. What I suddenly have remembered will not mean any changes in our relationships. And you two, Aunt Sonja and Uncle Mikael, automatically belong to my nearest circle. I've always loved you and will continue to do so.” Jenny smothers. "But I think I'm now old enough to stop calling you Aunt and Uncle."

Sonja and Mikael nod affirmatively.

”Now I´m starting to get hungry. Sven, please tell them to start with the main course now.” Jenny sits down on the chair. She's quite hoarse after talking for so long.

"I just want to add that you'll hear the whole story of what I've done during the time I've been missing. But ... let´s take a little break now before the main course arrives. So Sven, don´t tell them yet! "

CHAPTER 41

Mora, Sweden – 3 March 1974

Jenny and Maja suddenly meet inside the ladies´ room. Jenny notices that Maja has been crying. When she sees Jenny, Maja gets up and puts her arms around her.

"Dear Jenny, how wonderful that everything has now been solved regarding you. And for Ida, Sven, David and Anders as well. I just wish that even my own search would get the same happy ending."

Jenny, who from the very beginning has liked Maja, gives her a return hug and mystified looks at her. "Do you, too, have someone who disappeared?"

Maja sighs. "Yes I have. In fact, a whole family. I haven´t seen them since I was a teenager. And I crave for them. I can´t find them anywhere. We have even checked with Daddy's good friends in Australia, but they haven´t seen Wally for a long time. Anders is actually my dad´s best friend ever since they were teenagers."

"Sorry, what did you just say? Did you say Wally and Australia in one and the same breath? What did he do in Australia?"

"He panned for gold and searched for opals. And played adventurer, like so many others there." Maja does not quite understand Jenny's facial expression.

"What other family members are you looking for?" wonders Jenny intently.

"My brother and his daughter and son. I was so happy when I was recently told that I also have a nephew and a niece. Yngve and I have never been able to have children ourselves. "

"Come Maja, now we have to find Anders and Nicklas. There´s something I have to ask them."

Jenny takes Maja by her hand and drags her out into the lobby. Anders is standing at the bulletin board studying tourist information, while Nicklas is sitting in an easy chair browsing through a bundle of paper. He puts those into the attaché bag as he sees Jenny and Maja. Jenny, Maja and Anders then sit down together with Nicklas in the sofas. Jenny calls the head waiter and asks him to postpone the main course for a while. He sighs but nods affirmatively.

Jenny turns to Nicklas Burger. "Nicklas, I have an extremely important question. You and your company have also been my father's and grandfather's lawyers. Therefore you might be able to answer it. Can you tell me if my father had a sister? "

Nicklas nods. "Yes, he had. But for various reasons, I find it difficult to tell you about your father's family. You must first tell me why you ask?"

Jenny tells him about the conversation Maja and she had just had in the ladies´ room. She can see how Nicklas´ face looks more positive. Then he says: "Maja, can

I ask you to tell me a little about your teens? Did you do anything special or why did you lose contact with your family?"

"Yes, I did something very special, and that's the reason I haven't met them ever since. I ran away from home to join the Amish people. They didn't like that. I have realized only recently that it was because of love for me they tried to prevent me, because the Amish people don't think women should get any education. But at that time I was a young stupid teenager, who did not understand better." Maja stops talking and studies Nicklas' face. "Why are you looking so happy now?"

"I'll tell you later. Now it's apparently time for food again. I'm starving," laughs Nicklas and disappears into the dining room. The others follow him.

When the main course has been served and they have enjoyed it for a while, Nicklas suddenly stands up and grabs the red wine glass.

"Dear Jenny," he begins. "As your lawyer, I want to tell you that you have got a relatively large legacy after your father and brother. We'll talk more about that later because it contains many reservations and para- graphs and such. But ..." he adds, holding his breath for a moment, "you have also received something much more valuable today. I'm not talking about the diploma you received for skiing in the Vasaloppet. I'm not talking about your dear Sven or all your other wonderful friends. I'm talking about a new relative you got today. Get up Maja and Jenny! Hug each other really hard. Maja, you're Jenny's aunt. And you, Jenny, are Maja's niece. "There is absolute silence.

Then Maja and Jenny get up from the chairs and throw themselves in the arms of each other. The tears are spraying in all directions, not just from both of them. Everybody cries out of happiness.

"How could you know that, Nicklas?" asks Maja in a hoarse voice.

"Through what you told me about the Amish people. I´ve reviewed the family records in our archive. And it was mentioned there. And Jenny's grandfather was called Wally, and he had been looking for opals in Australia. There´s no doubt. You're Jenny's aunt. Unfortunately, you have now been told by Jenny that your father, your brother and your nephew are dead, but you have Jenny now. Are you happy?"

A warm and happy smile is the answer Nicklas gets.

Nicklas continues: "I want you both, Maja and Jenny, to know that both Wally´s and Johan's wills have now been found. I actually found them just a few minutes ago in a bundle of paper I received from my dad. You may not know that Wally's estate has been pending, waiting for us to find his will. And we have also been looking for Johan´s will. Let's meet tomorrow the three of us, so that you can hear more about it. And you Jenny also bring Mikael because you gave him a power of attorney. And Sonja is also welcome because you and Jenny are so close to each other. Maja, I can tell

you that Wally's will reflects the great love he felt for
you."

CHAPTER 42

Mora, Sweden – 4 March 1974

When a number of champagne bottles have been emptied and everyone has turned sweaty on the dance floor, Jenny tells about her experiences during the journey from Mora, Minnesota to Mora in Dalarna. Finally, however, the waiter comes to notify them that the restaurant is closed for the evening. Only then does the party leave the restaurant to continue to Anders´ and David´s flat.

Outside, a police car is waiting for them in the street. When the whole group is standing on the pavement, the police car´s main beams as well as the extra headlights are turned on. The company is suddenly bathing in a sea of light. There is a click in the car's loudspeakers and then a woman begins to talk.

"Everyone, just stay where you are and remain completely quiet and calm! I'm sitting in the car, and I´ve an automatic weapon aimed at you. I´ll shoot at the slightest movement. But don´t be afraid. If everyone is calm, it's just one of you that I want. Which one of you is Wally? Take a step ahead Wally! "

Anders immediately answers: "If you, lady, are looking for Wally, then you unfortunately arrived a whole year too late. Wally died in a heart attack after last year's Vasaloppet in Mora in America. "

"I was present when he died," cries Jenny. She suddenly feels completely dizzy and confused. That voice that she hears ... She has heard that voice before. Oh, that is the mean voice that has persecuted her for so long. The voice without a body that has scared her so terribly.

"You there, you bitch with the ugly hair, just shut up. Otherwise, I'll cut off your hair and make a doormat of it. I should have taken care of you when I was in Mora this summer. What a gaffe of me! No, I don´t believe Wally is dead. I'm Wally's daughter-in-law, Agnes, and I'll have my revenge on him, because he got me locked up in a hospital for ten years. "

"No, no, you're not my mom," screams Jenny upset. "My mom Agnes is dead. Dead, do you understand? She died when I was a little girl. There are no memories left. They´re also dead. Don´t do this to me! "

Jenny starts to cry, but then she pulls herself together and continues: "But what do you mean? Were you in Mora this summer? When Dad and Anton died?"

In the darkness of the police car, Agnes smiles: "Yes, little one, that's something you can keep thinking about. Oh, so you're that little toddler, who was ruining my nails with your pooh and used to scream every night. This may be your last memory of me. Your mother is not dead. She kills."

Jenny desperately screams:"Nooo! You cannot mean that! A mother would never do such a thing!"

"Oh yes, my little friend. Of course I can. It was obviously not good enough for you, my angel, to be christened to Veronica Strandberg after your birth at the Norrköping hospital. Do you really think that the name Jenny Johnson is more beautiful? Or… was it perhaps your darling Dad who was so afraid of me that he got you all into the Witness Protection Program? But I found you anyway, sweetheart!!"

Sven quickly calls out to his friends: "Note this down at once: Veronica Strandberg and Norrköping hospital. And also make a notation that she's talked about the Witness Protection Program."

In spite of the dangerous situation they are facing, Sven feels an enormous sense of joy. At last, his beloved Jenny might know a little more about herself?

Anders adds: "I'm Wally's best friend Anders. We've never met you and me, but we could try anyway. Can't we talk about this...? "

"Well, you're that bore, you say? But you look like Wally. He had a beard at that time, but you could have shaved it off. You're probably Wally. So you can take the bullet, even if you call yourself Jesus. Wait, I just need to unlock this bloody gun ..."

Rifle fire sounds and the police car's front window shatters. Anders, who has thrown himself down onto the sidewalk, almost immediately stands up again. Armed men, casting black shadows, come out of the darkness from all directions sprinting to the car, where they open the car doors. A man's voice, low but intense, cries "Secured!" After a few moments of silence a megaphone clicks.

"This is the police. We have just eliminated the threat you've been facing here on the sidewalk. But please remain at the very spot you´re now standing, for a little while, and do not touch anything. We only need to take some photos of your locations for investigation purposes." Sven recognizes Hellström's voice.

An ambulance from the hospital, driven by Doctor Larsson, turns into the street and stops behind the police car. Sister Gertrud jumps out of it, coming with a pile of blankets which she puts over the guests' shoulders.

Hellström cries, through the megaphone: "Could you, police assistant Martinsson, be kind to make a small break in your family life. You´re temporarily on duty now. Come over to us, your colleagues, for a while. I´ll inform you of what has happened, so that you can pass this information on to the other guests. "

Sven allows Anders to take care of Jenny, who is trembling and crying out of shock. He disappears over to the police, who are in full swing to get ready for departure. The ambulance has driven up next to the police car, so that nobody will be able to see when Agnes´ body is put on the stretcher and carried into the ambulance. Two police officers accompany the ambulance, which leaves without putting on the sirens.

Sven returns, assembles the others and says: "We have been extremely lucky. The police arrived just after we got out from Statt. A few days ago, the hotel manager thought that Agnes had run away without paying. Obviously she went to Stockholm then. So they called Hellström. The police matched her passport photo and got a hit in the register of wanted persons. She is said to have put a mental hospital in Switzerland on fire last year. Many patients were burned to death. It was a terrible story. She apparently did it just after she had been released from there and as a vengeance for the years she has been locked up. A gardener, who recognized her, saw her escape, and since then she has been internationally wanted. She was so sure that nobody knew she was the guilty one that she has even used her own passport. Tonight, some men were sent from Stockholm's police intervention force to pick her up calmly. She is, after all, extremely dangerous and capable of anything. The men in the police intervention group are specially trained policemen, who work with terrorism, robberies with violence, kidnappings and such. Some of the guys here were actually working with the drama at Norrmalmstorg last year."

"They had planned to group, when the hotel had closed, before going in to seize Agnes in her hotel room, but the police car was already in front of the entrance, when they arrived. And we had just come out on the sidewalk. When the men saw us outside, they were worried that they might not intervene in time. Doctor Larsson, who by that time had woken up at the hospital, phoned and told them about the police car.

"But now we have to move into a warmer place. Let´s go to Storgatan 12. There we can calm down and discuss what has happened here."

Jenny has been completely silent, just crying, since the shots fell, but now she says, in a weak trembling voice: "How could they ... how could they kill my mother just like that? She was mean, but she was my mother anyway, and she had not shot anyone yet. Her sentence should to be decided by the court, shouldn´t it? They shot her, killed her. Now I´ll never get a chance to meet her again. "

Anders clasps Jenny closer to him. "Sven, you´ve forgotten to tell us that Agnes is not dead at all. The police will not kill anyone unless they absolutely need to in order to save other people's lives. Here it was enough that one policeman with a riflescope put a bullet in her right shoulder. It hurts, but it doesn´t kill. I have good hearing, so I heard when he, the police over there, Hellström, informed you. You, Jenny, can certainly meet your mother when she comes back to her hospital in Switzerland. If she wants to see you. You can start by writing her a letter. "

The last 24 hours have been extremely difficult for all of them, both psychologically and physically, so after a cup of hot tea, they part from each other. They need a few hours of sleep before meeting again.

CHAPTER 43

Mora, Sweden – 4 March 1974

Nobody knows if Jenny is sleeping that night. Sven, lying next to her on the mattress Anders has given them, thinks she is asleep. Even calmer than usual. Jenny herself later in a conversation with doctors says that this is the night she sees the black truth and gets her mission.

At first she lies awake, thinking of everything that has happened in the past year. How the depression had pressed her into a deep darkness. How her whole person kind of disappeared, so that she had no memories left. How the memories resurrected in the Vasaloppet trail, like small chirping birds. The short triumph that ended with the police shooting her mother Agnes. That was when her memories quickly changed again, from small chirping birds to distorted monsters with many evil sides but no good ones. Dad´s oppression of her, for example. She had not been allowed to go on her own to the ball to become the queen of it, without being guarded by their neighbour, and she was not allowed to come home as late as she wanted in the evenings. She should always be kind and good. Had he never been young? And her horrible brother Anton, he had taken too much space. Had interfered so that all attention was not always focused on Jenny. She was best after all, was she not? The more Jenny thinks, the clearer it is to her that what had happened might have been the best solution. That Dad and Anton are gone. And Aunt Maja, by the way ... She's actually a murderess. If she had not run away from home, Jenny's grandmother would still have been alive... And dear beloved grandfather Wally, was he really so lovely? He had persecuted Jenny's poor sick mother and reported her to the police so that she had been imprisoned for ten years. That was not so nice, was it? No wonder Mommy wants revenge!

While Jenny is thinking about all these evil things, she gets a vision. But it's not God standing there, it is her own mother Agnes.

"I've come since you want me here," says she. "Now you´re the one who has to carry out revenge for both of us."

Agnes gets closer and kind of crawls into Jenny's ears. In the end, she's just a whispering voice which is to follow Jenny during the rest of her life.

"Everyone is trying to manipulate you, Jenny. Actually, everyone wants to harm you, but you're innocent, so defend yourself. You have to be cunning. Play your role and win friends. But at the same time plan their deaths. You´re the most beautiful and wisest one and should be at the centre. You have the right on your side. Be self-assertive, my dear."

Jenny sleepily stretches, making a grimace. She has definitely a headache. Next to her, lies Sven, on the edge of the mattress.

Sven also opens his eyes. "Where's Mum?" He asks worriedly.

"Don´t worry, honey. I´m sure she´s very OK with David," says Jenny, looking toward David's door. "Imagine if you get a little sibling. It is not at all incredible, given what I heard this night from David's room. It would be great, right? "

"I don´t want any siblings." Sven looks really angry. "She doesn´t need any man either. We´re fine as it is. That David is my adoptive father doesn´t give him any right to Mum. "

Jenny feels really cunning. Here is a crack she could use.

The door to David's bedroom opens. Heavy steps slowly approach the mattress. David's voice sounds a bit strange when he starts talking.

"Sven, my darling boy ... Ida and I have been talking and talking all night. She has told every single memory she has from your upbringing, Sven. It has been a wonderful feeling for me to feel part of your life. Knowing how you were and what you did. Ida fell asleep an hour ago and needs to sleep for a while. I feel she deserves to be awakened by lovely smells and good food. Would you like to help me?"

"So you didn´t sleep with each other?"

"But dear Sven, we prefer to keep to ourselves such parts of our lives. You should not ask that."

Jenny interposes: "But please David, don´t you see that we´re waking up. Leave us alone for a little while, huh!

Sven needs to rest. This part of our lives, as you say, we want to have for ourselves."

"You're a bit stubborn today?"

"Wouldn´t you, if you had friends who applaud the police for shooting down your mother? Do you do that in Sweden? You adults just seem to lie and hide your intentions. But I, I´ve nothing left you could steal. All my good memories are gone now. I only have bitter memories left."

"Oh I see, you're sceptical today, Jenny, aren´t you? But I´ll not take any mom away from you. Even if you are usually nice, I didn´t want to talk to you but to my son Sven. "

"What are you going to talk to him about?"

"It is really none of your business, but I´m going to give Sven a new mom and dad. Real, biological ones. Ida and I have been talking about this tonight. Nobody else knows about it. Not even Anders. He would never have approved of it. But Ida wants me to tell you. Now!"

Jenny is about to answer, but Sven stops her. "Don´t interfere, Jenny, you're not a protagonist now. Let Dad talk! "

"Ida is your biological mother, and I'm your biological father. You were made in the normal way. End of discussion! "

Sven gets interested. "Now you must explain what you mean!"

"Gunnel wanted children but could not get any after her pelvic surgery. It was she, who came up with the idea that we would do the same as so many other wealthy people did at that time. We asked our friends if they knew any woman who would give birth to the child. Of course against proper compensation. Our best friends´ maid, Ida, accepted. Everything went well, and she got pregnant at the first attempt. We already knew her before and knew that she was a good girl. Ida gave birth to you, got the money, went to sea for a year, and married a sailor who later died in an accident.

Ida deeply regretted that she had given you away. So she returned home and stole you back, when you were about two years old. We immediately suspected that she was the guilty one. She had then begun working full time with our friends again and was very accommodating in our investigations. The police made a house search at her home, but found no evidence that any child had been there. In the end, we had to finish the investigations. That's when Gunnel committed suicide.

Tonight Ida told me the truth. She was helped by her twin sister, who immigrated to the United States shortly thereafter. The first time after the kidnapping, you lived with the twin sister. Ida just turned up during the weekends. You resembled each other so much that no one reacted on the arrival and departure of two different women to the apartment. And you liked both of them. Ida didn´t want to acknowledge the money she received to feed you, so she saved them. Later she gave all the money to her twin sister so that she could start a new life in the United States. It is partly because of that I can forgive Ida. She did not care about the money we gave her. It was you, her son, she wanted.

And I'll also add one thing that might explain why Ida and I, so very soon after we met again after all those years, have got close to each other. Already at that time, I was very fond of Ida. If I hadn´t had my beloved Gunnel, maybe Ida and I would have been be a couple already at that time. Now that Ida has become a mature woman, she is even more delightful than she was then. And I didn´t immediately connect your mother Ida with my Ida, because Ida at that time was called Karin. That was the name by which I knew her. She was baptized to Ida-Karin, but now she prefers to just call herself Ida. "

Sven looks at David with a wrinkled forehead. "But why did Mom have to lie so much to me when she told me she´d kidnapped me?"

"But Sven, you have to understand that she was ashamed of having given birth to you - like on order against payment - and then giving you away for adoption. It was difficult for her to tell the truth. "

CHAPTER 44

Mora, Sweden – 4 March 1974

The sumptuous breakfast is eaten under almost total, serious silence. Everyone seems completely lost in their own thoughts.

Only Sven seems genuinely happy. He sits humming to himself, plays with the food and chuckling looks at David and Ida. It goes so far that Jenny twice sharply has to tell him to calm down. David holds up his hand to show her that she should leave Sven alone. He is only extremely happy about what he was told a moment ago. That he now has his own, very genuine and full family.

"Act like an adult, Sven! I'm tired of your childish manners!" Jenny exclaims after a while.

She has so many dark thoughts within that the mere sight of that drip makes her almost explode. How could she ever have fallen in love with him? And how did he manage to be accepted as a policeman?

"I find it strange that neither of you seems to care about what happened to my mom last night. How do you feel about what happened, Sven?"

"Yes, I'm sorry ..." Sven begins, and Jenny waits for the rest of the sentence. Perhaps Sven is still the man she is in love with? But then Sven continues: "... that the police did not aim better. Monsters like your mother don´t deserve to live. She should have been shot dead! I'm disappointed."

At that moment, hatred against Sven is born within Jenny.

Anders, who can see Jenny's flashy eyes, decides that it is time for Jenny to finally know the truth about her mom. It is not possible any longer to respect Nicklas Burgers´ desire for silence.

"Jenny. Honey, what you - and you others - still don´t know is that Agnes tried to kill you and Anton on two occasions, when you were really young. It was actually Wally who saved you both times. Nicklas found notes about this and told me. It was not meant for you to know. But ... I guess it confirms that Agnes is a monster, just like Sven said. "

"But why?" Jenny wonders, quite shocked.

"Well, she was obviously affected by a depression in connection with giving birth and it didn´t pass. And then she apparently became mad! She was diagnosed in Switzerland as schizophrenic. "

Hearing this Jenny turns completely crazy inside.

"And since when is a disease a crime? A crime to be killed for?" she exclaims.

No, now she had better control herself, not showing her feelings. "Thank you for the breakfast. I´ll take a walk for a while. See you later." She quietly rises from the table, takes her outerwear and leaves through the door. She can barely avoid banging it behind her but with an effort she manages to close it gently and carefully.

CHAPTER 45

Mora, Sweden – 4 March 1974

Jenny is sitting all morning browsing old magazines, though they do not really interest her at all. She is feeling isolated. Her outburst during breakfast was stupid. At that time even Sven had confronted her. They are all united against her. But shame on the one who gives up! In her ears, she can hear Agnes' hissing voice: "Be self-assertive Jenny. Don't let them win!"

Around 1.00 p.m., Anders declares that Nicklas Burger will soon be arriving at Storgatan 12, together with Maja and Yngve, Sonja and Mikael, to inform about the contents of Wally´s and John's wills.

Anders, David, Sven and Ida decide to have lunch at a pizzeria, so that the others can be alone with Nicklas. David's plan is also to tell Anders the truth about Sven's birth and about David´s and Ida's mutual plans.

Nicklas Burger arrives slightly late. As everyone is seated, Nicklas picks up a stack of paper from his attaché bag putting them on the dining table. Then he clears his throat and starts speaking: "Before talking about the wills I wish to inform you that I will immediately start the procedure of getting you, Jenny, a real passport. We now know for certain that your name is Jenny Johnson and that you were born in Norrköping. You should be able to get at least an interim passport within the next 24 hours. I will also, through my American police colleagues, check if you are indeed included in the Witness Protection Program. But the name you were originally given is of no importance just now. The most essential thing is to get you a passport."

Relieved, Jenny smiles. She will at long last get her identity in writing.

Nicklas continues: "I think we´ll start with Grandfather Wally's will. It contains a lot of tricky legal terms, so I´ll explain in plain words what his wishes mean. We can return to amounts and such when we´re back in the United States and I´ve had time to review all the accounts again. "

"The summary of Grandfather Wally's will is as follows. The assets, which are not insignificant, are divided into two equal parts between his children, Maja and Johan. Wally has not made any deduction for the legacy that you, Maja, have received earlier. If Maja and / or Johan are deceased, the estate will proceed directly to their children. However, no-one will have access to her/his legacy before completing an academic education or vocational training. Marriage or cohabitation is also not permitted before an education is completed and may lead to the inheritance being completely withdrawn. With this, Wally wants to avoid that you Jenny, for example, will put yourself in the same situation as Maja. Maja, you don´t have any education, Maja, because the Amish people don´t consider any more education than through class 8 is needed. Then there is, of course, some legacy to be paid for some worthwhile purposes, according to a list I have here. "

Jenny begins to look grim. She and Sven have, after all, decided to marry soon.

Nicklas goes on. "Unfortunately, both Johan and Anton are now also deceased. Half of Wally's assets should have gone to Johan. At Johan's death, that inheritance was divided into two parts, one for you Jenny and one for Anton. Because Anton is dead, also his legacy goes to you, Jenny. Johan has entered a similar limitation in his will. A fund will be set up for you, which will be paying for your education. As the education is completed, you´ll have access to the rest of the inheritance and will also be free to marry or get a partner. I also want to say that personal letters to both of you are attached to the wills. You´ll receive those immediately. Any questions?"

"I'm leaving for Stockholm early tomorrow morning to catch the United States flight home to Minnesota in the evening. You´ll have to sign some documents, but I´ll contact you from home about that."

When Nicklas has left the apartment, the rest of them are silent for a while. Maja and Jenny read their letters. Maja wipes away the tears that have fallen during the reading. Jenny, on the other hand, feels ice cold."But I don´t know what I want to be. I have no idea," she exclaims with simulated despair. "And I really don´t give a damn about the money. I want to marry Sven and go to Australia. That's all I want! But now it seems that I´m not allowed doing that. "

Maja looks serious. "Darling, off what would you live? I don´t think a foreign police assistant could get a job in Australia. Keep in mind that Wally and Johan have shown a lot of concern, putting those reservations in their wills. They really wanted your best. "

Jenny nods. "I understand that, but it feels difficult. You could help me with ideas. My mind is completely empty right now." But then her tone becomes increasingly accusatory: "All the fine memories that returned during the Vasaloppet, they are no longer there. They´ve disappeared. There is only a bundle of wills, in which the old and dead dictate what I should do with my life? I get so angry." Her voice is now shaking with anger.

"Calm down Jenny, let me tell you about Yngve´s and my plans for the near future. You may be able to get some ideas by hearing our thoughts. You understand, Jenny, we´re both tired of our boring life. We want to find something new and fun to do. Yngve doesn´t like being an accountant, and I´m just idle, with nothing to do, at home, because I don´t have any education. We both intend to get us a pilot license for small planes. In addition, I intend to go through a flight mechanic training. Yngve is quite handy as it is, but I´m so helpless regarding practical issues."

Now Yngve continues. "And I've always been very interested in rocks and minerals. Therefore, I believe I´ll go through some kind of shorter geology education. And maybe later also a gemmology training, because one of my hobbies is to shape precious stones. Sven and I have actually had very interesting conversations about rocks and precious stones, so maybe that might be something for him too. He already knows a lot." Yngve looks inquiringly at Jenny.

"What super ideas!" Jenny exclaims. "Flying is really something I would like to do. I´ve always loved aircraft, especially those with weapons. And that also makes sense with a mechanic training. Can´t I go the courses with you, Maja and Yngve? "

"Of course, dear. Nothing would make us happier, but then you´ll have to stay with us in Erie during the training. And when that´s finished, you'll have access to the legacy and can travel to Australia. But I didn´t know you were interested in weapons? "

"I´m not interested in arms as such. It´s the power and the authority that a weapon gives me that triggers me."

"We have another problem that needs to be discussed," says Sonja to steer up the conversation, which she feels is tracking out. "Tell me what you want to do with the villa at Mora. Do you feel like keeping it or will you sell it?" Sonja looks inquiringly at Jenny.

"No, I want to get rid of it as soon as possible. I can´t imagine living among all the memories of Dad and Anton. Now I want to live a real life."

Mikael and Sonja hesitatively look at each other. What's going on with Jenny?

Then Mikael says: "Jenny, we´re in fact looking for a villa for our son. They´re expecting another child and want to live near us, because Sonja and I will take care of the children daytime. Your villa would be perfect, and you would get a market price for it. Could that be something? Of course, there´ll always be room in our house for you and Sven, when you hopefully visit us in the future. "

"Wonderful! A concern less to take care of. I may occasionally arrange a quick visit by car in Mora to look for old friends, just like Mom apparently did this summer. Or whatever she did there."

Jenny has not yet allowed herself to think about what Mom had meant about being in Mora, USA, last summer. She feels she'd rather not know. That the truth could hurt too much.

"But Jenny ..." says Mikael cautiously, noticing Jenny's increasing aggressiveness.

"And Yngve and I and certainly also Sonja and Mikael would help you to pack and move," interposes Maja.

The doorbell is sounding and Sven enters, accompanied by mother Ida, father David and Grandfather Anders. They look significantly more alert than when they left and they are beaming of joy. They are now a whole and complete biological family. There is probably no place for Jenny in it, other than as a small, mousy daughter-in-law.

"Hello little Sven with your big family," she says in a sharp voice. "I've been told about my legacy now. I´m forbidden to move in with you, before I´ve a good education and I´ll not even be able to afford to travel to Australia, until I have that education. And Sonja has decided that I´ll be a pilot, and Maja wants the house in the States for her children so she´ll pack for me. Or was it the opposite?"

Then she abruptly changes the tone of her voice and kindly asks Anders: "What's the best thing you have in here?"

"It´s the photo of you and Sven in the goal area of Vasaloppet. I had it framed with glass yesterday."

Jenny raises, walks up to the photo, takes it up and delightedly laughs. "That is really nice. And my hair falls so beautifully. And little police assistant Sven is in it too." Then she lifts the photo and throws it straight into the wall, so that glass splinters are flying around. "But when I get angry, I don´t know what I'm doing."

Having let some of her anger out in this way, she coolly explains, "Do you know, my mother is not mean. You should feel sorry for her. Because Wally has been harassing her. I´ll get an education myself and take the money and use it to help her. And I'll follow in her footsteps. Bye! My lawyer Burger has given me a debit card for small expenses, as an advance of the inheritance. I´ll find my way out myself."

CHAPTER 46

Mora, Sweden, 4 March 1974

Still in a tantrum, Jenny hastily leaves the apartment at Storgatan 12 in Mora. She is dripping with sweat and can feel that her face is blushing red. She probably looks like a lunatic, which is exactly what she is feeling like. Absolutely mad with fury, her whole body is trembling.

How on earth was Sven capable of forgetting what the two of them had meant to each other? He was, after all, her best friend and her beloved fiancé. He had helped her through the difficult times when she had lost her memory and did not know anything about herself! It had been as if the two of them had been created for each other. Why had he now become so different? Well, perhaps she was no longer needed now that he had found his own, real, biological family. Obviously nobody wanted her to become a member of that family… She had suddenly become an outcast to them. Somebody they did not need any longer.

Shivering, she remembers what she has said and done, but she does not repent anything. She would happily do it all over again. And she will certainly take her revenge on Sven in a way that would really hurt him. He will suffer for throwing her out again − out of the group - into a life of loneliness. She has, herself, no family of her own and she has only known Aunt Maja for a couple of days − too short a time to regard her as a close relative.

Rage is still bubbling within her while the thoughts are whirling around in her head. Yes, she will at this very moment begin her revenge on Sven. She quickly zigzags her way through Mora to the tiny overnight apartment that Sven and she have retained after moving to live with Ida in Orsa. Having arrived, she starts her atrocities. She does not hesitate, not even for a second. The furniture is overturned, books and documents are torn out of cabinets and drawers, porcelain plates fall to the floor. There is no stop to her destructiveness. He is going to pay this price for what he has done to her. Finally she opens the small safe collecting her personal documents.

Having let off some steam, she sits down on the floor and starts crying, but after a short while thoughts are once again swirling in her head. Why did she also attack Sonja and Mikael? That had been so unnecessary and foolish of her. She does after all love them both so much and she ought not to have said the things she did. She should actually find them immediately and ask them for forgiveness. Make them understand that, given her foul mood, they had been included by mistake. That it had not been her intention to make them sad. And their idea was actually very brilliant, that their son would buy her house and furthermore to a market price. That would be very convenient both to them and to her. Oh, she misses Sonja´s big, soft and warm bosom so much and also Mikael´s reliable and trustworthy eyes! But she cannot approach them here in Mora without also meeting Sven and his family. Instead she had better return to the USA and see them there. Hopefully she would then be able to clear this misunderstanding and make peace.

Said and done. There is no time to lose. Jenny sits down at the phone table and calls Nicklas Burger. She tells him that after all that has happened she is feeling that she immediately must return to the USA. He promises her that she can pick up her new passport at Arlanda airport. Nicklas has, with his usual efficiency, already arranged a new one.

Thereafter, Jenny quickly leaves the small apartment. She does not want to bring any of her clothes or other personal belongings. You could always buy new ones. How lucky that Nicklas has provided her with a cash card! She hurries to Mora train station and is in time to board the train going to Borlänge. There she can change into another train for Stockholm.

Leaving Mora, Jenny feels such tremendous relief. She had expected to have a happy future there, but now she is feeling as if the village itself had betrayed her. Spending one more minute there would be too much.

Although Jenny's decision to return home has been made so abruptly that she has not had time to make any bookings, everything is working out perfectly and Jenny arrives in Mora, Minnesota, already within a little more than 48 hours. She had expected that she would draw a sigh of relief at the thought of being "home" again, but that does not occur. Getting off the bus she only experiences a strange emptiness and alienation. She does not belong here either! Less than a year has passed since she went to New York in order to start working at the *QE2,* but in spite of that short lapse of time everything feels so unaccustomed now.

Jenny recoils at the thought of meeting familiar persons on her way to the house. The thought of having to tell someone all that has happened to her is terrible and unthinkable. Therefore she sneaks home through, to her almost unknown, alleyways. It is unlikely that she will meet any acquaintances in those quarters.

She is afraid of entering the house. Afraid of the spooky voice and of all the memories of her dad and of Anton. And, very true, as soon as she has locked the front door behind herself, she once again hears that voice, whispering in her ear, but strangely enough it does not sound as horrible as earlier. Maybe that is because now she can finally connect a face to the voice. Now she knows that it belongs to Agnes, her mother.

Jenny is so tired, so dead tired that she does not even get afraid of the voice. The journey has been long; she has neither had anything to eat nor to drink during the whole trip, but she does not suffer because of that. She only notices that the air in the living room is very stale, so she quickly opens the window to its full extent. Thereafter, she summons all her courage, opens the door to Dad's room, runs up to his bed, in the fly grabbing the can containing sleeping pills, which is lying on his bed table. Quickly returning to the living room, she swallows two sleeping pills without even bothering to take some water with them and then lies down on the sofa. To sleep is the best thing she can do, she thinks, and within only a few seconds she is actually asleep in the increasingly cold room.

CHAPTER 47

Mora, Minnesota – 7 March 1974

Dear Maja,

First of all, I want to ask you to forgive me for my too short and maybe a little brusque telephone call the other day. I was in such a hurry but at the same time I was so anxious to let you and Yngve know that we had found Jenny. That she is here in Mora, Minnesota.

When Mikael and I arrived home we almost at once noticed a wide-open window in Jenny's house. We hastened over to it and found Jenny unconscious on the living room sofa. She was terribly cold and, as we were later told, had not had anything at all to drink nor to eat during several days. We at once called the ambulance and Jenny was admitted into hospital where they started giving her intravenous nutrition and also raised her body temperature. Now the doctors consider her, physically, well enough to be released so we are getting her back home tomorrow.

Maja, Jenny is in a very bad mental state. We have difficulties in making her talk, but what she has uttered so far shows that she feels quite abandoned and alone – having no fixed point in her existence. She locks everything inside and we are quite worried about how she is feeling. She says that she does not belong anywhere.

We have tried to convince her to meet you and Yngve, but at present she refuses. She says that if she gets too fond of you, you will certainly also one day abandon her – just like Sven did. For this reason I think you had better wait with your reunion until she has recuperated some of her trust in people.

Jenny is very eager to sell her house as soon as possible to Mikael´s and my son. We have set as a condition – which by now she has accepted – that we are allowed to refurnish our son´s old room into a room for her, so that she can always come to us, whenever she wants. We are, Mikael and I, after all, the only persons she has known for almost her entire life. To us she is the daughter we never had.

Regarding the future, we have started talking to Jenny about the possibility for her to meet young people of her own age if she were to study in Minneapolis, living in a student corridor. Maybe contact with young ones might make her feel better. She has not yet decided what to study but it seems she is inclined to be a fire technician. We will have to await her decision, when time is right.

I promise to keep both of you informed about Jenny´s progress but at the same time I must stress that I could not let her down by divulging any confidences.

With warm regards from Sonja

While Sonja is writing this letter to Maja, Mikael is in Minneapolis at the office of their advocate friend Nicklas Burger. During the joint search for Jenny, which has ended in Swedish Mora, both Nicklas, Mikael and Sonja have become close friends, and now they once more need Nicklas´ help.

Mikael has just explained to his friend all that has happened to Jenny and that Sonja and he are now desperately trying to make her feel better, make her feel some joy of life, make her able to trust people again.

"Nicklas, we need your help with a couple of things. Firstly, Jenny wants to sell her house to Sonja´s and my son. We´re going to be babysitting their children, and therefore it would be very convenient to have them close to us. Jenny herself hates the house and wants to get rid of it. She´s promised us that we can remake our son´s old room into a room for her. That way she´ll always feel welcome in our home. Could you please check if there´s anything hindering the sale? The price has to be a market one. And if you yourself could organize the sale we would all three of us be very thankful. What´s your answer?"

"Dear Mikael, of course I´d like to help you. As you know, I´m very fond of Jenny and it makes me sad to know that she isn´t well. Regarding the sale I can right away tell you that there´s no obstacle to that. Actually, Jenny´s father Johan transferred the house onto his children already several yours ago. Therefore it´s not included in the stipulations in Johan´s will. And Jenny will automatically inherit also Anton´s part of the house. I could ask a surveyor to look at the house and tell you the market value of it."

"Oh, that's so kind of you. And then there is another issue. We feel, both my wife and I, that Jenny's best chance of ever feeling better would be to hang out with youth her own age in another, funnier place than here in Mora – perhaps in a student environment. She's talking a lot about maybe becoming a fire technician. And, as you know, she'll not get access to her inheritances after Johan and Wally until she's completed an education. And being a fire technician to me seems like a good choice."

"In my opinion, a very wise choice", Nicklas interrupts. "But how could I help you in that respect?"

"We were thinking that you might try to find out as much as possible about the courses so that Jenny could get a clearer image of it all. And, after that, you hopefully could also look for cozy student lodgings. Like for example a room in a corridor with collective spaces. In such a place it would be quite difficult for her to sneak away alone. With a small apartment of her own, Jenny would probably isolate herself and that would be wrong. The girl must learn to laugh again. She must start feeling young, getting new friends. Do you think you would be able to do that?"

"I'm quite sure I would. I have many friends with student kids so it wouldn't be that difficult. But in which city would she study?"

"Here in Minneapolis, we think. Then we would be close to each other, should the need arise."

After some talk about Jenny´s fabulous accomplishment in the Vasaloppet race and about the capture of Agnes in Mora with her ensuing detention at the mental hospital in Switzerland, the two friends part.

It does not take more than a week before Nicklas, as effective as ever, has taken care of the issues Mikael has mentioned. The house survey has already been done and Nicklas suggests that he himself go to Mora to meet Jenny. He brings a preliminary sales contract and a lot of information, documents about the coming education program and also about student lodging in Minneapolis. He and Jenny sit down to study all this material together.

"You´re lucky, Jenny", says Nicklas. "There´s actually a vacancy in the class of future fire technicians and, although the term has already started, they´re eager to get you as a pupil. I´ve told them a lot about you. The fact that you´ve completed the Vasaloppet race made the headmaster very interested in you. The pupils must, after all, be physically strong – and you are. Go through the documents and if you´re still interested after reading them, you can tilt and drive. I´ve also found you very nice student quarters where there is an empty room for you."

"Lovely, Nicklas", answers Jenny. "Thank you ever so much for all your help! Now the sale of the house is next on line and, thereafter, I´m ready to start a new life. What a wonderful feeling!"

Jenny is in fact now getting out of her dormancy-like state. What is happening is so thrilling. Very concentrated she studies the documents regarding the education, finding that it would suit her so well. Living in a student corridor also seems so exciting.

Before the house sale, Jenny and Sonja rummage the house looking for things and furniture that Jenny would want to place either in her future room in Sonja´s and Mikael´s home or in her future student room. The two of them also make a two-day excursion to Minneapolis to buy lots of new and modern clothes for Jenny.

Quite suddenly the sale has gone through and Jenny has received a large amount of money. What a wonderful feeling. Maybe she might even be happy again?

The study time in Minneapolis is fun. Jenny very much enjoys being both with her class mates and her corridor friends. Suddenly she feels alive and positive. She quickly picks up her class mates´ lead and enjoys being able once again to use both her brain and her body in order to get good results.

It is only when Jenny, for some reason, starts thinking of Sven and the past that she feels like a lump of ice near her heart. An enormous anger. A feeling that she would be able to put a knife right into Sven´s heart, were she to meet him. That feeling terrifies her. Could she be mentally ill? Has she inherited the illness from which Agnes is suffering? That thought worries her quite a lot. As soon as she gets a chance to visit her mother at the Swiss hospital, she will try to get answers to some of the questions she keeps buried inside herself.

CHAPTER 48

Traineeship in Switzerland – Spring of 1976

When Jenny´s basic education is finished, she will have to go through traineeship in two different European countries. She chooses to begin in Switzerland. She has, after all, her mother there.

Jenny is very happy with her traineeship at the Fire Authorities in Geneva. She is welcomed with open arms, from the very first moment and is placed in one of the most important groups of fire technicians. She is very content that all her colleagues speak good English, since she herself – in spite of several good tries – has never gotten on well with the French language. Work is very interesting, and Jenny can feel that she, the whole time, is learning more and more useful things. The quality of her training in the USA is very high, but she still looks at the traineeship as a matter of giving and taking knowledge. Sometimes, she can contribute with something new, and sometimes she is the receiving party of new knowledge.

At the beginning of Jenny´s traineeship, there are a couple of horrendous arsons, which are really interesting from a work point. Those incidents, however, take so much of her time draining her from strength, that she already at an early stage, contacts her teacher in the USA, to ask him to extend her time in Switzerland with one more month. She also explains that her mother is in a hospital in the surroundings of Geneva, and that Jenny once in a while must have time enough to visit her. Shortly, an affirmative and compassionate answer arrives from her teacher.

As soon as her traineeship allows, Jenny goes to the mental hospital outside Geneva, where her mother has been admitted. She is really longing for a chance to solve the problem with Agnes, but, at the same time, she is feeling scared.

Jenny hesitantly raises her hand to knock on the door to patient-room number 11. She quickly glances at the doctor and the paramedic standing at her side. Both smile reassuringly at her. Then she summons her courage, knocks and opens. Takes a couple of steps inside. She immediately stops, noticing the patient´s angry face staring at her.

At her back she can hear the doctor whispering:”Don´t be afraid. She´s had a sedative, so she´s not dangerous. She might actually send you away at once, but be patient with her. Perhaps you´ll have to make several visits before she starts talking to you.”

”What are you muttering, you stupid doctor? If you can´t speak in a normal voice then you could as well go to hell! And you there, brat, why have you come here? Did I ask to see you? No, never ever! I´ve had enough of you, already before you were born. If only you knew how many times I was on the verge of putting a knife in my stomach just to get rid of you.”

Hearing the hatred in Agnes' voice Jenny feels like a stab in her heart. She wants to escape but she cannot do it. She has to get to know her mother. Know more about her. Why does her mother feel this hatred towards her? And also towards her poor brother Anton, whom Agnes has already murdered. She has to connect to Agnes – in some way. Therefore she has to stand her mother's evil words. So to say, turn the other cheek.

"Hi! But gosh, how beautiful you are! I had totally forgotten that. It's quite unbelievable that you can be my mother looking that young and fresh!" Jenny does not need to lie saying that. What she says is actually true. They could have been sisters instead of mother and daughter.

"Don't you ever believe that you'll be even half as beautiful as I." An involuntary smile is for a moment seen in Agnes' face, but then she once again turns moody. "What are you doing here? Did you come to taunt me for being confined here?"

"No, no, not at all. I was only thinking you might feel very tired of the situation and that you once in a while would appreciate having someone to talk to. And I could actually buy you fashion magazines and cosmetic products, if you would need such. I don't mean that you need any, but just in case..."

"That was nicely thought, you little scout, but you'll have to leave now. I'm fed up with you. But I'll think about it, if I want your services or not. You could actually be useful to me. Let´s see."

"Late as usual", Agnes annoyed exclaims, seeing Jenny standing in the doorway. Jenny has by now gotten used to Agnes´ tantrums and does not mind any longer. "Did you bring anything fun for me? If not so, then you could as well disappear at once."

"Well, this time it is a home furnishings magazine. I have already bought you all the fashion magazines published this month, but I am also bringing some photos that we could look at together."

"Photos – what kind of foolishness is that? I have certainly nothing worth remembering from my life." Agnes looks bitter uttering that. "And by the way, if those are really photos from my life, you could not have them, could you?"

"Yes Agnes. Looking through the house after Dad´s and Anton´s deaths, I actually came across a heap of photos that I hadn´t seen before. I felt that they could be important so I intended to bring them when I went to sea. But then I forgot them in the house. And later, when Sonja was searching for photos of me, before she and Mikael left for Sweden, she also brought these, giving them to me, as we met in Mora."

Agnes is looking doubtful. "Are you really sure that the photos are of me and my life?"

"Wait and see. There are a lot of photos that I believe come from your childhood. If that´s right, you might even smile at some of them. You had a rather lovely childhood, didn´t you?"

"OK, it was not too bad. Let me see!"

Jenny flips through the photos. The first one she shows is of a rather big croft, surrounded by birch forest and a lake. A maypole is decorated with beautiful summer flowers. A long table, festively laid, and sitting around it ten persons looking happy and satisfied.

Agnes looks surprised but at the same time happy. "Yes, you´re right, I guess."

"Tell me about these persons", asks Jenny.

"How nice to see this photo! I haven´t thought about it for a long time. I just know that we had a marvellous Midsummer and that everybody was happy — for once." This is the closest to laughter that Jenny has ever heard from Agnes. She looks quite excited. "Wait, we´ll see if I can remember who those persons are." She thinks for a moment and then continues: "That man at the short end of the table is my dear daddy. He was the best father in the world."

Agnes suddenly breaks into tears. Floods are running down her cheeks and her mascara soon looks like stripes on her face. Jenny gets quite miserable seeing her so sad. Agnes is usually grouchy, angry and harsh, never showing any soft feelings. Jenny feels a big and tender compassion for her mother. What horrible things could have happened to make Agnes start crying like this?

"Agnes, why are you so upset? Tell me so that I can try to help you. It´s terrible to see you this desolate. I care about you, so please let me help!"

"No, Jenny, nobody could help me. The photo you showed me was from our last summer as a happy family. Then such terrible things happened. I´ll try to explain when I´ve calmed down, but right now I need a pill from the doctor – in order to cope. Could you please call him? I´ll tell the nurse to call you, when I can bear talking more about this."

Nurse Louise from the hospital calls a few days later, saying that Agnes would very much like Jenny to come for a visit. She obviously has something to tell. Jenny rushes there and is met by a quiet and subdued Agnes, who actually gives her a welcome hug. The first hug that Jenny has ever received from her mother.

"Sit down, Jenny. Do you want coffee or anything else to drink? What I want to tell you will probably take a while, so you´ll have to tell me if you don´t have time today to hear it all."

Jenny is taken aback. What is this? Agnes has never before shown any interest whatsoever in others, neither in what they would want nor if they have time to be with her. She is really happy. Maybe the two of us could finally connect in a serious way, she thinks.

"Yes please, Agnes. A cup of tea would be really nice. And, by the way, I don´t have any plans for today, so you can have all the time you need. Don´t feel pressed. Tell me at your own pace."

Agnes interrupts:"Do you think that you´ll ever call me Mother? In a way, that would feel much nicer."

"Yes Agnes, I´m sure I will one day, but first I would prefer to get to feel that we – truly – care for each other and can trust each other. I´ve always longed for a mother, so when that moment arrives I can promise that I´ll be extremely happy. Could you be satisfied with that answer, for the time being, Agnes?"

With a happy smile, Agnes nods affirmatively in answer to Jenny´s question. After a moment, she starts going through the envelope with photos bringing out four of them. The rest she pushes to the side.

"Look here, Jenny! This first photo shows the farm at which I was born and where I lived until my early teens. As you can see, the farm is rather big. A big dwelling, some outbuildings and a huge barn. It looks pretty, doesn´t it? Our lands stretched along the sea and were, on the other side, enclosed by a birch forest and a little further down by a fir forest. Right now, I don´t remember the acreage we had but it was enor-mous. We partly lived off the income from all the ani-mals, partly from that of the forestry. Our home was located close to Norberg in Västmanland and we called it the Hundred Acre Croft. We had no labourers, man-aging most of the work ourselves. My dad was a hell of a man, being able to do the work of seven hired men, but in connection with the wood logging he sometimes hired some help. My mother was a true farmer's wife. She milked the cows, took care of the hens, collected the cattle from the fields and lots more. On top of all that, she loved to cook and bake. In other words, we were a truly happy family, and we were very close. And everyone contributed in some way or the other to the household."

Agnes catches her breath and looks at Jenny: "Don't you also think that this seems a perfect setting for a happy life? Almost as if taken out of a really old sugary book for girls, don't you agree?"

Jenny nods affirmatively.

Agnes drinks some water before showing the third photo. On it, you see a nicely dressed family, probably on their way to church. Five persons are visible. A man and a woman, both very handsome – and three children. One girl with copper red braids, a somewhat younger boy in trousers and an unruly cendré-coloured hair and then finally a still younger boy in shorts and with gaps between his front teeth.

Agnes wipes away the tears that have now started running down her cheeks. "Yes, this is my beloved family. Or, to say it in a truer way: This used to be my family. My dad was called Daniel and my mother Ingrid. My name you already know. And then, this boy in trousers is the older of my two brothers. His name is Sture. The charming little one, who has just lost his first teeth, is Laban. Oh, how I wish that I could return to those happy days!"

"Dear Agnes, I understand that something horrible must have happened. Do you really think you have the strength to tell me more today?"

Agnes just nods. Jenny can feel that this beautiful story will have anything but a happy ending, and she trembles at that thought. Poor Agnes!

"Agnes, are you really sure that you can deal with telling me more today? Shouldn´t I ask the doctor what he thinks?" ask Jenny concernedly.

"No, I had better get it all out of my system at once, now that you are here. I don´t think I´ve ever told anyone the whole story – except maybe to Johan, your father. You should also know that once upon a time I really loved him very much, but then something went wrong between the two of us.

Agnes continues:"This fourth photo is from our last happy Midsummer. Only a couple of months later, our family had been destroyed. What happened was really awful. And so horribly unexpected."

A new shower of tears makes her voice almost inaudible. Jenny sits down close to Agnes, holds her and rocks her the way you do with a restless child.

"No, I can´t postpone it any longer. I just have to tell you about the horrendous thing that happened. I might even find some peace doing so. This is what happened. The older one of my two brothers, Sture, became very jealous of my little brother, Laban, when he was born. Sture and I had never had any problems between the two of us, but when Laban was born Sture changed completely. He constantly tried to harm Laban, in different ways – both mentally and physically. I noticed this at an early stage and tried to protect Laban as much as I could. I even told my parents about this, but they never seemed to believe me. They said it was a natural thing for brothers to fight and quarrel.

Then this summer arrived, the one from the Midsummer photo. We owned a couple of bulls for breeding and they were supposed to mount our cows. As the first cow was to be mounted, my dad asked Laban to bring the bull out. Laban had a natural talent with animals and the bulls loved him. None of us knew that Sture, for a rather long period, had been badly harming the bulls, when they were in their cubicles, by nailing them with sharp sticks and similar things. So when Laban took the bull outside, it immediately attacked him. Laban got one of the bull's horns stuck deep into his body. My mother heard his cries and ran into the barn and the cubicle in order to try to save Laban. She was thrown right into the wall and got brain damage. Dad also heard the screams, jumped from the tractor and ran like mad up to the cubicle. The bull attacked also him, stomping his chest to pieces. Sture escaped into the forest.

I was away when all this happened. The village doctor was present, when I returned home, and he told me about it. By that time, both Laban and Dad were dead and Mum was very seriously injured. Sture was still hiding somewhere in the forest, so I couldn´t have the consolation of hugging him and sharing the grief with him."

"Oh, how completely horrible! And what a trauma it must have been for you being so young. What happened to you and Sture?

"Yes, Jenny, I myself had a complete nervous breakdown and was, for quite a long time, in a mental ward for children. As I, finally, was considered well enough, the social authorities arranged with a foster family for me. I lived with them for some years but as happens to so many other youngsters, I finally ended up in bad company and did some rather bad things. My next foster family was stricter and made me pull myself together. And then I met Johan, your father, and we moved in together. And we were, actually, quite happy for some time."

"And my uncle Sture, what happened to him?"

"Well, to begin with nobody knew where he was. He just disappeared into the forest and did not even show up for the funeral. After a couple of years I was told, by the social authorities, that Sture had been in Ibiza together with a gang of drug addicts and behaved so badly that he was kicked out of Spain. He ended up in some sort of reformatory in Värmland. I wrote to him but never got any answer. And then, quite suddenly about a year ago, I saw a newspaper article about a new sect or church in Sweden, of which Sture seems to be the leader. I think it´s name is Show Empathy To Africa or similar. People say it´s collecting money for the poor in other countries. So, Jenny, if you ever go to Sweden again, look him up. It´s quite possible that he´s improved.”

”But I have to ask you, Agnes, what your maiden name was? I have to know that in order to know my uncle´s name if I´m to find him.”

”Blomkvist. A long time ago I was Agnes Blomkvist so my brother´s name ought to be Sture Blomkvist. But this thing with surnames is a little tricky, isn´t it? When I read in the paper about your achievement in the Vasaloppet race, you had a quite different surname than the one you were given after birth. That is strange, I think. Do you know anything about that?”

”No, actually not. I can only remember that my name has always been Jenny Johnson, and that I have always lived in Mora, Minnesota. But there was something strange because Dad and Granddad never allowed us children to tell others about our lives or about our relatives. We actually found that rather annoying. We almost felt as if we were villains having done something ugly. We never had answers to our questions, neither from Dad nor from Granddad Wally.”

”Well Jenny, my name was definitely not Johnson during my marriage to your father Johan – and his first name was quite different from Johan at that time. And we lived in Colorado and not in Minnesota. The only explanation I could give is that you might have been included in the Witness Protection Program and that you moved as soon as I had been taken into custody."

"But Agnes, you said that already outside Statt…"

With an angry sputter, Agnes says: "Don´t you dare interrupting me! I know that I´ve already said that, but at that time it was merely as a joke. Now, I actually believe it´s true. And you should know that I actually enjoy the thought of being able to scare both "Johan" and Wally to that extent!" Agnes smiles sneakily. "But enough about that now. After all, they do not exist any longer!"

Seeing Agnes´ facial expression Jenny is not only scared but also sad. Tears are rising in her eyes and she feels that for the moment she cannot stand the sight of Agnes any longer. She suddenly remembers the happy memories of her own childhood and what a happy little family they had been, during all those years Agnes had not been a member of the family. She raises saying in a sharp voice: "No, if you´re to be like that, then you´ll have to do without my company for some days. I´ve had a very happy childhood with them. And that you murdered my father and brother is something that I probably could never forgive you. I´m here with you, because you are my mother, and I want to try to understand the things that happened. I know that you´re ill and that is probably the cause why I´m still hoping that we will, the two of us, one day be close. I´m now leaving for today – I can´t deal with any more spitefulness from you. I will return in a few days. Bye!" Having said that, Jenny hastens to the door.

During Jenny's following hospital visits Agnes seems laconic and in some ways absent-minded. Sometimes, without any visible reason, she also gets tantrums – often aimed at Jenny or at the paramedic. It is obvious that there is a temporary decline in her illness. It makes Jenny sad to see her that way, since the two of them have actually by now becoming closer, feeling more like mother and daughter instead of two strangers like they were at the beginning of their acquaintance. Agnes is sometimes so mean that Jenny just stands up and leaves. That is an awful thing to do but she must put some limits to what she can accept, but at the same time she has decided never to dwell on things her mother has said; never to bring up, at her next visit, the spitefulness she has been shown. Just ignore it instead of starting a time-consuming quarrel. She has to remember that Agnes is ill and that she cannot always control what she says.

On another visit, Jenny notices, already entering Agnes' room, that her mother is in a much better mood. Jenny Is welcomed with a hug and is asked to sit on the bedside to talk. Agnes speaks a lot about her happy childhood years – before the accident – and about a lot of funny experiences her family had met. But she never mentions Jenny's first years or anything from the years they had spent together. It is like she has erased those years from her memory. Neither does she talk about the deaths of Johan and Anton nor about Wally. On the other hand she asks a lot of questions about Jenny's education as a fire fighter and her additional training as a fire technician. Her curiosity about these subjects seems very strong. She wants to know as much as possible about different ways to start a fire and about the investigation of fire sites. Jenny, knowing that Agnes has once started an arson in Switzerland, tries to answer the questions as vaguely and evasively as she can without infuriating Agnes. Jenny is terribly afraid that Agnes, in some way or other, might get an opportunity to start a fire again, and therefore she absolutely refuses to give Agnes any more knowledge about fires.

As Jenny stands up to leave, Agnes asks: "And Jenny, what will you do, when your traineeship here in Switzerland is finished?"

"Well, then I´ll have to return to school in the USA and report all that I have learnt here. After that, I´ll have a couple of additional terms with technician studies in the USA and then I´m going to Stockholm for a short period. Having reported on my Stockholm experiences, I´ll be ready with my studies and can call myself a fire technician."

Agnes laughs out loud. "What a splendid combination we are together! I love putting things on fire, and you love extinguishing them! What a future we could have had together!" But then Agnes turns serious again and continues: "Jenny, you´re really both smart and tenacious. I want to ask you if you, at some point, could pass my home in Torrevieja. There are some documents and things that I´ll need, as it seems that I´ll be staying here for rather many years. Could you do that for me?"

"Yes, of course. But since I have to leave now we could perhaps talk about that next time I visit you. And please remind me that I also have some questions for you! Bye bye!" Having received a hug, Jenny leaves.

At Jenny's next visit, she asks Agnes about the things Agnes wants her to collect in the house in Torrevieja. Agnes has already prepared a list with small things she would love to have at her side: some small keepsakes. "But there are a couple of things among this that you can keep for you and take care of. A small ring that I got from my mother, when I was still a kid. I believe your fingers are slim enough for it. I guess you have inherited your beautiful fingers from me but, of course, I still have mine left!" she adds with a little laugh. "Then you can also take the gold necklace. Bring the rest of the jewellery to me. And there's also an envelope, on which is written 'Will'. Take that one and keep it safe until the day comes when It'll have to be opened. But Jenny, remember that if I get angry at you, I might as well write a new will. In such a case, you would lose my whole fortune. I'm so easily affected that that might well happen!"

"Yes, Agnes, I understand that, and I'm not expecting anything at all from you. I actually have no idea whatsoever what you own or don't own. I want us to like each other, I don´t hope for more than that. But I´ll do as you wish if only you give me your key!"

"Yes, here it is. The address is on the key fob."

"OK, but there are a few things I´d like to ask you, Agnes. It is quite possible that you´ll become angry but I´ll have to accept that. Is that OK?"

"Well, I can´t comment on that until I´ve heard the questions, can I? But go along!"

"OK, then I´ll start. My first question is whether you´ve ever told your doctor about the horrible experience you had when your father and little brother were killed? I mean, really told him how you remember it and how you felt inside? The reason for asking this is that it could actually be important for him to know, considering your disease."

"Jenny, if only I knew. People have told me that, as a kid, I absolutely refused to talk about the accident. That I shut it up inside me. Avoided to speak to people. And, as far as I know, I have never, as an adult, talked about it – with the exception of you. Whatever happened then is probably buried deep inside of me. It would be too horrendous to let the thoughts loose. Do you understand what I mean?"

"Yes, Mother, I do. I reacted in more or less the same way, when Dad and Anton died. It is too difficult to talk about such terrible incidents."

Agnes holds out her hand to caress Jenny´s hand. "Do you know that you just called me Mother?"

"Yes, Mother, I know. I think it´s about time to do that now. I can feel that we´ve become very close, but I also know that we´ll surely have arguments again, but that´s rather human and not so very strange, isn´t it?" She ponders for a moment before continuing. "Both of us have had very traumatic experiences, of which we don´t want to talk. I was thinking… I was thinking that the doctors might find a reason to why you feel the way you do. And I, myself, don´t feel too well either. I suffer from strange mood changes and such. Don´t you think you could be strong enough to tell your doctor about what happened? It might make a difference in the treatment you´re undergoing. I don´t know but…" She adds:"In any case, I´ll see a doctor and tell him how I reacted to what happened to me. There is something called Post Traumatic Stress Disorder. And I have read somewhere that it could co-exist with schizophrenia."

"Jenny, you´re a rather wise girl for being so young. And what you´re saying seems logic. I promise to consider your suggestion. But, as you know, I´ve now been diagnosed as a schizophrenic and that is hereditary. Are you not afraid that you´ll also be that? I would, of course, feel very relieved if they find that I don´t suffer from schizophrenia."

"Both yes and no! I have, of course, thought about that, but at the same time I´ve a feeling that there could be something else behind it. That´s why I´ve brought up the subject of PTSD.”

”And Mother, now it´s actually soon time for me to return to the USA for continued studies. My time here in Geneva has finished but before I move from here I´ll make a quick trip to Torrevieja to collect the things you have asked me for. Next time we meet, we´ll have to say 'Goodbye'. But…” Tears are welling up in Jenny´s eyes; she wipes them away and continues: “I will keep in touch with you and come to visit you as often as I possibly can.”

Agnes extends her arms to get a hug from Jenny, the daughter she has finally accepted as such.

CHAPTER 49

Traineeship in Stockholm – August 1977

After two more terms with studies in Minneapolis, Jenny has now arrived in Stockholm, the place she has chosen for her last traineeship. Her US teacher has been very happy hearing her choice, since Sweden is among the leading countries when it comes to technique in connection with fire investigations. Since he finds Jenny very intelligent and therefore very capable of absorbing possible news from the Swedish Fire Authorities, he is convinced that such news will be forwarded also to the American fire authorities, and the permission is granted.

Jenny has found herself a rented room with an elderly widow in central Stockholm, and she is now on the hunt for possible friends with whom she could spend her off-duty days. She has, during her studies in Minneapolis, learnt to appreciate the company of young people of her own age. Therefore, Jenny asks her landlady for advice about where to go in order to find youth. The answer is: To Nalen.

So, one of her first evenings, she summons all her courage and goes to Nalen –in Sweden a very well-known dance hall. Oh God, how boring! Intrusive men trying to be far too intimate. There is no lack of interested men, but they have no style. Imagine guys in knitted cardigans with belts and embroidered shirts. They actually look rather stupid in comparison with the cute boys at home. Only a lot of cocky youths behaving very badly. The music is so bad and prices are too high. To have to pay almost a fortune for a lousy drink could drive you crazy. Let down, Jenny walks out of there.

Jenny has, indeed, given up hope of meeting nice friends. But then, just by chance, a day later she meets a group of youth, seeming very nice. They start talking, finding pleasure being together. They are curious about her and want to know a lot. Jenny tells them about her strange experiences: the bear attack, the amnesia and the Vasaloppet Race. She, on the other hand, does not tell them about the curious voices she has heard, or about her tantrums and similar things. Those incidents might alienate them from her.

Jenny's new friends bring her to jazz clubs and good bars and restaurants, and also take her on different sightseeing walks in Stockholm. Jenny soon changes her opinion about Swedish people. They seem so stiff and formal, but once you get to know them, they are as nice as the Americans.

One night, having been with her friends, for a couple of hours, at Gröna Lund – the amusement park at Djurgården - Jenny suddenly feels very tired. She leaves the company, who wants to stay a little longer, and start walking towards her rented room in the lovely summer evening. The environment at Djurgården is very different. Old wood houses in long rows and then suddenly an odd palace-like building.

Walking on, Jenny suddenly sees firelight from an old wooden house. She stops. That does actually look like a fire, she thinks. She approaches the house and, true enough, she sees – to her horror – that there is in fact a fire going on. Jenny quickly runs up to a telephone booth, being quite close, pressing the SOS button. She shouts that there is a fire in a house quite close to the Tivoli and that she is going to enter it. When she is warned warned that that is dangerous, she rapidly explains that she is a fire fighter. Then she quickly hangs up.

Back at the house, Jenny breaks a window and enters. The fire is now getting more intense, but Jenny feels that she must check the whole house for possible inhabitants. She finds none, except in the last room she is checking. There she sees an elderly man lying on the floor and Jenny also notices that it seems as if the fire has started in this same room.

Hearing the sirens of the approaching fire engines, Jenny quickly searches for a water tap. Having found it, she soaks a couple of towels and puts one of them over her own hair and one over that of the man. Now she has to hurry up. The fire is increasing and the situation is becoming dangerous. She quickly grabs the man´s arms and drags him out of the room. She continues through to the next room where she finds the front door. It is bolted from inside but she opens it and, using her last powers, she succeeds in getting both the man and herself out of the house. Firefighters immediately take over control and two paramedics run up to Jenny and the man to help them.

When Jenny's paramedic has examined her, he says: "It seems you're OK but for safety's sake your lungs will be checked at the hospital. What do you know about the fire? Do you also live there?"

"No!" says Jenny. I'm a fire fighter and just happened to pass by. Seeing the fire, I called 90 000 and then I entered the house. Is the man alive?"

"What a fantastic thing to do! You have saved the man's life. My colleague gave him some CPR and then he woke up. He will, of course, also go to the hospital for a check-up."

"Does he know how the fire started?"

"Yes, he does", answers the paramedic. "He says he was in front of the TV, having a beer and some ground nuts. He had lighted a candle in order to have a cosy evening, but then he happened to get a ground nut stuck in his throat and fighting to get some air, he happened to turn the candle over and that caused the fire. And by then, he was so affected that he couldn't do anything in order to stop the fire. He thought he would die! And, by pure fear, the ground nut came out his mouth."

At the hospital, the doctor wants Jenny to stay the night – just in case. She has also had a couple of small burns that they would like to take care of. Before falling asleep, she is browsing a couple of newspapers from some days ago. At the front page of one of the newspapers, there is a photo of an elderly man. The headings are big as is also the photo. Studying the photo, she gets a feeling that she in some way recognizes him. She is pondering for a moment over where she could have met him, but then it suddenly dawns on her that the man very much resembles Agnes. When she, thereafter, quickly reads the photo heading, she sees that the man´s name is Sture Blomkvist. At his side, there is a younger man – of approximately Jenny´s own age – and the article tells that he is Sture´s son. But how strange! That must be her own uncle! And she evidently also has a cousin! Jenny gets quite happy and decides to try to find them. Reading the article, she sees that they are both being praised for having started a project, worth of earnest consideration. The project, having been named Show Empathy to Africa Association, although being very new, obviously already has a lot of members. The intention is to collect money for smaller good projects in Africa. The money is to be used for health clinics, medicine, women´s projects and wells etcetera. Everything meant to help the poor people in the African countryside.

Reading this, Jenny feels proud of both her uncle and her cousin. And Sture surely must have improved as a person since his youth! She would really love being part of this association. She has to check it. And she would feel so happy having a few new family members. For the time being, she has, after all, only Agnes left. Having also an uncle and a cousin would be so nice.

In the morning, just before leaving the hospital, Jenny has a visitor. A man, to her completely unknown, is suddenly standing in the door opening. He introduces himself as her future boss during her traineeship, congratulating her to her fantastic contribution the prior evening. Thereafter, he tells her that if she continues to live up to his hopes, he will offer her a permanent employment, as soon as she has received her diploma as a fire technician.

"I feel much honoured", says Jenny, "but couldn´t I be allowed to make an investigation of yesterday´s fire site in order to check the man´s story?"

"Of course", is the answer. "I´m really pleased that you´re so curious and meticulous. You´ll be in charge of the investigation, but – for safety – I want to have a couple of my technicians present. They could intervene in case you´re going astray,"

That same afternoon, the evening papers and the rest of media are busy reporting about the fire at Djurgården. Jenny has suddenly become a heroine, and the reporters have found out about her earlier success in the Vasaloppet race as Mora´s own Jane Doe, and that she before that had been attacked by a bear, losing her memory as a consequence.

Blushing, Jenny reads the whole story. She finds it a bit exaggerated. But, thank heavens, at least she is now mentioned with her name Jenny Johnson instead of the imaginary name Jane Doe. Whether she had been called something else at birth, as Agnes has said, is now of no importance whatsoever. She is Jenny Johnson – and that is it!

As Jenny finally leaves the hospital, to her astonishment, she sees a long row of old cars awaiting her. Her
new friends have come in their cars, equipped with big
signs with Jenny´s name on them, to collect her and
take her to a secret place for celebration.

Chapter 50

Uppsala, Sweden - August 1977

Sture Blomkvist, slowly, walks into the kitchen, in his housecoat and with dishevelled hair. In spite of having just showered, he is still not completely awake. With the movements of a sleep walker, he puts on the coffee maker – strangely enough he remembers to check if there is water and coffee in it. On his way to the kitchen, he has fetched the morning paper lying on the hallway floor. Sighing, he sits down at the kitchen table to make himself a couple of sandwiches, before reading the paper. Seeing the paper's front page, he gives a start. What is this? But how strange. He carefully studies the big photo on the page, pondering for a while. Then, suddenly, he understands what has made him react. The girl on the photo is actually so very alike his sister Agnes that they could have been cloned. As he continues reading the article, he starts to cluck internally. How wonderful!

No, he really has to stop spending late nights with his friends, on week days. He must remain smart daytime, because there is so much at stake, if only he succeeds with the plan he has set his mind on. And today's article makes it all much more live. No, no more night life with booze – he has to work.

A sudden bang on the upper floor tells him that his son Ove is coming downstairs to the kitchen. Oh, how he wishes that the kid, at least once in a while, would refrain from closing the door in that way. And, hearing his scuffing feet coming down the stairway, you could well believe that Ove were an 80 years old man. He is only 20 years of age, why cannot he move like such? He is so tired of his son that he, daily, considers the thought of exchanging him for someone better.

"Morning, Ove. What did you do last night? Did you drink alcohol as usual?"

"You shouldn´t ask that! How much did you, yourself, have – if you dare answer that question? You shouldn´t throw stones when you are sitting in a glasshouse. Remember that, Dad!"

"Show some respect, please! And don´t go to your traineeship without having showered, combed your hair and shaved. You look like something the cat has brought into the house. Don´t disgrace yourself and, above all, don´t disgrace me!"

"What does it matter? After all, there is nobody caring."

"But Ove, don´t you remember our big project?"

"Which one of them all? You have new projects almost every day …"

"No, we actually started one a couple of years ago, about which the newspaper has now written an article. I have been lying low on it, but now it is really time to kick it alive again!"

When Ove still does not seem to understand, Sture clarifies his answer. "I´m talking about the Show Empathy to Africa Association, the one about collecting money for the poor in Africa. You remember that one, don´t you?"

"Yes, but we are the ones needing money, don´t we? Why should we help others and not ourselves?"

"Yes, Ove, but you can´t always only think of yourself? Empathy means compassion. Imagine if everybody stopped helping people in need, then some countries would fall apart. Countries that also we need, countries producing things that are used even by us. And, furthermore, imagine that we − you and I − one day would need help. If we don´t help others, they might not come to help us the day we are in need. Do you understand?"

Sture knows, through an IQ-test he has convinced Ove to do, that Ove is not very smart, but he is still hoping to persuade Ove to join him in his plan.

"Ove, I´m going to make a few important phone calls today. If they work out well, then you and I will talk some more tonight. By that time, I might tell you something new. Something I think is rather nice. Now, go and have a shower and make yourself ready for work."

During the day, Sture calls the Fire Authority, asking to talk to Jenny Johnson. He is told that she is out working and that she cannot be reached. When he asks for her telephone number or address, he learns that the girl at the telephone exchange is not allowed to give out private details regarding the employees. But, on the other hand, he could leave his name and telephone number so that she can call him, if she is interested in talking to him. OK, it will have to do that way. Now he can only hope she will call him.

And then, in the late afternoon, there is suddenly a phone call. Sture has, during the whole day, been craving for a couple of whiskeys, in order to relax his nerves, but has decided to keep completely sober. So much could depend on the outcome of a possible call, that he does not want to risk it by not being sober. And he could blame his hoarse cigarette voice on a cold or something similar.

"Sture Blomkvist", answers Sture, in a friendly voice.

He hears a short inhalation in the receiver, followed by a happy laughter. "Oh, I'm so happy to hear that name", the voice of a young woman says. "I had really hoped to hear exactly that! Now it only depends on your next answer, if everything is going to be right. Do you have or did you ever have a sister? In such a case, what was her first name?"

Sture laughs. "What a different beginning of a telephone conversation with an unknown person. Yes, I have a sister, Agnes, but I don't know whether she's alive or not. Was that the right answer? And, by the way, why are you asking that?"

Jenny laughs again. She is bubbling inside of laughter and joy. "Yes, Uncle Sture, you just had a niece. What do you think about that?"

"Fantastic! Wonderful! It was with that expectation I contacted your employer. I saw your photo in the newspaper and thought you were a true copy of Agnes. I so much hoped that I would be right in that. And, wow, my son Ove will be so happy to have a cousin. I believe you´re both of approximately the same age."

"Oh, how nice! I´ve far too few relatives, so an uncle and a cousin are most welcome! We have lots to catch up on. When could we meet?"

"Jenny – because that´s your name, according to the newspaper article – I´m just leaving on a business trip and will be gone for approximately a week, and Ove has just left for a week long course, so I think we´ll, unfortunately, have to delay the meeting for between one week and 10 days. And then, of course, it also depends on your schedule. Is that OK?"

"Yes, of course, but I´m feeling a little baffled having to wait for a meeting, but I´ll have to accept that. I´ll call you again within a little more than a week. Have a good time until then! I look forward to meeting both of you!"

Having both put down the receiver, Sture takes some skips of joy. This could be a direct hit!

Appearing for dinner, Ove is very expectant. Dad has, after all, said that he would have something good to tell. What could it be?

"Hi Dad, what did you want to tell me? I´m so curious!"

"Sit down first, boy. First of all, we´re having a beer each and drinking it I´ll tell you the news."

Sitting down in the messy living room, they open their beer cans.

"Ove, reading the newspaper this morning, I saw something much unexpected. On the front page was a photo of a young beautiful girl – approximately of your own age – and an article about her. She, obviously, made a big contribution during the fire drama, taking place at Djurgården in Stockholm a few days ago. And she has, furthermore, earlier distinguished herself during the Vasaloppet race, etcetera. She is being described as a true heroin. Seeing the photo, I immediately reacted, because she looks incredibly much like my sister Agnes as a young girl. And now, this afternoon, I have talked to her – her name is Jenny – on the phone, and she´s really my niece and, therefore, also your cousin."

"Oh, how nice! But what is so remarkable about that? I mean, how would that affect our lives -if at all?"

"Well, Jenny is now a, more or less, well-known person. We have agreed to meet within a little more than a week. I postponed the meeting, saying that I´m leaving on a week-long business trip, and that you had just left for a week-long course. I wanted us to have a chance to prepare ourselves before meeting Jenny."

"What do you mean: prepare ourselves? What is so important about Jenny?"

"Wait, I´ll explain. She is bang on the right person to help us to re-launch the Show Empathy To Africa Association. Everyone admires her and she could probably, through her celebrity status, make people donate money to the poor in Africa, but we can´t show ourselves as we are today. We have to better ourselves in order to give a better impression. I will dedicate the time until the meeting with Jenny to make the flat look better and, of course, myself too. New clothes, less to drink etcetera. You must also, yourself, undergo a change, Ove. And I´ll let your mother help you with that."

"Mum? She doesn´t want to help you, does she? You´re not exactly on friendly terms."

"No, you´re right in that but she adores and loves you. Therefore you are to contact her, telling her that you want to change your way of live. That you want to have further education in order to be of help in the Show Empathy to Africa Association, and that you, for that reason must get a new image – a new look and behaviour. That is to say, getting a completely new style: new hair cut, new clothes, help to learn a little more on how to behave and – not the least – help in quickly learning about help projects in Africa. You´re, after all, rather technical so you should perhaps read about technical solutions, solar energy and such. And you know how much she raves over help projects for suffering people. She will be so jubilant, don´t you think? And you could, actually, suggest that she also join the association. What do you think about that idea?"

”It sounds quite clever. But … what will the advantages be for you and me? What will we win on this? But, by the way, let me see the photo and the article.” Having read the interjection, he nods. “Yes, she is really cute.”

”You just wait and see. Trust me, Ove! This is something from which we will also profit.”

Chapter 51

Meeting with Association members in Uppsala – September 1977

Sture initiates the meeting with the following words: "I welcome all of you to this meeting. I will start by letting Jenny Johnson have the floor. Some of you might already have read about Jenny in the newspapers, in connection both with the Vasaloppet race, a couple of years ago, and also in connection with a fire drama in Stockholm. She´s a good person, feeling a lot of empathy with all the people suffering in this world. Since it´s difficult to help everyone on the globe, she has decided to concentrate especially on Africa. Jenny´s idea of how to help was actually born as she happened to see one of my bad consciences – my cellar. And here comes Jenny!"

Now Jenny takes the microphone and starts speaking: "Hi everyone and thanks for coming here today. As Sture just said, one of his bad consciences is everything he has collected in his cellar. I´m sure that a lot of you are also having a bad conscience like that, regardless of it being a cellar, an attic or some other storage area.

Our thought is that some of all the things we collect might be better off in a trash container. But … among all that we, ourselves, regard as trash or want to throw away, there is also much that can be of use in other countries. Things the poor could either use or maybe take parts from when, with local methods, producing something new. There are many examples of how they, using simple rubber material, can produce primitive shoes or sandals. Or how they, from sheet metal, produce wheelbarrows – which can be used for normal work as well as for transport of sick people on muddy roads where no cars can pass. Cloth could be used as diapers. Stuffed animals could comfort a sick child. You could continue this list forever…

Let us suppose that we clean away all our bad consciences, collecting all those items in one place, for example in Sture's garden – where we could put up a tent so that they are not destroyed during rainy weather.

But to sort and send all those things to Africa also costs a lot of money and the association could not yet afford that. Our idea is that you also give away some other things that you don´t need any longer or can use. Fashion also changes and so does taste. When you refurbished your bedroom or the kitchen or the garage, I´m sure some things were left that don´t any longer fit into your environment. A lamp, a toaster, a painting, the old TV – things worth a little more money but not enough for you to bother with your time or your money in order to get rid of them yourself. And it might even be things that you understand can´t be used in an African village, where there is still no electricity, water, or health care center. In such cases, please remember that through an auction, organized by us, those things could generate money for both transport to Africa, clean water for villages, medicine, blankets, health care centers etcetera. Things that poor people need so much.

Therefore, our suggestion is that you search your stashes carefully for all the things you don´t want to keep as you no longer need them. Pack the things you think would give money at an auction, so that they will not break, marking on a paper the contents. We could put up two tents in Sture´s garden, so that the things can be divided according to type – broken things that could be sent to Africa and unbroken that could be sold at auctions. If we get a lot of things, this generosity from your side could mean a lot for the chosen African villages.

You can get posters to put up in your own domicile in order to spread the message. And maybe you could organize some local collection places. Ove, Sture´s son, could also, if need should arise, come with a truck to recollect whatever has been given.

And remember – the better things collected, the more money could help our African friends. And they really need help in order to survive. And at the same time you´ll also get rid of your bad conscience!

”Well, my friends, what´s your opinion about this proposal?”

In answer, Jenny gets a resounding applause from the audience. Warm-hearted Ove is standing beside Sture, wiping away his tears, clearly affected by Jenny´s speech. Sture does his utmost to look, also he, touched, but internally he is cheering. Jenny has performed so well! This could really mean money!

Jenny is quite moved by the enormous positive reaction from the audience. After a short while, she, however, holds up her hand in order to silence them. Then she, once again, starts talking, but with a very serious facial expression. "The speech I have just given has been written by Sture, but now I´m going to add my own thoughts. Yes, I too was feeling very happy and positive about the ideas of Sture and Ove – because they didn´t come from me – about how you could Show Empathy to Africa. But then I started to think. The more I was thinking, the more hesitant and dubious I became. I looked at the photos of the wells that have been dug, with the help of this association, and I found some details that puzzled me. I´ll not go into more details about this, but the consequence was that I went to Africa on a quick visit, to the villages in which the wells ought to be. And there were, of course, neither any wells there, nor any knowledge, whatsoever, about this association."

Sture has now scuttled from his chair, trying to tear Jenny away from the microphone. Ove is still sitting in his chair, but with a startled open mouth. A man, from the first row of chairs rushes up to Sture snatching him away in order to let Jenny continue speaking.

"Yes, dear association members, I´m sorry to have to tell you that you´ve all been subject to fraud. An ugly fraud, where your money and the valuation of what you´ve given away, has all gone back into Sture´s own pocket. Not even one dime has gone to the Africans, nor to any wells or other things the association claims to have done. I´m awfully ashamed of what my uncle has done and I do hope that he´ll have his punishment! When it comes to Ove, my cousin, I actually believe that he has not known anything about the fraud. Please, go on being open-handed, helping the poor suffering Africans – but please do it through one of the older and more trustworthy collecting associations. Thank you!"

Now there is complete chaos in the hall. People are running towards Sture, trying to tear him down on the floor, but within a few moments a number of police-men enter and try to re-establish order. They put handcuffs on Sture and take him away. Crying and pro-testing that he does not know anything at all about the fraud, Ove is following his dad.

Jenny feels relieved. She absolutely refuses to become involved in such shady business.

After the Show Empathy to Africa Association´s scandal, very appreciative articles once more appear in the press about Jenny and her decision to notify the police about the fraud her uncle has committed. Jenny is feel-ing uneasy about this and would just like to be left alone.

She feels sorry for Ove, who has actually shown him-self as a rather caring person, and she therefore looks him up. She finds a pale and depressed cousin. It is hurting to see him like that.

As Ove sees Jenny, he at once exclaims in a miserable voice: "Jenny, you mustn´t believe that I knew about the fraud! I absolutely did not! I was so happy at thought of helping African people in need. I was looking so much forward to getting the chance to go there to help them on the site! I´m so miserable and also ashamed of Dad´s betrayal against all the kind people!"

"Dear sweet Ove, I know that you´re kind hearted and also that you´re innocent. Do you still want to go to Africa to help?"

"Yes, there´s nothing I´d like more", Ove says with emphasis.

"Well then, let´s arrange that. You see, I´ve inherited a couple of persons, now that I´ve finished my education. I´ll give you some money so that you´ll be able to go, but there will be demands on the accounting of the money. How do you like that idea?"

"Wonderful", says Ove, tears in his eyes. "I´ll not let you down, I promise that!"

After discussions with different well-known help organizations, Jenny is able to send Ove to East Africa, where he will be working as a volunteer for a year in the name of one of the organizations.

Working in Stockholm, Jenny makes some visits to Agnes in Geneva. Agnes has summoned her courage and told the doctor about the horrible events she had gone through as a child. As a consequence, the medicine is changed and Agnes also starts having therapy sessions with a psychologist. An improvement is actually visible rather soon. The doctors believe that Agnes is partly suffering from schizophrenia but cannot rule out that also Post Traumatic Stress Disorder could lie behind Agnes' former tantrums.

When it comes to Jenny, her doctor says that solely the dark events, caused by Agnes during Jenny's early childhood, could have caused her mood swings – that is to say PTSD. He finds no evidence at all that Jenny would have schizophrenia.

Jenny has decided not to tell Agnes anything at all about Sture's fraud. Agnes is having enough problems as it is. Therefore, she only tells Agnes that she has not been able to find Sture.

At the beginning of 1978 Jenny gets a message from the mental hospital telling her that Agnes is dead. She has been murdered by another patient. Jenny mourns Agnes but at the same she is also feeling that what has happened might have been best for Agnes. She had, actually, had so many years left of her hospital stay. Such a long time until she would have been released.

After Agnes' funeral, Jenny goes to Torrevieja. She has also asked Nicklas Burger to come there in order to assist her in issues regarding the almost unbelievably big fortune she has now inherited. The house will be sold and the money she gets from it will be placed in a fund, destined to help the really poor in the Torrevieja community.

Furthermore, Jenny sets up a fund for Ove to help him with money for his charity work in Africa. He has, after this time, proven that he is in the right spot – that he is completely suitable for this work. Therefore, he will now get a salary and also some employees. But there will, of course, also be included a demand for accountancy to Nicklas.

Having finished all these arrangements, Jenny decides to go to Australia. She is still planning revenge on Sven, and she has, through Sonja and Mikael, been told that Sven – who now has a family of his own – and the others are in Lightning Ridge.

Chapter 52

Lightning Ridge, Australia – 4 March 1978

It's pitch-dark outside. Up in the sky, millions of stars are blinking. In the vicinity, you can hear subdued voices chatting, at times mixed with laughter.

Sven and his wife are sitting outside their big caravan, having a cool beer. They have just returned from a meal, consisting of a big piece of meat, at Diggers' Den, with their friends. Before that, they have all taken a nice hot bath in Bore Bath. When their young son, Wally Junior, after the meal started to get annoying, they had to go home to put him to bed. Now he is in deep sleep.

It has been four years since the traumatic drama in Mora was unravelled. During those years, Jenny has completed her education – she had finally decided to be a fire technician – had got her heritage and moved to an unknown place.

Sven has, finally, accepted Gertrud's proposals and married her. They have a son, Wally Junior. The name is a tribute to grandfather Anders´ old friend Wally.

Gertrud works as a nurse for the Flying Doctors, often in team with Maja, who has trained as a pilot. The two of them love to fly and are quite busy. Every day is exciting. And the nasty memories from Mora begin to disappear.

Sven has also had training. As expected, the geology education was something that really suited him. Together with Yngve, he now runs a successful consulting firm. With Yngve's airplane and pilot knowledge, they travel to the various mineral fields to provide advice and education.

Ida, David and Anders have started a small business with supplies for fortune hunters. They sell gasoline, milk, meat, preserves and all other necessities needed to live a good life in the bush. Ida also runs a caravan park for visiting adventurers.

Today, they have received a message from Nicklas Burger. A message that, although it is nasty, has calmed them all. The mentally confused murderer Agnes, Jenny's mother, has herself been murdered at the psychiatric clinic to which she had been returned after the events in Mora! The possible future danger is over. Now they can all continue to live without worry and devote themselves to enjoying life and friendship.

Maja stops her car in front of the caravan. She is on her way to the hangar, where her aircraft is standing. Sven and Gertrud have been allowed to put their caravan on the small airport field so that Gertrud can quickly get to the plane when there is an assignment.

Sven goes down to Maja's car to talk a little. Gertrud goes in to check on her beloved little Wally.

"Have you heard that there is a wave of fires in mental hospitals in Europe?" says Maja.

"Yes, a fire engineer education provides many work opportunities," laughs Sven. "Such mother, such daughter! Who knows if Agnes´ fondness for fires may have been inherited? Jenny said she would follow in Agnes´ footsteps." But seeing Maja's horrified expression, he quickly continues: "Sorry, I just joked. But it's good that Jenny has remained in Europe."

Gertrud suddenly stands in the doorway, completely white in her face. "Little Wally has disappeared. The crib is empty. Someone has kidnapped him. Do something, Sven! "

In the next moment, Maja sniffs the air. She recognizes a familiar smell that is quickly spreading. Then she exclaims: "It smells like smoke, burning gas! Damn, the hangar is on fire. The whole town could burn down! "

While Maja throws herself in the car to go down to the hangar to try to save her aircraft from the flames, Gertrud and Sven run around the caravan in the direction of the opal mines. They are terrified. Completely horrified by the thought that little Wally could have fallen into one of the deep mining holes. In such a case it is impossible to survive.

"Have you seen a little three-year-old guy here somewhere?" calls Sven to a woman who is doing this and that outside a caravan at some distance from theirs. Sven is heavily sweating and his heart beats double strokes.

"Yes, I saw him passing here a little while ago, together with a red-haired young woman. They each had a flashlight to shine with. They walked over towards Four Mile Deep, you know that big dump heap with a deep shaft in the middle," says the woman, pointing.

Gertrud is now at Sven´s side. Together they run, as fast as they can, to the heap. Already at a distance, they notice that the night silhouette against the sky looks different. The plate cover over the shaft is gone! Somebody must have moved it. The fear of what this might mean almost makes them stop.

At that very moment, a sweet child voice cheerfully cries out: "Look Daddy!" It's Wally Junior sitting on a dump heap, right at the side of the hole, proudly holding up a rock. When he shines on it with his small flashlight, Sven can see a big black opal in his hand.

"Mom, Dad, the Aunt fell into the hole!"

Chapter 53

Lightning Ridge, Australia - 4 March 1978

In the moonlight beside a dump heap, a movement can be distinguished. At the same time, there is a low sigh, followed by a sobbing inhalation. Jenny is on the verge of waking up from her almost unconscious doze, but she is frantically fighting the awakening. She just wants to sleep. To die. Only forget the horrifying thing she had almost done. What a monster she is!! Yes, really a monster. Exactly what Sven had once called her mother, several years ago. And that time Jenny had become furious with him, finishing their engagement. But now, suddenly, she understands what he had meant.

Yes, what could actually be more horrific than killing a small child? How could you even have such a thought in your head? Then you are not a normal sound person – you are simply a monster. MONSTER Jenny, that is who she is.

Once again, she bursts into tears. It feels as if she would never ever be able to stop crying. Everything is so horrible. Why had she not committed suicide instead of just pretending to do it? She had dedicated a long while to tear her trousers and shirt apart; she had even pulled big flocks of her copper-red hair. All this, she had thrown down into the deep mine shaft in order to get people believe that she had jumped into it herself. A couple of days ago, she had even been at the shaft to scout. At that time, she had noticed there could be a riverbed at the shaft floor. Her body could have been washed away there, if people, however unlikely, would go down there to search for it.

She had planned everything so well but – at the last moment – she had neither been able to push the little boy into the shaft, nor to commit suicide as punishment for her evil thoughts. She had, instead, in the dark night, half naked crawled a couple of hundred meters to hide behind another dump heap. Here she had been lying since then, cold and crying hysterically for several hours. She was obviously incapable of doing anything right – neither good nor evil.

Jenny suddenly notices something moving beside her. She can, in the moonlight, see an elderly man getting on his feet at the next heap. He stretches out his hand to help a small boy getting up. Thereafter, the man salutes her with his hand, like a farewell salutation, and disappears. Now she can see that it is an old aborigine. The boy carefully approaches Jenny. He might be around nine or ten years of age and is also an aborigine. For a short moment, he stands silent and quiet beside her and then he sits down at her side.

"Riki", he says cautiously, extending his hand to Jenny.

"Jenny", she answers, accepting Riki´s hand. They look, examining each other.

"I don´t speak very good English, because I´ve not gone to school. You see, I belong to a walking family. But I know some nice Aussie children, who try to teach me English." The words are coming out haltingly, and he often has to search his memory for the words he needs. When he cannot find the words, Jenny helps him along suggesting a word.

"My old man", says Riki, "that is my father´s father, says that you have ache in here." He points at his heart. "He wants to help you. We aborigines don´t talk very much. Instead we direct good thoughts at the person that doesn´t feel well. Thoughts can help."

"Riki, your grandfather is a good man. He is right saying that I have ache in my heart as well as in my soul. I´m happy to sit here with you. I think that would do me good."

After a moment of silence, during which both of them are contemplatively looking at the moon, Riki says: "Jenny, you and me, in a way, belong to the same family. My Grandfather´s blood brother – his best friend – is called Wally. And Grandfather believes that Wally and you belong to the same family. Grandfather, however, thinks that Wally is not walking on this earth any more. Almost five solar turns ago, Grandfather felt that he could no longer reach Wally with his thoughts."

Jenny blinks away some tears, caused by thinking about her grandfather Wally. "You´re so right, Riki. My grandfather died almost five years ago. But how can your grandfather know that I´m related to Wally?"

Riki is almost looking proud, as he answers: "You see, seeing you, he at the same time saw Wally´s face, feeling his presence. My Grandfather knows these things. And he says that there is possibly yet another person in the surroundings, also belonging to Wally´s family."

Yes, that could be true, thinks Jenny. Wally´s daughter, Maja, actually also lives in Lightning Ridge.

Jenny sits silent for a while, thinking of this. How is it possible? Do the aborigines have an extra "gift" within them – to be able to look into other people´s souls? Oh, she would really like to know more about them!

Riki has, with interest, been studying Jenny´s shifting facial expressions during her thinking. Then he gets an idea. "Jenny, you´re cold and hungry and sad, but you also have anger inside. Come with me and meet my grandmother. She can make you feel better. She says so many wise things."

"But Riki, you said you people don´t usually talk. Does your grandmother speak?"

"No, I´ve hardly ever heard her talking. But she´s exceptionally good at sending her own thoughts to the brains of others. The other persons can feel her thoughts inside themselves. Let´s go to her now."

A group of aborigines are sitting at the partly demolished mine entrance, sheltered behind a part of the door. In front of them they have a warming fire. The men are sitting around a big rock they are using as table, while the women are in a long row on the ground along a wall.

Riki´s grandfather lifts his hand, greeting Jenny, but he does not say anything. Riki guides Jenny to the row of women, where she sits down as the last in the row. Within a moment, a young girl hastens up to Jenny with an old dented tin mug filled with hot soup. Smiling, she hands it to Jenny. Another girl puts a warming cloth over Jenny´s shoulders.

The soup is so thick and good. It has probably been made of herbs and other things you can find in nature. Jenny feels refreshed by it. Warmth, gradually, returns to her body and her worries start decreasing.

Having now finished their soup, the men stand up and disappear outside. A somewhat older girl arrives putting a bundle of clothes on the ground in front of Jenny. She smiles amicably, points at the clothes and thereafter at Jenny. Then she disappears outside, together with the other women.

The only ones left are the oldest of the women - Riki´s grandmother – and Jenny. Grandmother sits down at Jenny´s side and takes her hand into hers. It is old, dirty and wrinkled but so comfortable to hold. Yes, it ought to have been just like this, holding the hand of her own grandmother, but she has never done that. Grandmother had died long before Jenny was born.

Jenny slowly relaxes, in the heat from the fire and the wonderful friendly silence. Then she suddenly hears a voice inside her. A whispering and comforting voice.

”Life is difficult, my girl! It´s difficult for each and every one of us and sometimes it gets extra hard. Like it is for you now. You have many black thoughts in your heart but also quite many positive ones. Make use of the positive ones and you will soon feel much better. Remember that it was the positive ones that won earlier this evening, when you chose not to kill the little boy!"

Jenny can feel how good the friendly, inaudible, or inner voice is for her soul. Yes, the voice is right. She has actually won over the evil within her – the devil did not get hold of her. Her good sides have won. She feels this is like a big victory but she is, at the same time, extremely afraid that the evil forces will take over at a possible new black moment and that they will, at that time, be stronger. How should she cope in order to diminish the black and evil thoughts and, at the same time, make the good ones increase?

As if Jenny would have said this aloud to the old woman, she almost immediately, once more, hears the inner voice answering her questions. "Don´t be afraid. You have so much goodness inside. You´ve suffered a lot and that has created bitterness and some vindictiveness in you, but you could correct that. It will take some time, but if you follow my advice, everything will eventually be good.

It feels so good to hear that inner voice express such positive trust in Jenny´s future that Jenny instinctively presses the old woman´s hand.

Jenny can once more feel how the woman´s thoughts enter right into her soul. "You and I will meet at Uluru within two lunar months. You can go there in any way you prefer. I myself will wander there with my tribe. When we meet again at Uluru, we will, the two of us, sit together for a couple of days in the shade of our sacred mountain, and I´ll then try to make my soul mix with yours. Try to give you answers on how you will get internal peace."

When the old woman and Jenny part, Jenny decides to stay in Australia until her next meeting with the woman. She has heard about Coober Pedy, where people live in caves. Instinctively, she knows that a stay in such an environment could give her the peace and time for consideration she needs. She has to disentangle her thoughts. Try to understand how she should react. Understand why her Psyche goes up and down like a roller-coaster.

But in what way should Jenny go to Coober Pedy? She does not feel like going on a tourist coach, having to socialize with a lot of unknown people. No, it will instead have to be by car. That way, she will have more time to ponder over her life. She is, after all, not in any hurry and can stay overnight, if she finds cozy places along the way.

Said and done. Jenny buys a second hand cab with the intention of reselling it, when no longer needed. She packs some eatables for the journey, a big jerrican of drinking water and a couple of extra jerricans with petrol. Lastly, she also buys a map of Australia.

The journey feels so exotic. The deep blue sky against the orange-coloured sand is so beautiful. Along the road: kangaroos, lizards and high termite nests. In one place, she sees a couple of wild dogs – dingoes – and a herd of wild horses. A tree here and there but very few houses. Sometimes, she sees big burnt-down areas, telling about the fires that once in a while occur in Australia, and also proof of past floods. Occasionally, she drives along worse roads, finding small exciting groups of houses and the odd bar, where you can stay overnight.

Jenny is in no hurry. She does not arrive at the goal – Coober Pedy -until five days later. Signs are showing that this is the capital of the opal industry. The landscape is hilly, and in between the small hillocks you can see big opal fields. Very few houses are seen but soon Jenny understands why. The people live inside the hillocks, in dug-out caves.

Having searched for a while, Jenny finally finds the Tourist Office. There she asks for a guided tour of Coober Pedy, with the possibility to also see the interior of some caves. She has been expecting a scanty living but becomes flabbergasted seeing how neat it is. New and comfortable with nice furniture – exactly like in a normal house. And it must certainly be nice and cool living like this, when the Australian heat strikes. As the tour is finished, Jenny asks if she could rent a little cave for some weeks and the guide arranges that quite quickly.

Weeks pass with Jenny sitting in her cave opening, meditating. She thinks back to everything that has happened to her during the last five years. She is also pondering over the future, wondering how to proceed with her life. She has a profession and lots of money, now that the inheritance has gone through. But how would she learn to socialize again? Learn to trust others? Not always expect to be let down again?

In spite of all, Jenny now understands herself better. She has, probably not, like Agnes, schizophrenia. She is presumably suffering from Post Traumatic Stress Disorder, but she is sure she could get treatment for that. As soon as she has returned to Stockholm, she intends to look for a specialist. The only inconvenience she notices is that she, thinking about Sven gets like a node of ice in her heart region. She feels a desire to kill, but maybe that is not so strange. She has after all been abandoned by him, sent away to a life of loneliness. It is only natural that you feel anger and impotence after such treatment… But the aborigine woman might help her to get rid of that feeling.

Gradually Jenny forces herself to start leaving the cave, to join the people down there. She avoids getting friends, because she still does not trust such, but she makes an effort when it comes to talking to others. That way she can get acquaintances for which it is enough to exchange a few words or to say hello to her when she is passing them.

When the time for the meeting with the aborigine woman at Uluru is approaching, Jenny decides to go by tourist coach this time She will take this as a trial of herself. If she can deal with being so close to others, then she is probably on the road to recovery.

With a feeling of regret, Jenny says goodbye to Coober Pedy. She climbs the bus and sits down in an empty chair beside an American woman. The bus journey turns out to be very exciting. The guide decides that every one of the travellers periodically must change seat in the bus, so that they all get to know each other better. At first, Jenny is hesitant to this, but she soon notices that the atmosphere in the bus gets much nicer. She is still rather reserved towards others, but she can feel how she slowly gets more and more relaxed.

The first night is a complete surprise to all of them. In the middle of nowhere, the bus stops and everyone is told to get out of it. Thereafter, one of the bus boots is opened and sleeping bags are distributed to them all. The guide explains, to the surprised group of travellers, that the night will be spent outdoors. They are to spend it in the same way as the Australian Bushmen, which means that they also will have a real bush meal. It turns out to be a strange but very fun evening. Big desert-barbecued steaks are served together with glow grilled sooty potatoes. At intervals also alive maggots and larvae are offered. At those times you have to open your mouth, shut your eyes and swallow, because who would like to be a coward in front of the others, not testing this Australian delicacy! An elderly couple, who at the beginning were very reluctant at the thought of spending the night in the open, is suddenly the happiest and most positive of them all. After the enormous but excellent dinner, the socializing is ended as they get some traditional Billy tea – a big tin can is swung around in the air a few times, before the nice but very smoky tea is served.

At the end of the evening, the guide shows them in what direction to go for any private needs. Then he adds:"Don´t forget to tell one of our bush friends, if you need to go there. It is important that he first check if there are any venomous snakes in the neighbour-hood. It is just as in African tourist camps, where you should ask the guard to check that there are no hungry leopards in the trees above the toilet space."

A terrified murmur is heard from the group. The guide laughs, telling them that he just wanted to give them a feeling of adventure. It is, in reality, very seldom that you meet dangerous snakes at night.

After a rather chilly night out in the open, underneath the glimmering starry sky, the group continues towards Ayers Rock – or as the aborigines call it: Uluru. Jenny is feeling very well, both mentally and physically. Being close to other people is, after all, not as bad as she has imagined.

A big part of the following day is spent on the bus and those who have not slept well during the night are tak-ing advantage of the possibility to doze. Towards the afternoon, Jenny suddenly sees a formation of domed rounded cliffs further to the left. The guide tells them that those are the Kata Tjuta Mountains, by westerners called The Olgas – also this place is sacred for the aborigines. A stop is, of course, made here with the possibility to take a walk among the exceptionally beautiful mountains.

After another 25 kilometres, they arrive at Uluru. With a glass of champagne in their hands, Jenny and the others admire the spectacular sunset over the mountain. From one moment to the next, the play of colours over the mountain is changing. Jenny finds it very impressive.

After sunset, the bus takes them to a hotel, and a sumptuous dinner finishes this wonderful bus trip. Before parting from each other, the travellers exchange addresses. Also Jenny takes part in this, since she is feeling that there are several persons in the group, whom she would like to meet again. Almost supersaturated of all the beautiful sights and events during the bus ride, she falls asleep in her bed already within a couple of seconds, sleeping completely dreamless the whole night through.

Next morning after breakfast, Jenny catches a cab from the hotel to the Uluru Mountain. Hearing the voice of the aborigine woman saying inside her: "Stop here!" she asks the driver to stop and let her out. She is very much looking forward to spending time with Riki's grandmother.

The two days Jenny stays with the aborigine woman prove very important to her. She notices that when she thinks about the different horrible happenings she has experienced during her life, she is getting a response from the woman. Not even one syllable is uttered, but just the same Jenny can in a strange way hear the woman´s thoughts and answers within herself. Jenny is feeling calmer and more harmonic for every hour that passes.

As the two part from each other, Jenny gets an advice from the woman: Jenny should look up her former friends in Lightning Ridge, tell them about her thoughts and say "I will be seeing you" to the ones she still likes and say a definitive "Goodbye" to those that have let her down. She should tell those that she is now feeling well again and that she from now on will live her own life, not caring about them or their trouble. This is, according to the woman, exactly what Jenny needs in order to get a good life.

It is difficult for Jenny to part from the woman, but she is feeling very content and grateful for the silent advice she has received from her. Now she is ready to face her difficulties. She knows how to cope with them. The only thing left is to face reality, not being afraid. She will cope!

Having anchored this decision deep inside, Jenny takes a bus to Alice Springs and from there a mail plane back to Lightning Ridge. The moment has now arrived. Now she will prove to herself that she has enough courage to confront the others.

CHAPTER 54

Farewell

Having arrived in Lightning Ridge, Jenny sends a message to Maja, informing that she would want to see the whole group in the usual bar the very same evening. Everyone turns up but they seem ill at ease.

Jenny starts the conversation by saying: "I have understood that you all believe I started the fire here, about two months ago. I can assure you that my biggest interest is to stop fires and not to start them. It might well have been sun reflexes passing through a piece of glass that caused the fire."

Ida scornfully looks at Jenny and exclaims. "Like mother, like daughter! Don´t deny it, you´re the guilty one!"

Jenny quickly turns to Ida, hissing: "I´m not even going to respond to that accusation." And then she asks, in an ironic voice: "Ida, how come that you according to yourself have never been to the United States, can speak such perfect American? I´ve heard you speaking to Americans inside the shop. This is actually something I´ve been asking myself for quite some time."

Surprised and dismayed, Ida just stares at Jenny. She is obviously totally incapable of uttering a single word.

Sven is next in queue to be the object of Jenny´s attacks. She contemplates him for a moment, and then she thoughtfully says:"Where is the real Sven whom I used to love? That one was a good-looking and straightforward policeman, who was also caring and sweet. But now, looking at you, I see a meek without any pride whatsoever and without any free will! Yuk! And imagine that you married a woman you hate – just because Ida told you to do it. I remember quite well that you used to call Gertrud Dracula. And, by the way, who gave you the right to steal the name you gave your son. You know very well that I used to say that my first son would be called Wally Junior – and still you gave your own son that name."

"But it was Gertrud who decided that…"

"Once again you are showing signs of meekness. And…"

She is interrupted by Anders, who indignantly exclaims: "Jenny, I tried to stop that. I didn´t feel they had any right to christen the boy with that name. They are, after all, not related to Wally!"

"And you, Sven", continues Jenny, "Did you never wonder where your aunt is? She was of such importance to Ida that she gave her sister all the money she received for giving birth to you, so that her sister could move to the States. As you know your aunt is an exact copy of Ida. How come Ida never speaks about her? In your place, I would certainly look closely into that matter. And who knows, maybe it has actually been your aunt fostering you and not your mother? But I´ll let you solve that possible mystery all by yourself."

An expression of horror is reflected on everybody´s face, as they gradually understand what Jenny has just said and what that could implicate.

"Well, I´m now leaving Australia and you – as I hope be forever. As you surely already know, my mother Agnes has died, so now it is time for me to live my own life."

Jenny walks up to Maja and Yngve, giving each of them a hard but very loving hug. "On the other hand, I hope to see a lot of you two in the future. Please forgive me for being unpleasant also to you. I will better myself in that respect, because I have now – finally – found inner peace. Please let us keep in contact through Sonja and Mikael."

Lastly she approaches Anders saying:"Since you and my grandfather Wally were such close friends, I will always love you too. May I give you a "see-you-soon"-hug?" She interprets Anders' tearful eyes as affirmative and hugs him. Thereafter, she turns her back on them heading for the waiting car.

Pirate Jenny Lyrics

German original lyrics by Bertolt Brecht (from the "Threepenny Opera", 1928)Songwriters: NINA SIMONE / Pirate Jenny lyrics © Warner/Chappell Music, Inc.

You people can watch while I'm scrubbing these floors
And I'm scrubbin' the floors while you're gawking
Maybe once ya tip me and it makes ya feel swell
In this crummy Southern town
In this crummy old hotel
But you'll never guess to who you're talkin'.
No. You couldn't ever guess to who you're talkin'.

Then one night there's a scream in the night
And you'll wonder who could that have been
And you see me kinda grinnin' while I'm scrubbin'
And you say, "What's she got to grin?"
I'll tell you.

There's a ship
The Black Freighter
With a skull on it's masthead
Will be coming in

You gentlemen can say, "Hey gal, finish them floors!
Get upstairs! What's wrong with you! Earn your keep
here!
You toss me your tips
And look out to the ships
But I'm counting your heads

As I'm making the beds
Cuz there's nobody gonna sleep here, tonight
Nobody's gonna sleep here
Nobody!
Nobody!

Then one night there's a scream in the night
And you say, "Who's that kicking up a row?"
And ya see me kinda starin' out the winda
And you say, "What's she got to stare at now?"
I'll tell ya.

There's a ship
The Black Freighter
Turns around in the harbor
Shootin' guns from her bow
Now
You gentlemen can wipe off that smile off your face
Cause every building in town is a flat one
This whole frickin' place will be down to the ground
Only this cheap hotel standing up safe and sound
And you yell, "Why do they spare that one?"
Yes.
That's what you say.
"Why do they spare that one?"

All the night through, through the noise and to-do
You wonder who is that person that lives up there?
And you see me stepping out in the morning
Looking nice with a ribbon in my hair

And the ship
The Black Freighter
Runs a flag up it's masthead

And a cheer rings the air

By noontime the dock
Is a-swarmin' with men
Comin' out from the ghostly freighter
They move in the shadows
Where no one can see
And they're chainin' up people
And they're bringin' em to me
Askin' me,
"Kill them NOW, or LATER?"
Askin' me!
"Kill them NOW, or LATER?"

Noon by the clock
And so still at the dock
You can hear a foghorn miles away
And in that quiet of death
I'll say, "Right now.
Right now! "

Then they pile up the bodies
And I'll say,
"That'll learn ya!"

And the ship
The Black Freighter
Disappears out to sea
And
On
It
Is
Me

Blue-eyed in Luhya-land

by Gunilla Fagerholm

A rather normal middle class Swedish couple in their fifties left their suburban life in Sweden in search of something new – a contrast to the secure Swedish Welfare State. They sold their small house, packed their belongings in a shipping container, and left Sweden behind. They went to Africa.

This book tells the true story of how they, during five years, lived as the only Europeans in a small village at the edge of one of the last rainforests in Kenya. They moved from a stressed life to a simple one, a clay hut on a maize field in Western Kenya, without any of the modern conveniences. On their own, they built a small rainforest hotel as the start of a new life. But life turned out difficult; corruption, tribal traditions and witchcraft hindered the blue-eyed couple in their efforts to help the suffering villagers.

The story reflects this turbulent time with a lot of positive and negative occurrences, arising in the meeting of contrasting cultures and traditions: Swedish meeting tribal Kenyan.

Please visit www.medialib.se if you want to see photos etc from our life in Kenya!